Praise for the novels of Jaclyn Reding

The Secret Gift

"Reding is at her very best with this deftly written story of the heart and soul of Scotland and the man and woman who find each other there. An elegant and moving story."
—Catherine Coulter

"A delicious contemporary debut . . . pure romantic fun!"
—Mary Jo Putney

"A compelling contemporary romance that warms the heart and satisfies the soul."
—Patricia Rice

"Reding similarly endows this new generation with courage, resourcefulness, and determination in a deliciously detailed story of an inheritance lost and found."   —Booklist

The Adventurer

"A fine Scottish plaid expertly woven of romance, history, and legends, the second book in Reding's *Highland Heroes* . . . is sheer magic. Readers who enjoy such books as Connie Brockway's *McClairen's Isle* series and Diana Gabaldon's *Outlander* won't want to put this one down."
—Booklist

continued . . .

White Knight

"I'd be a damsel in distress any day if this white knight was in the vicinity. Don't miss Reding's latest goodie."
—Catherine Coulter

"Jaclyn Reding spins a tale of love like no other! Highly recommended!"
—Under the Covers

White Magic

"With her superb knowledge and admirable skill, Reding captures the romance and grace of Regency England."
—*The Literary Times*

"This very satisfying historical romance runs the gamut of emotions; it also leaves just enough unsaid to make you want to read the next book in the quartet." —*Rendezvous*

White Heather

"Captivated me from the start . . . a charming combination of mystery, murder, romance, intrigue, and legend . . . a magical journey to romance." —Scottish Radiance

"Rich in historical detail, endearing characters, compelling stories—Jaclyn Reding has it all. This is a writer to watch."
—Linda Lael Miller

The Second Chance

Jaclyn Reding

A SIGNET ECLIPSE BOOK

SIGNET ECLIPSE
Published by New American Library, a division of
Penguin Group (USA) Inc., 375 Hudson Street,
New York, New York 10014, USA
Penguin Group (Canada), 90 Eglinton Avenue East, Suite 700, Toronto,
Ontario M4P 2Y3, Canada (a division of Pearson Penguin Canada Inc.)
Penguin Books Ltd., 80 Strand, London WC2R 0RL, England
Penguin Ireland, 25 St. Stephen's Green, Dublin 2,
Ireland (a division of Penguin Books Ltd.)
Penguin Group (Australia), 250 Camberwell Road, Camberwell, Victoria 3124,
Australia (a division of Pearson Australia Group Pty. Ltd.)
Penguin Books India Pvt. Ltd., 11 Community Centre, Panchsheel Park,
New Delhi - 110 017, India
Penguin Group (NZ), cnr Airborne and Rosedale Roads, Albany,
Auckland 1310, New Zealand (a division of Pearson New Zealand Ltd.)
Penguin Books (South Africa) (Pty.) Ltd., 24 Sturdee Avenue,
Rosebank, Johannesburg 2196, South Africa

Penguin Books Ltd., Registered Offices:
80 Strand, London WC2R 0RL, England

First published by Signet Eclipse, an imprint of New American Library,
a division of Penguin Group (USA) Inc.

First Printing, February 2006
10 9 8 7 6 5 4 3 2 1

In memory of my brother,
John Adamowicz.

You were like a candle that couldn't help but burn too
brightly, shining your light on the rest of us despite the
danger of melting too fast.

I'm so grateful I was given the gift of knowing you.

Chapter One

Castle Wrath, Scottish Highlands

"Flora, you know I wouldn't ask this of you if there were any other way."

Flora MacCallum took a breath and braced herself for what would undoubtedly come next.

It couldn't be good. Surely at any time throughout history, whenever such words were spoken, they had never been followed by anything positive. And as she stood there, facing a woman whose belly was swollen with nine months and nine days of pregnancy, Flora could only hope that it wasn't . . .

"The baby?" she asked.

"No, no," Flora's friend and employer, Libby Mackenzie, answered quickly, waving her hand. "It's nothing like that at all. The baby's fine, just a little shy, it seems, and not at all eager to greet the outside world. No. My problem has to do with the house."

"The house," Flora knew, was Libby's childhood home, an old Federalist-era ship captain's house that stood above the sea on Massachusetts's north shore. It had been left to her when her mother passed away a little more than a year before. Even though she now made her home in Scotland, Libby hadn't been able to part with the place where she had passed her happy childhood. Nor could she bring herself to leave it sitting empty but for the few times since then when she and her husband, Graeme, had managed to visit. So Libby had decided that she would turn the place into a bed-and-breakfast, and had undertaken to transform the house from a family home into a tourist's out-of-the-way haven on the New England coast.

"The project," as the house's makeover had come to be called, had become somewhat of an obsession, even after Libby learned she was expecting her first child. Once traveling back and forth was no longer an option, she'd simply overseen the work from a distance, relying on the family's attorney in the States, James Dugan, to see to the details. That is, until he apparently . . .

"Slipped a disc in his back," Libby told Flora. "Swing dancing of all things. Seems he 'swung' himself straight into traction. And as if that wasn't bad enough . . ."

The pause that followed was more pregnant than the woman who uttered it.

"Apparently the Howards, that couple Dugan hired to run the place, have decided not to run the place after all. Going off on an RV trek across the United States instead," Libby muttered under her breath. "Of course, they didn't think to tell us this until—she glanced at her desk calendar—*three weeks* before our first guests are due to arrive. So it's either cancel the reservations we've already accepted, which at this late date would likely prevent these poor people from finding alternative accommodation and ruin their holidays, or . . ."

Flora simply stared at Libby.

"I know it's short notice and all, but I . . ." Libby glanced at her husband, Graeme, a handsome Scottish architect, and noble lord to boot, who was sitting beside her. "*We* were wondering whether you might be willing to travel to the States to take over the final preparations and then stay on to open the house for the season."

"Me?" Flora let go her breath in a rush. "You want *me* to travel to the States?"

"Flora, I know it seems a lot to ask, but you can hire someone to do the cooking and the cleaning for the guests, and Dugan can help set up someone for bookkeeping. You'd simply be managing the house just as you do the estate here." She paused, her voice thickening. "I just don't know what else to do. This couldn't have happened at a worse time, what with the baby coming, or rather *not* coming, and me getting bigger by the second." She splayed her hands over her swollen belly. "The doctor assures me that if the baby doesn't make his appearance by next week, we'll issue him an invitation he cannot refuse."

Flora reached for Libby's hand. She was a petite woman with shoulder-length dark hair, held back in a headband from her classically pretty face. Something about the energetic American brought out a protective affection in Flora. In truth, Libby had become the sister she had never had. Yet despite her seemingly boundless optimism, Flora knew the pregnancy hadn't been easy for her at all—going from the early weeks when morning sickness had lasted all day to swollen ankles and lower back pain now.

Having had three very easy, very eventless pregnancies of her own—water breaking at or nearly on her due dates—Flora could only imagine Libby's fears. And it was made all the more desperate by the fact that the child she carried—a son—was the heir to a rather grand English dukedom, not to mention an additional Scottish earldom, and would become, the very moment he was born, both the Earl of Westonleigh and Baron Conybeare at once.

It was an event the entire British press corps was waiting for.

To the rest of the world outside the village of Wrath, a tiny hamlet tucked away on Scotland's northwestern coast, Libby's husband, Graeme Mackenzie, was known as the Marquess of Waltham. He was once one of the UK's most eligible bachelors. To say it had made headlines when he married Libby, a previously unknown, certainly unexpected, American, would be an understatement. Suddenly Libby couldn't go out for tea in London without it appearing in the next morning's editions. But those in the village knew that Libby Mackenzie was about as unaristocratic as a lady could be, a girl who would rather spend her days in ragged blue jeans, pulling weeds in the gardens, than hidden behind the ridiculously large brim of an ascot hat under the queen's tent at the yearly races. Somehow, though, she managed to do both—gardening because she loved to, and attending the races because she was expected to as Graeme's wife.

"I don't know how you do it," Flora had once said to her.

They had been sitting in the parlor at Castle Wrath, Libby and Graeme's "house," the oldest part of which was a thirteenth-century tower keep complete with lofty turrets and cobwebbed secret passages. Libby had been sitting cross-legged on an antique Aubusson carpet, wearing a Boston College sweatshirt whose cuffs and collar had gone ragged from wear and faded jeans with a missing back pocket. A Brown Betty full of Earl Grey sat between them while they filled literally hundreds of colored plastic Easter eggs with pence coins, candies, and various other surprises in preparation for the Easter egg hunt that would take place in the castle's gardens later that week. Libby had begun the event for the children of the village as a means for her and Graeme to become more a part of the community. Unfortunately, once the press got wind of it, the event also became a BBC news item, with paparazzi flooding the village in hopes of an exclusive snapshot.

"It's simple really," Libby said, shrugging it off. "Didn't you ever play dress up when you were a girl, pretending you were a princess?"

"Of course," Flora admitted. "All little girls do at one time or another."

"Right." Libby smiled. "The difference is I get to do it now as a grown-up, too."

It was that same practicality that helped Libby cope with being the wife of a future duke. As Graeme's uncle, the present duke, often proclaimed, "She will make a right fine duchess."

"But the kids . . ." Flora said, bringing her thoughts back to the present and giving the most obvious reason why she couldn't make the journey to the States that Libby was asking of her. "School . . ."

"I've already spoken with Headmaster MacNeil," Libby answered. "The children can finish their studies a week early and be on the first flight over little more than a fortnight after you. That will give us time to make the arrangements for their passports and any other necessary travel documents. We've talked to Angus and he has offered to bring the children over to meet you in the States himself. He'll even stay on for a while to help you at the house. Consider it a working summer holiday for you and the family, all expenses paid."

As if on cue, Flora's brother, Angus, walked in. "I've a'ready spoken to the widow MacNamara and she's offered to watch the wee one whilst the older two are in school and

I'm at work, just as she does when you're working here at the castle. I'll take care of them in the evenings, get them fed, bathed, and up in time for school in the morning. I've watched you do it every night now for the past three years. I know your routine with them."

Flora was running out of excuses. "But why me?"

"Who else would we ask?" Libby answered. "You've done such an incredible job here managing the estate, and this will be quite similar. If all goes well with this project, Graeme and I are thinking of converting several of the old stone crofter's cottages and maybe even the old stable block here at the castle into holiday cottages to help attract more tourism to the village. Right now, the only other accommodation this far north is at Miss Aggie and Miss Maggie's B and B, but they told me they're thinking of retiring. If we did convert the cottages, they would be self-catering to start, but perhaps in time we would expand into a bed-and-breakfast, too. We've got to do something, Flora. Without any places for tourists to stay, local businesses will suffer, and the village will fall off the map completely."

Though her first instinct was to insist she couldn't possibly do this, Flora found herself hesitating in her response. Wrath Village was her home. It was where she was born, where her children were born, too. Her ancestors, Libby's ancestors, as well, had lived in that tiny corner of Scotland for centuries, surviving wars, harsh living conditions, even the terrible Clearances back in the nineteenth century. But farming, or "crofting," was a waning livelihood, and twenty-first century villages had come to rely more and more on outside support. Their location at the most northwesterly point of the Scottish mainland made it a challenge to appeal to tourists. As such, shops and commerce were constantly struggling, and some villagers were even beginning to move elsewhere. Without villagers, there would be no village. With no village, all that history would be forgotten. Flora would do anything she could to help Wrath Village survive.

"Come on, Flor," Angus said as Flora sat considering every aspect of the offer. "If for no other reason, do this to give yourself a well-deserved break from here. You've been a single parent, doing it all on your own, for too long now."

Had anyone other than her older brother spoken those words, Flora's temper probably would have bristled, even though she knew what he said was true.

Since the death of her husband, Seamus, on a North Sea oil rig more than three years earlier, Flora hadn't been able to take the time to treat her kids to anything more than an occasional jaunt to the cinema in Inverness. But this? A holiday to the States for all three of them? She'd never be able to afford it otherwise, and her eldest, Robbie, was quite keen on all things American these days. In fact, he swore that as soon as he turned eighteen, he planned to leave Wrath Village, dubbed "The Most Boring Place on Earth" in his eleven-year-old opinion, never to return. Of course, having never been any farther from the village than Inverness, Robbie had never known homesickness.

For Flora, it was a little different. Even though the village had been her home for all her life, it had also become for her a daily reminder of all she'd lost. In the months since that horrible day when she lost Seamus, she had existed in a sort of limbo—going about her business day to day—getting a job, struggling to support three children on her own, and all the while seeking to find a rhythm to her suddenly out-of-tune life. Flora hadn't allowed herself to do anything but attempt to fill the void left in her children's lives without their father, even as she knew that no matter what she did, she could never take that emptiness away from them.

And now here Libby sat, offering them all a much-needed holiday, a working holiday, yes, but a holiday nonetheless. And actually, the idea of running a bed-and-breakfast was something Flora found interesting.

But could she *really* do this?

She kept coming back to the kids. They were her life, and she'd never been away from them, ever, not even for a day. Could she really leave them, put an entire ocean between them, even for the short time before they came to join her?

"Flor . . ."

Angus came up beside her, taking her shoulders. "Listen to your big brother, now. I'm older and far wiser in these matters."

Though he winked, his face, so like their father's with its dimpled cheek and twinkling eyes, quickly took on a more serious expression. "The past three years have not been a'-tall simple for you. I've watched you. It's doing something to you, this determination you have not to crumble. I canna remember the last time I saw you smile, truly smile." He pointed to her heart. "It's killing something in you. You havna allowed yourself the time to come to terms with what happened. But you canna ignore it forever. Your grief for Seamus needs to be dealt with, but staying here and burying it behind your responsibility to the kids winna make it go away. Trust me. It isna good for you, and it certainly isna good for the kids. They need to see their mum as the beautiful, brilliant, laughing woman I have always known her to be, not this shadow, this substitute who has come to take her place while she hides from the darkest part of her life. I . . ." He glanced at Libby and Graeme. "*We*'ve come to realize that it is something you just cannot do here in the village—where every day everywhere you go and everything you do is a reminder of what happened."

Flora closed her eyes as the pain of her loss knifed through her, tightening her throat and burning at the back of her eyes. She'd pushed that feeling and any feeling that might come after it away for so long that she'd become an expert at it. It was like turning off a lamp, watching the glow of the bulb dim, fade, and finally go cold. All she had to do whenever those feelings began to burn was click off the light and embrace the darkness, armor herself with it until she was safely numb once again.

Still Flora knew Angus wanted only what was best for her. And Libby . . .

Flora glanced at her friend, who merely nodded, her eyes filled with concern.

Angus tipped Flora's chin up to face him. "Do this for me. For the kids. But most importantly, please, do this for you."

Flora looked at him, her dear brother. He'd always been her protector. Though she didn't want to admit it, she knew he was right. From the day Seamus died, Flora had locked her own grief away, hoping to shield the kids from having to see their mother completely unravel before their eyes. But keeping her emotions under lock and key was definitely taking its toll on her. In the past six months, maybe more, she had noticed a tendency in herself to withdraw from certain situations, particularly when she was around Libby and Graeme, who still acted very much like newlyweds and were both quite openly over the top at their impending little arrival.

Love.

Marriage.

Children.

It was all Flora had ever wanted or ever dreamed of. Flora loved Libby and Graeme both so dearly, and she was so happy for their joy, but watching their open affection for each other day in and day out couldn't help but cause a twinge deep inside of her. A twinge of envy, yes, and a twinge of sadness at the loss of the love and the life she had once shared with Seamus.

God, how she missed him. She missed the most looking into his eyes and seeing the heat of his stare when he watched her doing something as simple as hanging the wash on the line. She remembered times when that wash had been left to wrinkle in its basket—when Seamus would come from behind the cover of a sheet flapping in the wind, grab her about the waist, and pull her down into the heather for a sun-kissed romp. Flora smiled. Her daughter Annie had been conceived during one such romp. Seamus, her youngest, was the result of one particularly cold winter night by the hearth. And Robbie . . . he had been conceived on their wedding night, born nine months to the day later.

If only it could have been a bad dream. The truth of it was that a part of her still hoped they had been wrong somehow, that the helicopter crash hadn't really taken him, and that one day he'd come walking down that crooked pathway to their tiny cottage as he always had, whistling some made-up tune with his hands in his pockets and that tweed hat slanted over his eyes. But no matter how much she wished for it, no matter how many times she stared out at the starry night sky and begged the heavens for just one more chance, Flora knew she had to accept that Seamus wasn't coming back to her.

Ever.

Flora took a deep breath, and imagined herself at a crossroads. One direction led down a road that looked familiar but at the same time was utterly empty, no trees, no flowers, only miles of nothingness stretching before her. The other road turned a curve leading into the unknown. But there was a certain light beckoning from around that bend. It called to her, that light, offering the warmth, the promise, of the summer sun.

Flora let go her pent-up breath and nodded. "All right, then. I'll go."

That night, after the supper dishes had been washed and all three of the children had been bathed and pajamaed for the night, Flora sat with them in the middle of her brass bed surrounding her atop the thick goose-down duvet. She lowered her face against her daughter Fiona's—known more familiarly as Annie—hair, colored the same shade of red as her own, and breathed in its freshly washed scent. The seven-year-old sighed softly and leaned back against her mother in drowsy contentment. Wee Seamus, still her baby though he was nearly three, was tucked up against the crook of Flora's left arm, his thumb fixed firmly in his mouth, while Robbie sat cross-legged at her feet, reading from a favorite storybook.

"Are you quite certain you're okay with this?" Flora asked when Robbie had finished and wee Seamus's eyes had begun to droop.

One condition of her accepting Libby's offer was that the older children must agree to it. Otherwise, Flora wasn't going.

"Yes, Mummy," Annie said first, smiling her freckled angel's smile. "It will be an adventure for us, like one of those reality telly shows where families have to meet challenges and pass tests. Uncle Angus has promised to let me do all the cooking and the wash while you're away."

"Eating your cookin'? That'll be a challenge a'right," Robbie muttered, earning him a stern stare from his younger sister.

"Really, Rabbie . . ." Flora said. "I'm serious now. How are you with it all?"

" 'Tis fine . . ." He sighed loudly, rolling his charcoal eyes beneath a tousle of chestnut hair and looking far too much like Angus when he'd been that age.

Flora read the obvious lack of enthusiasm in his response. " 'Tis fine, but what?"

"I just dinna think it's fair we have to wait to go until after you. Why canna we come with you? We dinna do anything in school the last weeks anyway . . ."

"You'll stay and you'll finish your studies. That's the agreement. Otherwise, we don't go a'tall. Any of us."

He frowned, but nodded in resignation. "Hoch aye . . ."

"Mummy?"

From the big yawn that followed, Flora could see that Annie was fading, too. It was nearly an hour past their bedtime, but she'd made an exception, knowing she'd be away from them so soon.

"Aye, m'wee dosh?"

"Auntie Libby said there was a bakery near where she lived in New York that made biscuits as big as a pizza." She yawned again. "Do you really think what she says is true?"

Flora smiled and kissed her sleepy daughter's forehead. "Well, Annie, I'm sure if Aunt Libby said so, then it must be true."

"Can you imagine it, wee Seamus?" Annie said, her eyes blinking, going as wide as could be. "Can you imagine a biscuit as big as this?" She held her arms up as if she were cradling a pizza pie.

Seamus blinked, his tiny brow furrowing as if he couldn't quite grasp the notion, before he closed his eyes again, his mouth working sleepily on his thumb.

"Can we get one when we come to America, Mummy? Please? And can I eat it all m'self?"

"For certain, Annie dear. Off to bed wit' you now, aye, whilst I take wee Seamus to his cot."

Flora watched as Annie headed for the door, the hem of her nightgown dragging on the floor behind her.

Robbie, however, lingered behind.

Flora saw that he had taken out the atlas, that Angus had given him, and had turned to the page that showed a map of the state of Massachusetts. He pointed to the small dot that marked the village of Ipswich-by-the-Sea, just northeast up the coast from the larger dot of Boston.

"Is this where we're going?"

"Aye, 'tis," she answered quietly.

Robbie turned to the back of the atlas then, to a larger map that showed all of North America, as well as Europe. With a finger whose nail was black from playing football out on the peaty Highland soil, he traced an arc from Massachusetts across the Atlantic to the very tip of Scotland, where their village lay nestled in relative obscurity. Flora needed no words from him to know what Robbie was thinking.

"I'll only be there a fortnight afore you, Rabbie. Then your uncle will bring all three of you to join me and we'll have the grandest summer holiday you can imagine, filled with adventures. Dinna worry, aye?"

Though he tried very hard to mask it, his eleven-year-old eyes shone with a glimmer of fear—the fear that only comes from losing a parent at a tender age. Bravely, though, he took a breath and nodded.

"Now off wit' you, and scrub that dirt from under those fingernails afore the entire village thinks you've been raised in a byre."

Flora smiled at him and watched as he went, her heart tightening at the vulnerability of her firstborn son, who wanted so badly to be thought of as a man but at the same time—especially at times like these—couldn't deny the boy he still was.

After she'd tucked Seamus beneath his favorite blanket and watched him curl up on his cot, Flora walked the length of the cottage, turning off the lamps, the telly, and the radio that the children had left on. She slid Angus's supper plate on the rack to warm in the oven and then headed off to bed herself.

She tugged off her jumper, rolling her head from one shoulder to the other to ease the tightness that had settled in her neck. It had been a long day. As the estate manager at Castle Wrath, Flora spent most of her time making arrangements for deliveries and setting up the various restoration and maintenance work that was needed both for the castle and its extensive gardens. It was a seemingly endless undertaking, owing to the fact that the castle had been left uninhabited for some time before Graeme and Libby took up residence. The roof slates were in sorry need of repair, the stucco walls needed refinishing, and the seawall needed reinforcement. The gardens, once the pride of the whole northwestern coast of Scotland, had gone wild, the antique roses tangled from decades of neglect. And that was just the outside work.

For the inside, Libby had spent months poring through every document and engraving she could find moldering in the castle's garrets. She was determined to return the labyrinth of rooms and twisting hallways to their former glory. The necessary fresh paint, new plaster, and paneling would take years to complete, but once finished, the estate and castle of Wrath would be a true jewel in the crown of

Scotland's northern coast. It was a thrill for Flora to be a part of it.

The night was chilly, and Flora took out her thickest flannel to slip on before turning to reach for the lamp beside the bed. She caught a glimpse of Seamus's photograph sitting on the night table—she saw those eyes in one sense or another in each of her three children. Normally, whenever she happened to notice the photo, she would quickly look away, banishing the twinge that inevitably came at the sight of it. Tonight, however, she picked up the tarnished silver frame, sat at the edge of the bed she had once shared with the man pictured there, and studied his image closely.

How well she knew his every feature, from the crooked bump on the bridge of his nose to the rasp that grew along the line of his jaw when he hadn't shaved. How she longed to feel that rough chin brush against her cheek just once more when he kissed her, as it had so many times over the years they had been together. Had she known then that this one simple pleasure would be taken from her so much sooner than she'd expected, she would have savored it much more while she had him.

She'd met Seamus when she was seventeen, an *innocent* seventeen who had scarcely ever been kissed. Even though he was the only man she'd ever been with, Flora had never once regretted pledging her life to him. He had stolen her heart the very moment she saw him.

She would never forget that long-ago night. She'd been standing with some of the other village lasses at a ceilidh. And while most everyone had been dancing, reeling beneath the lights strung overhead in the village hall, Seamus had locked eyes with her and hadn't let go. He'd been new to the village, having come from Glasgow to take a job on an oil rig drilling some three hundred miles out on the North Sea.

He worked four weeks on and four weeks off. Most of the rig workers spent their time off traveling as far from the rig as possible, escaping to Inverness, even Edinburgh to spend their hard-earned pay. But not Seamus. He'd rented a room at the widow MacNamara's and came to the ceilidh on his first free night, making the acquaintance of some of the villagers before setting his sights on Flora.

He'd asked her to dance and they'd shared a waltz beneath a canopy of fairy lights. He'd been nineteen, ready to enter adulthood, and from the moment his eyes smiled down into hers, Flora had been his. It was the way of the world in the village of Wrath. Young men met young women. They courted. They wed. They had children. Life carried on, generation to generation.

Within two years, Flora and Seamus had been married.

They spent their wedding night on the very bed she sat on now, with the sound of the North Sea that broke just down the hillock from their small cottage the music to which they had danced and clung to each other. Seamus had been a gentle lover, patient and thoughtful. Flora became pregnant before the honeymoon was over; in fact, Seamus had always teased her about it, calling her his "Fertile Flora." In truth, it seemed he only had to look at her and she would end up carrying his child. Had he not made their living out to sea on that oil rig, gone all those weeks at a time, she'd probably have had at least a half-dozen children or more in their short marriage.

But neither one of them could have known that their time together was limited.

It had been a bleak November night when the village constable at the time, Jamie MacNeill, had driven his checkered patrol car up to her cottage. His arrival hadn't caused Flora any alarm. Jamie had been a schoolmate of both herself and Angus and often stopped by to share a cup of tea when he made his patrol about the village. This time, however, the look in his eyes when she'd gone to meet him had been enough for Flora to know . . .

" 'Tis Seamus," she'd said, facing him at the front door even before he'd closed the garden gate behind him.

Jamie had simply nodded, his face shadowed by the dread he felt at having to perform this particularly undesirable task.

"The helicopter taking him back to the rig went down shortly after taking off, Flor. Witnesses said it broke into pieces afore it even hit the water." He'd looked at her then before finishing, "There were no survivors."

Angus had been away, having gone to the States to train as a fireman with FDNY. It had been his dream, getting that job, but after receiving Flora's call, he'd been on the first flight back home to Scotland.

Only a week later, Flora discovered she was carrying Seamus's last legacy, their youngest son. When he was born, she named him for his father. And Angus stayed on to help her, eventually taking Jamie's place as village constable when Jamie moved on to district headquarters.

Setting Seamus's photograph aside, Flora walked to the tall pine dresser that stood in the far corner of their small bedroom. She hadn't touched it in more than two years—hadn't opened a drawer, hadn't moved the three pounds and fifty-seven pence that her husband had left lying atop it the last time he'd been home.

Wrapping her fingers around the tarnished brass fitting, Flora tugged the top drawer open and blinked down at the small stack of neatly folded shirts tucked away inside. She could feel every breath she took lifting her chest, rushing out of her nose. Before she could talk herself out of it, she took the topmost shirt and lifted it up by its worn, well-laundered collar.

Flora buried her face in the fabric, breathed in the faint scent that was Seamus. Somehow, amazingly, it still clung to the shirt even after all this time. She quickly unbuttoned the loose shift she wore and let it fall to the floor. She took off her bra, slid free of her panties, and then let the shirt envelop her bare skin. The fabric was soft, the sleeves fell well beyond her wrists, and the shirttail brushed the back of her bare knees as she sank slowly onto the bed. She put out the lamp, stared at the ceiling, and lay there alone in the darkness with the moonlight reaching in through the window to trace its shadow along her figure.

Flora closed her eyes. She could feel the heat, the burn, of her tears. The grip her emotions had on her throat tightened with every breath.

God, how she missed him.

How she missed what their life had been. It was simple, unexciting, but it had been theirs.

For the first time since the day Jamie MacNeill drove up to her door, Flora gave herself over to her tears. She let down the armor she'd taken on, the armor that had kept her strong for her children. She cried for Seamus, for what they'd had, and for what could have been, weeping silently into her pillow so as not to awaken her children. Her body rocked with each sob until her chest ached from the strain of it and her eyes were swollen from the salt of her tears. And then after the tears no longer came, she closed her eyes, and for one last night, before she left the home they'd made together, before she turned that crossroads and headed for whatever lay ahead, Flora slept with her husband's shirtsleeves wrapped around her, holding her, keeping her warm.

Chapter Two

Ipswich-by-the-Sea, Massachusetts

"Get you a warm-up on that coffee, Mr. Matheson?"

Gavin turned from the window to glance at the waitress, a young brunette named Jules. He gave her a half nod, watching as she topped off the spider-veined ceramic mug he'd been palming over the past two hours.

"Jules . . ."

"Yeah?"

"I come here every day. Sit at this same table. Drink bottomless cups of your father's coffee. I think you can drop the 'Mr. Matheson' stuff by now and just call me Gavin."

"Sure thing, *Mr. Matheson.*"

Jules winked and gave a tip of her head in the direction of her father, who stood behind the front counter. He was an apron-clad, barrel-chested Italian who looked a bit like Danny DeVito, actually—squat, balding, with dark ferret-like eyes. Even though he was busy chatting with some of his other patrons, it was obvious from the glance he gave his daughter that he managed to keep one ear and one eye on the goings on in his café at all times.

The surest sign of a shrewd businessman.

"Well, then," Gavin said, "Mr. Matheson it is."

"Uh, yeah."

She was a good kid, Jules, and pretty in a tomboyish sort of way, made all the more so by the faded jeans and baggy sweatshirts she typically wore. Just out of the local high school with a 4.0 GPA and a mind for math like a computer, she had her pick of the Ivy Leagues along with any number of West Coast universities. There was Harvard, of course, thirty or so miles down US-1 in Cambridge. And Yale, a couple of hours away by train. Problem was, she couldn't make up her mind on any one of them. So, instead, she'd decided to take a year off to wait tables at her old man's coffee shop, where the locals were more than happy to offer their "suggestions."

New Englanders on the whole were an opinionated lot and never shy about speaking their minds, be it which school was the better choice, or the chances of the Red Sox winning another World Series. Although Gavin had tried to steer Jules toward his alma mater, Columbia, the current favorite among the other café customers was, of course, the local Harvard. It was also her Sicilian father's choice because it would keep his only child closest to the home nest.

"Thanks, Jules," Gavin said as he sipped the freshly warmed coffee.

"Anything else? Bowl of chow*dah*?" she asked, cocking her head to one side, her voice flat with the distinctive New England accent. "Piece of pie? Ma made a *crostata di fragole* this morning that'll melt in your mouth. I'm telling ya, it's wicked good."

Gavin smiled and shook his head, although the pie did indeed sound "wicked."

"Just the coffee for me, Jules. Thanks."

The skinny brunette sighed, shaking her head with a

swish of her ponytail as she headed off to freshen the cups of the other café patrons.

The coffee shop, called Common Grounds, stood on the fringe of the town's central green area, or "common" as it was called. It was next to the post office, adjacent to the pizza takeout owned by Jules' uncle Tino, and just past the whitewashed bandstand where the local chamber music society held concerts in the summer. It was the sort of place that was always busy no matter the time of day, the local watering hole where everybody knew everybody else and greeted them the minute they came through the door. If you needed to find a good plumber or know which farm stand on Route 133 offered the freshest produce, you could ask pretty much anyone and be sure of getting an honest answer. The pastries, cakes, tortes, and biscotti, too, were Italian and incredible, made fresh each morning by Jules's mother, Maria. The coffee, prepared most any style one liked—espresso, cappuccino, latté, or even "American style" drip—was always hot, made with the best beans Italy could send across the Atlantic, and prepared by Jules's father, Sal, himself.

Sal Capone.

And, yes, that was his real name.

The tables, of which there were about a dozen, were numbered and clothed in red-checkered linen—the regulars definitely laid claim to their favorites. Number 4, by the window, was the meeting spot for the local garden club each Tuesday afternoon, when polite gray-haired ladies would share an assortment of teas and almond biscotti over heated discussions of crocuses and gladiolas. At Number 3, the local selectmen met for lunches of prosciutto panini and iced tea topped with scoops of lemon ice, discussing such things as the town's new DPW Garage or the latest upcoming zoning bylaw. The local cop on duty perched at Number

1, near the door, where he could hear his car radio if a call came in, while the trio of young mothers who walked together each morning took Number 5, which offered ample room for parking their collection of jogging strollers.

Gavin, however, preferred Number 7, because it was set away from the others and commanded the best view of the bustling waterfront beyond the village common.

Outside the café, the May sun was high and a good breeze blew in off the scenic bay. Pleasure sailors were preparing to go out for a skim on the Atlantic while fishing boats, battered and rusted from the salty sea, were already coming in with that morning's early catch.

With a history of trawlers, gillnetters, long-liners, and lobstermen that stretched back nearly three hundred and fifty years, Ipswich-by-the-Sea was one of the last true fishing villages in New England. Also known as Little Ipswich or the more local acronym of IBTS or "Ib-its," it was situated on a rocky neck of land with the only access to it coming by way of one winding two-lane road. This, and the fact that it didn't offer any public beaches, kept it tucked away from all but the most discriminating of tourists' eyes.

The village had been built and had survived upon the hardworking lives of seamen—fishermen, boat builders, and even one purported pirate. Thus far, the townsfolk, traditional to the core, had remained steadfast in their refusal to tear down the old waterfront docks and replace them with bustling hotels and trendy eateries in lure of the tourist's dollar. The closest thing to a souvenir shop was the village pharmacy, which did offer a small stock of IBTS T-shirts and picture postcards alongside the cough medicines, Band-Aids, and assorted tubes of toothpaste.

It was precisely that unspoiled, small-town character that made the village all the more attractive to those seeking a hideaway from the rest of the world. Artists and writers, even executives from Boston and New York, had come to Ipswich-by-the-Sea to refresh and be inspired, renting beach houses and trading tailored suits for drawstring pants and Birkenstocks. The village had certainly appealed to Gavin, who had taken up residence in his friend's summerhouse for the past several months. He hadn't intended to stay so long. A weekend, he'd thought. Maybe two. But, somehow, from the moment he'd arrived in Ipswich-by-the-Sea, Gavin had felt that this place would prove to be his salvation.

He just had to wait for it.

Day after day, Gavin came to this same café and sat at the same table, seeking something of the spark of inspiration in the sight of the gritty, weathered faces of the fishermen who went out to earn their living upon the dark waters of the North Atlantic. Hadn't the same thing worked for Billy Joel? Hadn't a number of his lyrics been inspired by the fishermen of his native Long Island? The only difference was Gavin wasn't looking for lyrics, or the poetic, meaningful play on words.

Gavin was looking for music.

There were no papers spread out before him on the café tabletop, no synthesizing keyboard tucked inside his bag. When it worked, Gavin heard it—the notes, the melody—playing in his head. The process was inexplicable, unable to be forced, and unwilling to be controlled. When it did come, floating in to deliver its mystifying measure, it was almost magical.

And that "magic" had given him a career most could only dream about.

Gavin Matheson, the composer, had been writing songs since back in high school in the Baltimore suburb where he'd been born and raised. Together with lyricist Alec

Grayson, his partner since Columbia, he had created dozens of respectable commercial hits like "Always Annalise" and "Lost in You Again" while dreaming of Grammy gold. They had worked with artists both up-and-coming and established. It was a career that allowed him the excitement of the limelight without the glare. His anonymity preserved his private life. Songwriters and composers weren't pictured on CD covers. Their names usually appeared beneath the song title, sometimes even after the lyrics, an afterthought. Paul McCartney walking down Broadway buying a hotdog from a street vendor would most certainly be noticed, but Gavin Matheson would not be. At least, that was the case until the day Gavin lost his then-six-year-old son, Gabriel.

"Lost" wasn't quite the right word when it came to explaining why Gabriel was no longer in his life. It implied that Gavin had had some measure of control over it, as if he could have done something, anything, to prevent it from taking place. Had he known, had he even suspected, he would have done anything, faced down the devil if he'd had to, in order to prevent it.

It had been a sticky, humid, late summer day in the city, without even a hint of a breeze to stir the air. The sun had burned down on the Manhattan asphalt jungle while air conditioners chugged and churned from apartment windows, dripping onto the sidewalks. It was the sort of heat that brought out the worst in people, the sort that made them do crazy, unthinkable things. And one of those people had been his then soon-to-be ex-wife, Miranda.

Gavin was in the studio when the call came in on his cell. He'd answered it, still listening to the playback as the song that would prove to be his breakout success was being recorded by an artist whose career had soared nearly the minute the track hit the airwaves. It had won him that longed-for Grammy, as well as almost every other applicable award. But Gavin hadn't been there for the resulting accolades. Alec accepted the collection of golden plaques and statuettes for him. Despite the success it had meant for him, from that streamy summer day on, Gavin couldn't stomach hearing that song. Each time he caught it on the radio or heard it playing through an open apartment window, it served only as a bitter reminder of the day his son had disappeared.

The caller had shown as UNKNOWN with a 718 area code on his Caller ID, indicating that whoever was calling was in the greater New York City area outside of Manhattan.

"Gavin."

It was Miranda on the other end of the line.

"Am I late?" Gavin had said, immediately glancing at his watch, hoping it hadn't stopped since it showed he still had two hours before he was supposed to pick up Gabriel for their court-scheduled weekend.

"No. You're not late."

Gavin heard background noises, a muffled voice echoing over the buzz of an intercom. "Where are you?"

She didn't immediately answer, but he could hear her breathing heavily into the receiver.

Finally she said, "I'm at the airport."

"Airport? What are you—?" And then he felt his pulse jump into the back of his throat. "What are you doing, Miranda?"

"I'm leaving, Gavin. I just wanted to save you the trouble of going to the flat since we won't be there."

We. That meant her—and Gabriel.

"Where the hell do you think you're going? Where's Gabriel? Put him on the phone. Let me talk to him. Don't even think you're taking him with you . . ."

She knew damned well their court appearance was scheduled for that Monday, when the judge would rule on the issue of Gabriel's custody. As it was she'd changed the date and then neglected to appear so many times before that the judge had warned her if she didn't make this appearance, he'd find her in contempt of court.

It was one of the main reasons their marriage had failed. No matter what Miranda ever might have been expected to do, be it as a wife, as a mother, or in any other role she might play, she always—*always*—did the opposite. If she had an appointment for ten o'clock, she breezed in at eleven fifteen. When she volunteered to chaperone an event at Gabriel's preschool, she couldn't be bothered to show up, leaving the entire class no choice but to cancel their field trip. She'd even married Gavin, he had little doubt, simply because her parents hadn't wanted her to marry an American, fearing they would lose her to the other side of the Atlantic. She just refused to do anything that might even remotely resemble "conforming."

But even Gavin couldn't have expected what she'd do that day.

"Miranda, just tell me where you are and I'll come and get Gabriel. You can go and do"—he chose his words carefully—"whatever it is you find yourself needing to do at this moment."

"What I need to do at this moment, Gavin," she ground out in her clipped British accent, "is take my son and leave."

"*Our* son, Miranda. Gabriel is my son, too."

She had launched into a familiar vitriol then, accusing him of treating their son like a possession. Christ, no matter what he did, what he said, she always found a way to turn it around. She was a true master at painting him in the worst possible light.

Usually, whenever Miranda started in on him, Gavin would just hit the END button on his phone. He no longer lived under the same roof as she did, so he didn't feel obliged to stand by gritting his teeth while she doled out one of her famous tirades. This time, however, Gavin let her rail, doing everything he could to keep her on the line, quickly scribbling a note to Alec that read simply:

Miranda. Have to go. Now.

Underlining the last word three times, Gavin grabbed his jacket and ran for the studio door.

Miranda was still shouting at him through the earpiece of his Nokia as he frantically hailed a cab. When the driver looked at him in the rearview mirror, obviously wanting to know where he intended to go, Gavin hesitated.

Which airport was she calling from?

JFK or LaGuardia?

With the 718 area code, it could be either one.

He certainly couldn't ask her, so he covered the mouthpiece and told the driver the one that seemed more likely.

"JFK. And there's an extra hundred in it for you if you get me there quickly."

As they raced down Delancey Street on their way to the Williamsburg Bridge, Miranda had gone on, citing her laundry-list litany of reasons for why their marriage hadn't succeeded. Every one of them, of course, was Gavin's fault. It had been that way from the start.

He cared *only* about his career.

He was *never* home.

He was *always* working.

Miranda only ever saw things in extremes. And the list had grown to book-sized proportions in the seven years they'd been together.

The fact that he'd rearranged the recording schedule of a

major artist so that she could attend a week-long retreat up-
state to "rejuvenate" after having Gabriel had disappeared
from her memory completely, yet she recalled every occasion when Gavin hadn't been able to accommodate her
whims.

And then, suddenly, Miranda had stopped talking.

Sitting in the back of that stifling cab in the middle of
Manhattan traffic under that blazing sun, Gavin had prayed
his cell phone hadn't dropped the call.

"Miranda?"

"I gotta go," she said then. "They're calling our flight.
Good-bye, Gavin. Have a brilliant life."

"What the—"

Gavin heard the clank of the pay phone hitting its cradle
before he could get out his frantic, "No!"

And then the line went dead.

God, just let him make it to the airport before she left.

Unfortunately, Miranda had chosen the peak of the Manhattan rush hour to call him. The Williamsburg Bridge was
bumper-to-bumper, and traffic was absolutely crawling on
the BQE.

Gavin pounded his fist on the cab's armrest in frustration.
"Dammit!"

By the time they arrived at the airport located just fifteen
miles from Manhattan, an hour had passed since she'd
called. He couldn't find any trace of Miranda—or Gabriel.

It took Gavin until the following Monday, nearly three
days later, before he could even begin to try tracking them
down. Gabriel had a valid passport, and since there was no
formal order of custody yet, Miranda was within her rights
as his mother to take him. Until she didn't appear for their
court date. Given the urgency of the situation and the fact
that Miranda had already provoked him by playing havoc

with his court calendar several times before, the judge made good on his threat to find Miranda in contempt and then promptly awarded Gavin sole custody of his son for good measure.

But then the real work began.

Within the first week, Gavin, with the help of his attorney, was able to confirm that Miranda and Gabriel had indeed left JFK on a flight, but unfortunately that flight had gone to Rome, which turned the case from a domestic to an international parental-child abduction. To make matters worse, it was a slow news week. Given Gavin's recent, albeit somewhat behind-the-scenes celebrity, the media quickly glommed onto the story.

"AWARD-WINNING COMPOSER'S CHILD ABDUCTED," screamed the *Post*'s headlines.

And there went his comfortable anonymity.

Reporters began calling for quotes. Photographers camped out on his doorstep. Gavin decided it was better to give the media his full cooperation, reasoning that the more Gabriel's photograph was published, the better his chances for finding out where they'd gone. He did interviews and made appearances on the morning news shows. He even set up a hotline for tips and sightings. Meanwhile, he filed the necessary reports and made all the mandatory appearances, working his way through the State of New York's woefully overworked family court system.

Terms Gavin had never heard of before, such as "Hague Treaty" or "decree of sole custody," became unfortunately familiar in his vocabulary. From that ill-fated day, Gavin went from being Gavin Matheson, the somewhat renowned, award-winning composer, to something else entirely, something he never would have dreamed of in his worst nightmares.

Gavin became the "left-behind parent."

And he hadn't written a note of music since.

Oh, everyone had been watching, thinking he would create some Claptonesque tribute to his lost son, but Gavin had resisted that, resisted the comparisons that would undoubtedly result, resisted what writing a song like that would make him feel. Instead he focused all his attention on finding Gabriel and on getting him back. When the trail went cold somewhere between Italy and Austria, Gavin hired an international private investigator. The man was amazing, producing copies of receipts and even the occasional grainy photograph to which Gavin clung in desperate hope.

But every time they caught up with Miranda—zeroed in on her location—she seemed somehow to sense it, and fled.

Days stretched into weeks.

Weeks blurred into months.

When the first year passed, Gavin reluctantly accepted that he would have to get back to work. It had been at least three months since they'd had any solid verification of Miranda's whereabouts, and then it had been a small seaside village in Greece, which she'd vacated even before they could get the local authorities to respond. After that, the trail had gone cold and for the first time Gavin had faced the possibility that he might never see Gabriel again.

He turned to the only thing he had left—his music.

But when he sat behind the piano and stared down at those black and white keys, every aspect of the creative process, something that had been as much a part of him before as breathing, felt suddenly foreign to him.

He realized it was because he'd lost his inspiration.

From the moment he'd come into Gavin's life, Gabriel had changed everything. Gavin could spend hours just watching him sleep, his tiny hands balled into fists. He'd been the one to take the midnight feedings; Miranda just *had* to have her ten hours. But Gavin hadn't minded. He'd loved those quiet times in the rocking chair with his son. Just watching that little face in the light of his teddy bear nightlight had sparked Gavin's creative muse. Often, once Gabriel had gone back down in his crib, Gavin had slipped off to the piano, composing until the sun came up over the East River. He'd written the best music of his career then, including that last song—his professional triumph.

How could he possibly find his way back to the music? What had he done before; how had he written without him?

Before Gabriel came into his life, Gavin had traveled often and his music had reflected the places he visited. When he couldn't concentrate at home in New York, he wondered if perhaps a change of environment might help and started traveling again. He'd gone to San Francisco, but the foggy mornings and equally foggy evenings had only served to further depress him. In Hawaii, the sunsets had seemed somehow colorless to him, as if painted in black-and-white. Italy had only pushed him into the wine bottle, from which it had taken him six months to emerge. Nothing had helped because everywhere he went, in the face of every child he encountered, he searched for Gabriel.

And fell farther into the darkness.

Then there was an article in *Rolling Stone* that insinuated that perhaps Gavin Matheson's creative genius had left him.

Thank God for Alec. His partner and his closest friend, he had caught up with Gavin in LA just a few months after the second anniversary of Gabriel's disappearance. He'd found Gavin lost in the blurry bottom of a bottle of Absolut. It had been Alec who brought Gavin back to reality. It had been Alec who first told Gavin about the little unknown speck on the map called Ipswich-by-the-Sea.

"We've got a summer house up there now, Gav. Right on the North Shore."

"A summer house? When the hell did you buy a fucking summerhouse?"

Alec had looked at him, frowning. "Almost a year ago."

"Christ . . ." Gavin muttered, running a jittery hand through the beard he had long before stopped bothering to shave. "Where the hell was I?"

Alec just shook his head. He didn't answer. "Listen. This isn't some touristy place like Cape Cod or Nantucket. In fact, there isn't a hotel to be found. The people there are real. They're hard-working boat builders and fishermen who actually still fish for their livelihood on Cape Ann. No one will bother you. The press doesn't even know the place exists. Go there. Dry yourself out and get your head on straight, because we both know this isn't the way you want Gabriel to see you when he comes back."

The words had hit Gavin like a fist in his gut.

Alec had left the keys sitting on the counter of the bungalow Gavin had shut himself away in at the Beverly Hills Hotel.

Two days later, when Gavin emerged from the haze of his intoxication, he decided to take Alec's advice. Deep inside, Gavin had known he would never find Gabriel, or the spark that had been his life's work, at the bottom of a fifth of vodka. The drinking had been nothing more than a way of numbing the pain, but even as he'd been guzzling himself senseless, the saner side of Gavin's brain had realized it was only a temporary fix, a short-lived relief from the pain.

So Gavin had taken up the keys Alec had left, checked out of the bungalow, and headed east.

To *New* England.

For a *new* start.

That had been over three months earlier. Massachusetts had been in the grip of one of the coldest winters on record and Gavin had spent the better part of February locked away from the rest of the world as he conquered the beast of his alcohol addiction. Winter had turned to spring. He'd watched the sprouting of the local tulips, the greening of the trees. He had yet, however, to once again hear the music that had filled his world.

So he waited.

The people of Ipswich-by-the-Sea emerged after the winter's thaw, slapping fresh coats of paint on picket fences and throwing open the shutters to welcome the springtime. The newness of the season had even sparked a seedling of optimism in Gavin. Each day he woke with the hope that he might take that stroll into town and see something, hear something, that would trigger the faintest sound in his long-silent head.

Maybe it would be a wind chime moving in the breeze.

Or a seagull soaring overhead.

Once, in the early days of his career, Gavin had been inspired by the sound of a New York traffic jam.

That was the magic of it, his music. It could be anything, anywhere, at any time—except apparently it wasn't going to happen for him that day.

Giving up, Gavin got up from the café table and fished five bucks out of the pocket of his Levi's for the coffee and Jules's tip. He'd go back to the house to sit behind the keyboard for an hour, and if that didn't work, maybe take a walk down to the shore. He was just turning to leave when the tink of the bell above the café door caught his attention. He couldn't say why. That bell had rung literally hundreds of times during the hours and days he had spent at that front window, sitting at that table, and he'd scarcely ever noticed it. But this time there was something, some odd echo in the late-spring breeze that rushed in through the open door, that had Gavin lifting his head for a look.

A second later, he heard it.

Four notes.

Four little notes, soft as a summer wind.

Four little notes that actually stole his breath.

And so did she.

Her hair was the dark red of a garnet. Her face was like the marble of a Michelangelo sculpture. She walked in, stopped, then glanced around the café. Obviously lost, she crossed to the front counter, holding a rental car agency map that clearly had been the victim of at least one crumple of frustration. She wore a long skirt that swept against her booted ankles and a knotted, oversized fisherman's sweater, the sleeves of which were pushed up to her elbows—she was dressed far too warmly for May in New England. Her hair, that riot of red that framed her face, was tied loosely behind her, dropping to midback in a fall of twisting corkscrew curls.

Gavin stood in the middle of the coffee shop, watching as she quietly asked Jules's father for help in finding her way. He couldn't hear what she was saying, but that was only because the music in his head was still playing. It was a style of music that was completely unfamiliar to him. Exotic. Almost ancient. It was unlike anything he had ever heard before.

The woman thanked Sal for his help and turned, glancing at Gavin with a whisper of a smile before she drifted back through the door. The moment she'd gone, the song fell silent, breaking Gavin from his trance.

It had lasted scarcely a moment, but that was long enough to remind Gavin of what once had been.

The magic that he called *inspiration*.

"Mr. Matheson? Gavin? You okay? Something else you needed?"

Only then did Gavin realize he was standing in the middle of the café, staring at the door where she'd left.

"What? Uh, no. Thanks, Jules."

He turned to leave. Then he stopped and turned back. "That girl who was just here. What was she looking for?"

The waitress returned a sly grin. "Pretty thing, wasn't she?"

Truthfully, she was. He would even say she was beautiful. But her looks had been secondary to the music that had swelled through him the moment she had come in.

"She was looking for the Hutchinson place, the one with that odd name up on the bluff. You've seen it. That old sea captain's place . . ."

Gavin knew the house well. The windows of Alec's summer house looked right onto that windswept bluff.

"The blue one with the black shutters and the widow's walk that looks out over the bay?"

Jules nodded. "One of the oldest houses in the village. No one's lived there for well over a year now, not since the last owner passed away. We all expected it would be sold, what with the Hutchinson daughter moving away like she did. Sad, too, since it's been in the family for centuries. The talk around the village lately is that she's decided to turn it into a B and B. The first one in town. Took a lot to convince the Town Council, but they decided a B and B was the better option to having her sell the place off to some real estate developer who would slap a housing development or a strip mall onto one of the village's oldest properties."

Jules shrugged. "Who knows? Maybe the one with the map is coming to stay there."

Gavin was already halfway out the door.

By the time he reached Main Street, however, the girl, the woman, that *vision* that had been his first inspiration in over two years, was gone.

Gavin tossed his keys on the hall table and walked across the Italian marble floor to the wide bay window that faced out onto the Atlantic.

Outside, the mid-day sun was sparkling on the waters of Ipswich Bay, where sailboats skimmed the surface with white sails flapping like a parade of elegant swans. It was an image worthy of a postcard, but Gavin gave it little notice. Instead he turned the old brass and wood telescope, which stood on its pedestal before the window, up the coast, toward a distant house that stood high above the sea.

It wasn't the first time Gavin had trained the eyepiece on that house. From almost the day he'd arrived in the village, he had been drawn to it somehow. It was the sort of house that you just knew had a story connected to it, some long-ago tale that had been lost in the shuffle of generations past. But this time Gavin wasn't looking at the house. Instead he looked for her, hoping he could catch a glimpse of her out on the balcony or through an open window.

Just hoping he could hear that music again.

He waited.

He watched.

He listened.

But all he heard was the sound of the surf echoing through the open windows beside him.

A mile or more of Massachusetts shoreline away, Flora set her bags on the weathered planks of the wraparound porch and fit the key into the lock of the lace-draped front door.

She had certainly never expected that it would refuse to turn a moment later.

She tried it again. Took the key out. Put it back. Jiggled it. Turned it.

Nothing.

After a full minute, and several more attempts, Flora stepped back and said out loud, "Now what am I supposed to do?"

There was, of course, nobody there to answer her.

Libby's attorney, James Dugan, was still out of commission, and out of town, while he recovered from his line dancing mishap. His assistant, Kathleen, was to have left a mobile phone, cash, and all the other information Flora would need in the coming days at the house for her. They were undoubtedly locked up safe inside. Every detail had been thought of, and planned for, except . . .

They hadn't considered the possibility that the key wouldn't work.

Flora checked the house number again, even though she knew she was at the right place. Libby had talked of her childhood home so often and with such detail, Flora felt quite as if she'd been there before. In the yard, beneath the boughs of a huge oak, hung the weathered rope-and-plank swing where Libby, determined to fly, she'd said, had broken her arm when she'd been just a girl of nine. All along the porch line were the heathers her mother had lovingly planted in remembrance of her native Scotland. They were just coming to bloom alongside brilliant bright pink azaleas and budding wild roses whose perfume spiced the late-spring air. Though no one had lived at the house in over a year, Libby had made certain that the place was kept up—most particularly her mother's garden, which had been the elder Hutchinson woman's dearest pride.

Leaving her bags at the door, Flora took the steps down to the crushed stone pathway that wound around to the back of the house. A seascape that was unrivaled by any others she'd ever seen stretched as far as she could see on three sides. It was a hot day and the May sunlight sparkled brilliantly on the water. The wool of her sweater, coupled with her irritation at the key, was giving her an unpleasant itch. How she wished she'd dressed more comfortably.

Flora circled to the back of the house and tried the key in the back door, then the porch door, even the bulkhead that led down to the cellar—any other place it might turn. But in each lock, at each door, the key simply refused to budge. She looked at the key. It was a copy of the original, newly cut—and obviously cut wrong, too.

Flora studied the windows then, her eye catching on the upper floor, where one window had been left slightly open. A length of trellis, wound with rich, dark ivy, stretched beneath it. She needed to ring Libby up to ask how she could contact Dugan's assistant to get another key. As Flora saw it, she had two choices. She could either get in the car and drive back into town to find a pay phone and place an international call to Libby, except that she had perhaps only a dollar and change left from the small stash of American money she'd brought with her. The rest of her spending money, she'd been told, would be waiting for her once she arrived.

Or, she thought, eying that trellis again . . .

Fortunately for Flora, keeping house while chasing three young children around had helped to keep her in fit physical shape. The trellis, though obviously installed generations earlier, held sturdy under her weight as she hiked up the wool bulk of her skirt and fitted the toe of her walking boot into the first foothold.

She was halfway up to the window when she heard the sound of fabric catching and ripping, followed by an unyielding tug as the hem of her skirt got caught on one of the slats of the trellis.

Bloody hell.

Flora tried to lower herself a bit on the trellis to loosen her skirt, but it didn't budge. She looked over her shoulder and saw the reason why. The fabric was snagged on a rusted nail.

She felt a trickle of nervous perspiration work its way down her neck, falling between her shoulder blades beneath the heavy sweater. Gripping the weathered wood with sweating hands, Flora closed her eyes and let out with the most colorful curse word she could think of, one Angus had taught her when they were kids and which she only ever used when she knew she was completely alone and couldn't possibly be overheard by one of her children. She let it out loud and she let it out strong, closing her eyes and dropping her head back as she turned her face to the sun that was blazing into her.

It did help, just a little, to ease the tension and frustration of the day.

Until . . .

"Well, I'll have to remember that for the next time I feel like having an old-fashioned cuss. It was a good one."

Flora started, nearly losing her grip on the trellis at the sound of the unexpected voice coming from below. She looked over her shoulder only to find a man standing at the corner of the house, watching her.

He looked familiar. Hadn't she seen him earlier at the café where she'd stopped for directions?

She'd never even heard him walk up. She couldn't imagine how she must look, dangling from the side of the house like a broken shutter.

"I beg your pardon. I know this looks a bit peculiar, but there really is a perfectly logical reason for me to be here hanging from this trellis."

At least it had seemed perfectly logical at the time.

"I'm sure there is," he said. "Listen. I'm not sure how things are done where you come from, but most people find the front door a more useful means of gaining entrance to a house."

Nearly suffocating beneath her clothes, Flora was in little frame of mind for his teasing. "Really? Well, I certainly ne'er would have thought of that . . ."

She heard him chuckle to himself, and she gritted her teeth.

"You wouldn't perhaps care to make yourself useful and go find a ladder or something that might help, instead of standing there, deriving your afternoon's amusement at my expense . . ."

He shook his head, crossed his arms, smiled. "I suppose I probably could. . . ."

Flora tried kicking at the skirt to free it from the nail again, but with no success. Out of frustration, she loosened one hand from the trellis and gave the fabric a good hard tug but instead of the skirt tearing free, she felt the trellis creak beneath her. Heart pounding, she grabbed on to the nearest slat.

"You're going to tear the whole damn thing down," the man said, stating the obvious. "Stop bouncing around like that. Let me see if I can at least climb up a few feet from here and loosen that snag for you."

The wind off the coast blew her skirt and Flora could feel

it fluttering, lifting to expose her legs. The cool rush of air was a welcome distraction, blissful really, and she stilled for a moment to savor it. Until he approached the trellis directly beneath her, giving himself a clear view up her skirt, all the way, no doubt, to her pink-pantied bottom.

"No, don't—"

The second he put his weight on the trellis, she heard one of the slats crack and then give.

"Shit," he said, stepping back. "It's not going to hold me. And I'm beginning to think it's not going to hold you much longer either. Certainly not long enough for me to go back to my place and dig out a ladder."

Flora had no intention of "hanging around" that long to find out. Grateful that she could no longer see him standing below her, she loosened her grip from the slat she was holding onto, unfastened the two buttons that held the skirt at her waist and let the fabric slip over her hips. Thank God her bulky sweater fell long enough to cover her hips.

Standing on the lawn beneath her with his mouth hanging open, Gavin got a clear view of a most attractive pair of shapely white legs and a hint of rounded bottom as she resumed her climb to the open windows.

"Okay . . . now does someone want to tell me what the hell is going on here?"

Only something such as the authoritative voice of the police officer who had just come around the corner of the house could induce Gavin to tear his eyes away from the delicious sight above.

Well, *shit*.

"Oh. Hello, Officer. We were just, uh . . . hanging around."

"Yeah. I can see that," the cop said, then lowered his mirrored sunglasses on his nose, looking up to the top of the trellis where the skirt fluttered like a tartan banner.

"Ma'am, I'm going to have to ask you to come down from there now."

"I'm afraid that's impossible, sir," she answered.

"Is that so?" he said. "And why *exactly* is that?"

He had his answer a moment later when the trellis jerked, and with an audible groan, started to pull away from the house.

Chapter Three

"Name?"

They were sitting in a small back office of the Ipswich-by-the-Sea police station. The officer who had driven Flora there in the back of his police car was at that moment sitting before her asking her name, waiting to type it into his computer. He had assured her she wasn't being arrested.

Yet.

At least he hadn't dragged her in wearing just her underwear, she thought in an attempt to find something—*anything*—positive about the situation.

Instead, she wore a pair of denim trousers that she had quickly fetched from her bag—that is, after she'd fallen from the trellis, dropping straight onto a thicket of Libby's mother's heather. Bless that woman's soul for having had the foresight to plant it there, in that precise spot, and not something else, something prickly like an assortment of tea roses. The trellis, unfortunately, had suffered the worst of Flora's venture. Having stood for probably a hundred years or more, after just fifteen minutes in her company, it was now hanging from the house with its ivy clinging to it like threads to a dangling button.

Flora exchanged a glance with the policeman over the top

of his computer monitor, sighed and then tried again to explain why he'd found her, swinging from the trellis, wearing a sweater and her panties.

"Officer, I know it looks very suspicious, but I can assure you I do have the owner's permission to be at the house."

The policeman responded with a doubtful blink. "Right. And that would explain why you had to climb up to an open window to gain entry."

"I already told you the key I'd been given didn't work. I think it must have been cut improperly, or something. You see, I've come here to open the house as a bed-and-breakfast for the season. I've been hired by the owners to manage it for the summer."

"According to what my chief was told by Mr. Dugan, the owner's attorney, a couple by the name of Howard is going to be managing the place."

"The Howards *were* going to manage the place. However, they decided rather last-minute against taking the position after all. It's been left to me now, and I've got little more than a couple of weeks to get the place ready afore . . ."

Her voice fell off when she noticed the man sitting beside her—designated her "accomplice" by the police officer—staring at her from his chair. He had his legs crossed casually and a stupid sort of grin pasted on his face.

What did he find so bloody amusing?

She scowled at him. "I'm pleased you're enjoying this. I'm most certainly not."

"Oh, come on. You have to admit, it is at least a little bit funny. I mean, it's not every day around here someone takes on a trellis in her underwear."

Given her present predicament, Flora was finding it hard to see any humor in the situation.

The police officer simply looked at them both, gave a tired sigh, and tried again. "Name?"

"Flora. Flora MacCallum," she answered. She glared at the other man, still sitting in his chair, legs still crossed, still grinning that fool's grin, and muttered the word "idiot" in Gaelic.

"How do you spell that?" asked the officer.

"A-M-A-D A-N . . ."

"No, ma'am. Your name. M-A-C—"

Flora spelled her last name, then added, "Just as it reads on the passport that you confiscated from me."

The officer ignored her sarcasm, glanced at the other man, and waited for his response.

"Gavin Matheson, Officer Faraday, sir," he responded, reading the cop's badge. Then he spelled his name with all the obedience of a dutiful schoolboy.

Flora rolled her eyes.

"Officer Faraday," she tried again, "if you would please just phone Mr. Dugan, I'm sure he can sort this out quite easily."

"Well, that's going to be a bit of a problem, Ms. MacCallum, as Mr. Dugan is currently convalescing out of town and we have no way of reaching him." He added, "I'm afraid, until we can verify your story, we have little choice but to hold you here at the station."

Good God.

"Am I . . . under arrest?"

"No. But considering that both you and your accomplice were caught in the act of breaking and entering, we have every right to bring you in for questioning . . ."

"He's *not* my accomplice," she reminded him. "I have never seen this man before today. And I wasn't breaking into the house."

He just looked at her.

"Well, I suppose *technically* I was breaking into the house, but certainly not with the intention to rob it. Why would I do that when I'm supposed to be staying there for the next several months? I mean, does that make any sense to you at all?"

"Ma'am, it's been my experience that those who break the law rarely use common sense."

"Yes, I suppose if they did, they wouldn't be criminals."

Flora shook her head, unable to believe what was happening to her. Though she'd gotten rid of the wool skirt, she still wore the sweater, and the heat of the day coupled with her escalating anxiety had brought out a nasty rash on her arms. She tightened her fingers into a fist to stop herself from scratching.

"May I at least make a telephone call, then? I've watched enough American police dramas on telly to know I am supposed to be allowed that. I'll simply ring up the house's owner for you and she can get this sorted out for you."

The officer turned his black desk phone around to face her. "Dial nine for an outside line."

Flora reached a little unsteadily for the receiver. Although she was furious at the absurdity of the situation, she was a good deal frightened as well. After all, she was completely out of her element, a foreigner in a foreign land, who now somehow found herself sitting within ten steps of a steel-barred holding cell. In all of her thirty-two years before that morning, she'd never so much as received a citation for speeding. Now here she sat staring at the very real possibility of spending the night behind bars.

Dear God, please let Libby get her out of this mess.

Flora pressed the requisite nine, then quickly added the

international exchange for Scotland, followed by the number for Libby and Graeme at Castle Wrath.

She waited through a series of rings, then another. After another, she gave up. "No one is answering."

Officer Faraday merely stared at her, clearly not believing her. He was young, midtwenties, and had obviously taken his instruction in intimidation police tactics very seriously. His dark eyes bored into hers from across the well-ordered desk top. In fact, he only looked away when someone called to him from across the room.

"Chuck. Mrs. Moultrie is up front to see you. Her neighbor's dog was digging up her petunias again."

Officer Faraday exhaled loudly as the man went on. "Oh, and the chief's back from lunch. He wants to see you when you're done."

Faraday sighed a second time, nodded, then looked at Flora and Gavin, resting one hand on the pair of handcuffs fixed to his belt. "I trust I won't need to lock you two up while I go see to this?"

Flora squeezed her aching forehead. What did he expect she was going to do? Take the whole station hostage with her nail file?

"Would it be at all possible to get a glass of water so I might take a Disprin?"

"Disprin?" Officer Faraday asked. "What's that?"

"Aspirin," Gavin Matheson explained. "UK version."

"Jim," Faraday called to his colleague, "would you get the lady some water while I go see to Mrs. Moultrie?"

Flora fished in her handbag for the small bottle of Disprin she'd carried with her on the plane.

She didn't say a word to Gavin Matheson while they sat and waited for Officer Faraday to return. His colleague Jim brought her the water. After swallowing two tablets, Flora busied herself with studying the Wanted flyers that papered the bulletin board behind the desk, unwittingly comparing the grainy images of the criminals with that of Gavin Matheson. For all she knew, the man could be a serial killer.

Though he certainly didn't look like one.

His dark hair was a little on the longish side and fell back from a tall forehead as if he'd done nothing more than finger comb it while it was wet. There was a bit of it falling over his eyes. Eyes, Flora reminded herself, that thus far had done little else other than laugh at her. She'd never met anyone so cool, so calm, and so utterly infuriating. Even now, sitting in the middle of a police station on the verge of being arrested, he seemed as completely at ease as if he were out to tea. He certainly looked a good deal more comfortable than her, in his jeans and button-down shirt, the sleeves of which he had rolled up over a pair of well-muscled forearms.

Just who was this Gavin Matheson, she wondered.

He wasn't an overly large man or as densely built as Seamus had been. Seamus always had the look of a rugby fullback, his hands knotted and scarred from the physical labor of working on an oil rig. In contrast, Gavin Matheson's hands were well-formed, with long fingers and neatly kept nails. Whatever he did, it certainly wasn't anything that required working with his hands. She'd noticed this because she'd been staring at them all the while he sat beside her in the back of the police car, counting his fingers, noting the absence of a wedding ring, anything to avoid looking at him.

Flora knew from having walked beside him into the police station that he was tall, well over six feet, with long legs and a lanky build. Yet, he moved with a rhythm, a natural, grace. He'd held the door open for her, so he was—or at least at that moment had been—a gentleman. His voice was deep and cultured, indicating he'd been well educated. But there was a suggestion of ruggedness in his face, in his sharp nose, in the line of his jaw, which was shadowed by a day's growth of beard.

Flora realized then that while she'd observed all these things about him, one thing she hadn't taken notice of was the color of his eyes. Now, as she sat cataloging his every feature, she found herself wondering what color they were.

Brown? Probably. Simple, unflappable brown.

She stole a look a moment later, only to find that he was staring at her, too. Her pulse jumped and Flora felt her face go flush and quickly looked away, toying with the Disprin bottle inside her handbag.

They were blue, his eyes. And startling.

Officer Faraday returned, and Flora actually smiled to see him. He was accompanied by another, a senior-looking colleague who carried Flora's passport.

"Might I try the call again, please?" she asked.

"No need to, ma'am. We were able to get ahold of the local police constable back where you come from in Scotland. An Angus MacLeith. He confirmed your story, said he would vouch for you."

"I should hope so." She didn't bother to tell them that the police constable was also her brother.

"We also got ahold of Mr. Dugan's assistant, Kathleen Spencer-Brown. She has to take her kid to soccer practice but will drop another key by the house for you on her way. She said she'll leave it under the mat."

The older officer handed Flora her passport, then extended his hand to her. "Police Chief Barrett, Ms. MacCallum. Please accept my apologies for the"—he glanced at the younger officer—"*overzealousness* of Faraday. He's new to our department, up from Boston. Guess he needs to realize we're not as used to big-city crime around here. While I'm sure you can appreciate that he was only trying to do his job, to serve and protect the citizens of this town, I assure you we don't typically welcome visitors to Ipswich-by-the-Sea by hauling them down to the station for questioning. I hope you'll allow Officer Faraday to give you a lift back to the house. Again, our apologies."

Flora wasn't much fond of the idea of another ride in the back of a police car, but she didn't have any choice. The SUV Libby had leased for her was still at the house. "Thank you, Chief Barrett."

"What about me, Chief?"

Gavin Matheson had been so quiet, Flora had nearly forgotten he was still there. "Think I can be released on my own recognizance?"

"Yes, Mr. Matheson. We also got in touch with Mr. Grayson, who confirmed that you're looking after his place. I admire your work, by the way, especially the one you did with that group Metro. Got anything new coming out anytime soon?"

Gavin frowned, and for the first time, Flora noticed a crack in the shell of his easygoing demeanor. "Nothing right now, no. I've, uh, taken the last couple of years off."

The chief nodded. "Yeah, read about all that in the papers. It's gotta be rough. Sorry to hear of it."

At that, the crack all but shattered. The change in him was immediate. Gone was the cocky grin. His expression grew dark and his eyes lost their light.

He immediately got up to leave.

As Flora watched him go, she thought to herself that whatever the chief had brought up, it must be something that carried a particularly difficult burden for Gavin Matheson.

*   *   *

"Would you like me to wait until you've checked inside to make sure everything is in order?"

Officer Faraday pulled his police car up the drive that circled around in front of the house, got out, and opened the back door for Flora to exit.

"No, that's quite all right," Flora said. "I'm sure everything will be fine now. Thank you, Officer."

Truth was, at that moment, she wanted nothing more than to yank off that stifling sweater and lock herself away from the rest of the world. The stress of flying across the Atlantic and being alone for the first time, so far from home and without her children—with the added upset of the past few hours spent in the police station—had left her ready to collapse from sheer nervous exhaustion.

She dropped her suitcases in the very spot on the porch where she had earlier and quickly retrieved the key Kathleen had left under the mat. She exhaled out loud when it turned easily in the lock. She waved to the waiting Officer Faraday and watched as his car rolled down the gravel drive, turned onto the street, and vanished.

Silence greeted Flora as she stepped through the front door into a paneled entryway that was peaceful and still. She stood for a moment poised on the threshold and just listened to that silence, letting it embrace her and welcome her inside.

A table stood at the bottom of the stairway that led upstairs, and there she found the things Libby had arranged for her use. There was an envelope with enough money to cover her starting expenses, and an ATM card with a note that indicated it could be used either at a machine or as a credit card. A ring of keys and a small mobile phone were lying atop the local phone directory.

Flora took up the mobile and punched in the international

exchange, dialing the number for Castle Wrath. She had promised Libby she would call when she arrived and had been surprised when there was no answer when she'd called earlier. She was even more surprised when she didn't receive a response now. She tried Graeme's office phone, thinking perhaps he was working and hadn't heard the house line ringing. But his answering machine responded, urging her to leave a message after the tone.

Which she did.

"Hullo, Graeme. 'Tis Flora. I tried the house line, but no one answered. I've arrived at the house in the States. There was a bit of a mix-up with the key, but it's all been sorted." She hesitated, thinking of Libby and the baby. "I hope all is well there. I'll try back in a bit, but if you should get this message, please ring me on the mobile. The number is . . ." She looked at the phone. "To be honest, I don't know what the number is. Hopefully Libby has it. Ta for now."

She folded the phone to end the call.

Flora glanced at her watch. Though she'd left London late morning UK time, with the six-hour flight and five-hour time difference, it was only midafternoon now that she was in the States. But back in Wrath Village, the kids would already have come home from school would be sitting around the kitchen table completing their homework as they awaited their supper.

She flipped open the mobile again and dialed the number to her cottage. But she received no answer there, either. Now something really began to feel wrong. She told herself not to panic, fighting back the niggling fear that something might have happened to one of the children.

Her last resort was the constable's line.

Flora closed her eyes when she heard her brother's voice respond on the second ring.

"PC Angus MacLeith."

"Angus, 'tis Flora."

"Och, the international cat burglar herself, aye?"

His teasing tone set her fears immediately at ease. If something was wrong with Libby, or with one of the children, his manner wouldn't be so easy.

They spent the first few minutes talking about the children, Flora checking that all had gone well her first day away from them and Angus reassuring her that it had. Then Angus explained that the reason she hadn't gotten a response when she phoned the castle looking for Libby and Graeme was because they'd gone to Inverness for an appointment at her obstetrician's office.

"Where are the kids now?" she asked.

"I sent them o'er to Widow MacNamara's for a spell whilst I went out on a call to the MacNeil croft. Soon as I finish up this paperwork, I'll be heading off to pick them up."

"You'll have them ring me as soon as you get them home, aye? I'm going to have a bath first, to wash away this travel dust and unwind a bit, so give me till half eight afore you ring. No, on second thought, I'll ring you. I haven't quite figured out what the number is for this mobile yet."

"Aye. Oh, and hey, Flor? Can you stand a bit of advice from your big brother?"

"A' yea . . ." she said, almost dreading the answer. "What's that?"

"I meant what I said t' you afore you left. I know you think you need only the kids to be happy, but I'd hate t' see you sentence yourself to the life of 'what was' out of some misguided sense of loyalty to Seamus's memory. He winna have wanted that for you and you know that."

She closed her eyes, knowing if she didn't she'd probably start to cry. "Angus, I'm fine. Really."

"Nae, you're not. You've fallen into a 'condition' of sorts. It's as if you're so determined to be the mum, the da, and everything else you can be to these kids, that you've forgotten what it is to be anything else."

"What is it you're trying to say?"

"These next two weeks are an opportunity for you, no' to be 'the Mum,' but to shed the widow's weeds and see what it feels like to live again. What I'm saying is afore I come there with the kids, sometime in the next two weeks, I want you to have yourself a right good shag."

Flora mearly dropped the phone. "Angus MacLeith!"

"I don't care how, when, or with whom. I don't care if it's just a one-night stand, or if you find someone to have a fortnight fling with. Just make sure it's safe and make sure you enjoy it, because if you waste this on some bumbling blunkart, I'll ne'er forgive you. You're a young bonnie lass. Surely you can find at least one jock willing to do the deed."

An image of Gavin Matheson flitted through Flora's thoughts but she quickly pushed it away, even shaking her head to be sure it vanished completely. Was Angus completely out of his mind?

She even told him this. "It's daft y' are!"

"Nae. I'm a brother who doesn't want to see his sister forget what it is to live."

"I could be saying the same thing about you, y' know. It's not like you're out there looking for the lassies either."

"That you know of."

"I beg your—When? Who? Or for that matter *where*, considering that you live with me?"

"I'm not a man to kiss and tell, but suffice it to say I manage to find time and opportunity to see to the more basic human needs on occasion."

Flora's mind began to race through a list of the available women in the village. "It's Jennie Wheeler, aye?"

"Flora . . . I'm no' going to tell you."

"Katie MacNeill?"

"Flora Catriona MacCallum! 'Tis *your* love life that needs tending to. Not mine. I know you always thought Seamus would be the only one, and 'tis a noble thing, would have been a noble thing had fate not seen fit to take your man far, far earlier than it should have. But that's the way it worked out, and now you must stop living in the past and start thinking about the future. *Your* future. I talked to Libby and Graeme and we all agree. So get yourself prettied up and go down to the pub. Libby suggested you might start at the local café, some place called Common Grounds. All the local lads apparently hang out there. Oh, and Janet MacNeish says to wear your hair up. Shows off your neck, it does."

"Good God. What'd you do? Call a meeting at the village hall to see what could be done about Flora MacCallum's terminal celibacy?"

"Of course not, Flora. But Libby and Graeme, and me especially, we care about you. I'm serious now. You canna go through the rest of your life forbidding yourself from the intimacy, the release, of a physical relationship. It'll wither you inside. I'm no' saying you have to get married or anything. But its no' only lads who benefit from a little sowing of the auld oats. Just think about what I've said. Promise me you'll do that much, aye?"

"Fine."

She would have told him anything to have him drop this incredibly embarrassing topic of conversation. What was her life coming to when her brother of all people was giving her sex advice?

After she bade Angus good-bye, reminding him she'd ring back at eight thirty so she could talk to the kids, Flora took up her bag and set out for the nearest bathtub she could find.

Nearly two hours later, bathed, lotioned, and changed into her dressing gown, Flora felt like a new woman.

Outside, the sun was just beginning to set, shining through the lace-draped windows and casting everything around her in a soft, comforting glow. Before she got in the bath, she'd opened the windows and had let the gentle rhythm of the sea set her frazzled nerves at ease. Afterward she put the kettle on for tea, measured out the leaves, and left the pot to steep. Then, hairbrush in hand, she walked slowly from room to room, exploring the rest of the house as she combed through the tangles in her damp, curly hair.

It was indeed a lovely old place, the sort that felt like home the very moment you stepped through the door. Gleaming oak-paneled walls reflected the sunlight of the waning day, and the scent of the gardens outside drifted in through the open windows. It would have been a beautiful house to grow up in, and Flora could just picture Libby coming of age there, taking piano lessons on the rosewood upright that stood in the corner of the front parlor, dangling her five-year-old feet from the bench as she practiced her scales.

Libby had told Flora that the origins of the house were a bit sketchy. The first recorded owner was an ancestor of her stepfather's who had been a shipbuilder from England. There was mention in town records of another house on the site that dated back far earlier. Since the Hutchinsons had lived there, however, successive generations had altered or added to the place, each making their own mark. The most recent renovation had come around the time of the Civil

War—lifting the low ceilings, adding Victorian crown moldings, arched windows, even a turret.

Libby's mother, Matilde, had given the house its name in the Scottish tradition. She changed it from "the old Hutchinson place" to the more romantic "Thar Muir"—pronounced "Har Moor," which was Gaelic for "across the sea." Flora rather liked the touch.

On the ground floor, Flora strolled over honey-colored hardwood floors that stretched to a gleaming polished staircase. It had heavy balusters worn smooth over the generations and stairs that split midway to the upper floors, angling both right and left beneath a brilliant arched stained-glass window that peered down from the first landing. The parlor was the smaller of the front two reception rooms, the sort of place where Libby's mother would have sat to take tea with her friends from the local garden club. It was papered in a cheery splash of cabbage roses, and as she peeked in the doorway, Flora envisioned a quiet retreat for their future guests in the evenings, with a fire burning in the fireplace during cold weather and a soft breeze through the tall windows on balmy summer nights. There were shelves of old books for getting lost in, a games table for cards or other amusements, or for those inclined, there could always be music had from the piano.

The second of the two front rooms was a more formal living room, with tall sashed windows and a door that led to the back section of the house's wraparound porch. Flora saw this as more of a reception room, where guests could be greeted with tea and scones, where they would find literature about the local area, and could acclimate themselves to their surroundings upon their arrival.

Moving toward the back of the house, Flora returned to the kitchen, painted a bright yellow and located beside a pass-through door that led to the large dining room. Flora knew from having helped Libby with the preliminary planning for the B and B that this room had been enlarged from the former cozy dining room to accommodate the mealtime needs of a dozen or more guests. Small café-sized tables and chairs were scattered about the place, but Flora's immediate reaction to it was not very agreeable. In fact, it was all wrong. It gave the room more the look of a restaurant than a dining room, and she decided she would move the café tables out onto the porch where they would better serve for games of checkers or taking afternoon coffee. A large, long, preferably antique table, with mismatched chairs, would be more the thing, intimate and homey. Guests could gather together there for breakfast each morning and it would provide a better opportunity for mingling and getting to know one another.

Back in the kitchen, new stainless-steel appliances had replaced the old ones for functionality purposes, but even with this modern addition, the quaint, country feel of the place remained. Rows of dainty teacups lined the far wall and tea tins were stacked haphazardly atop the cabinets. Flora could just imagine Libby standing at the center butcher block, cutting out cookie shapes with her mother each Christmas while the winter sun struggled to shine through the windows that faced onto the back garden.

Off the kitchen, at the back of the house, a new addition had been built to provide living space for the innkeeper's family. It was nearly large enough to be considered a house on its own. There were three rooms that could be used as bedrooms or living space as needed, and a large airy bathroom with both shower and tub, which Flora had availed herself of earlier.

Upstairs, there were six guestrooms on two floors, and

though most rooms had already had their own hearth, each of them had been outfitted with its own private bath as well. The renovation had taken up most of the past year and had been done with the strictest eye for period detail. All the loos were equipped with antique pull chains and the tubs were claw footed. The modern conveniences of heated towel bars and soft recessed lighting had been added, disguised as best as possible so as not to intrude on the illusion of timelessness. Televisions were hidden inside antique armoires, and telephones and broadband connections were disguised by reproduction desk boxes. Each guestroom had a cabinet, which housed a small refrigerator, stemware, dishes and cutlery for in-room dining. Music could be had by stereo systems built into the wall. Libby's main objective was to have the guests of Thar Muir feel as if they had stepped back in time to a more gracious era, back before the buzz and flurry and noise of the twenty-first century.

In addition to the main house, there were two outbuildings, formerly the original carriage house and stable block. They both had been renovated into larger, more private suites; one suitable for families, complete with a laddered loft, and the second was more secluded with a four-poster bed, stone fireplace, and an oversized bathtub for honeymooning couples.

The furnishings and fittings of the rooms had been filled to Libby's specifications, and every possible guest need had been anticipated. Still Flora couldn't help but notice that there was something missing. Where were those little touches that would make each room unique and memorable to the guests? What would have their visitors requesting their favorite rooms time and time again?

During the plane ride over, Flora had the idea to individualize the rooms, giving each a specific theme and then decorating it to fit that theme instead of simply differentiating them all by a number on the door. In Scotland, other bed-and-breakfasts often did this by color, or sometimes by different clan names. Since this house was in the States, but had a Scottish name and connection, Flora had thought to designate the rooms by things such as the Heather Room, the Thistle Room, the Tartan Suite. She would even have little placards made up for each bearing the name in both English and Gaelic, to make it more unique.

Plans were practically buzzing through her head. Colors, textures, scents. But could she really do everything she hoped to achieve in the three weeks she had before their first guests were scheduled to arrive?

One thing was certain, she thought as she remembered her conversation with Angus earlier. She was going to be far too busy getting the house ready to go off looking for someone to relieve her of her "condition."

Chapter Four

It was three o'clock in the morning and Gavin sat at the piano—a Steinway that was grand, black, and glossy. Papers lay scattered around him, some scribbled with pencil marks to show the notes, others crushed and tossed to the floor. Those on the floor looked to outnumber those on the piano six to one.

He didn't work on a computer, or, God forbid, over the Internet with faceless names for collaborators as some of his colleagues did. His was what some might call an old-fashioned way of composing, for he did it as Beethoven and Mozart had, note by note, bar by bar, marking, erasing, scribbling, and sometimes cursing out loud. He crossed out more than he kept, but it was what worked for him, what had worked for him throughout his entire songwriting career.

He'd been at it since he'd gotten back from the police station, barely stopping long enough to wolf down the ham-and-cheese sandwich and handful of chips he'd slapped together for his supper. And for all his effort, he had one bar of music, just one short combination of notes written on a page.

But it was a start.

Like the writer who began with a word, building to a sentence, then a page, and eventually a chapter, Gavin had begun with the notes.

B . . . E . . . G . . . F

Beauty.

Elegance.

Grace.

Fire.

It was all he could remember of that unusual music that had drifted into his head at the café earlier that day.

When *she* had come in.

Flora MacCallum.

Beauty.

Elegance.

Grace.

Fire.

He'd even made her name the working title of the composition, scribbling it across the top of the page.

Since then, Gavin had spent hours trying to re-create the unusual music he'd heard. He'd sat at the piano, thinking of her, remembering the way she'd breezed into the café, how she'd dropped her skirt up on that trellis, the fear she'd tried so hard to hide when she'd been sitting in that police station.

B . . . E . . . G . . . F

He'd played it over and over, trying countless combinations of notes to follow.

But nothing he'd come up with had been right.

He could remember every detail about her, from the scattering of freckles that sprinkled her nose to the way she had chewed her lip while sitting so nervously at the station. He knew just from the short time he'd known her that she preferred tea to coffee and tied her shoes by knotting them twice. Yet no matter how he tried, he couldn't seem to find the music that should come after those first lonely four notes.

Damn.

He should take a break, in fact probably should've taken one hours earlier, but it had been so long since he'd felt it, the buzz of his creativity, that he was reluctant to leave the piano in case it should leave him once again. Frustrated, at the same time he was filled with promise. Even though he had just those four obscure notes to show for his efforts, it was more work than he'd done in the past two years.

Downing the last of his iced tea, he took up his keys and headed for the door. Maybe a walk in the pre-dawn air would help clear the muddle from his head.

Outside, the moon was full and hanging low, ringed by clouds. Gavin followed the sea stairs down from the house's high deck while a soft breeze swept in off the water, rustling the tall grasses lining the pathway that meandered along the rocky line of the shore. It was a well-worn trail, used for generations by those who owned houses along that particular stretch of New England coastline—for walking dogs, or just plain walking. Along the way there were tidal pools bobbing with the small colorful buoys that marked the lying spots of the locals' lobster pots and huge granite boulders that tumbled down to the water's edge where gulls and other bird life perched. Every so often, the path would pass a tiny stretch of sandy beach where locals could be found when the tide was low, digging for the clams that were unique to this part of the coast.

No one paid any mind to property lines; it was an unwritten courtesy, that pathway, so long as no one abused it. Gavin usually watched the comings and goings of his neighbors from his favorite lounge chair on the deck. When they noticed him, they always waved. Nothing too animated, just a gesture of acknowledgment, a halfhearted lift of the hand, which he always returned. He had no idea who they were, and they had no way of knowing who he was, but they always waved. And he always waved back.

At this hour of the morning, however, before the sun had risen, before the day had dawned, Gavin walked the pathway alone.

The weather was warm enough, even with the breeze that blew in off the water, for the jeans and loose shirt he wore. He'd stuffed his bare feet into a pair of leather loafers that were cracked from wear and saltwater but so soft they fit like a second skin. In another two hours, the sun would rise over the same ocean that now looked black, bottomless, and asleep. Now, the waves lapped at the shore like an old man snoring while the whippoorwill gave its distinctive call from the shelter of the trees that grew up to the very edge of the sea.

Out in the bay there lay the string of islands known as the Witch's Cauldron, looming in the hazy glow of a single distant lighthouse. The beacon stood on Hathaway Island, the largest of the four isles, and had been built in the late 1700s, when it was fueled by oil and had been tended to by a keeper who lived in the small stone house at its base. But before that, the islands had had a much darker history, one that stretched back over three hundred years, when a hysteria had swept across this part of New England and culminated in what would become a true witch hunt.

Accusations of witchcraft had cropped up from time to time almost from the very day the Puritans had arrived to settle the colony on Massachusetts Bay. In the waning years of the seventeenth century, however, the fears and suspicions and fascination with that which couldn't be explained came to a boiling point. Accusations were made. Trials were conducted and many were condemned to die. Though the trials are forever linked with the town of Salem some fifteen miles to the southeast, Ipswich Town and its smaller sister village of Ipswich-by-the-Sea had also played its part in those long-ago events.

A good many of the accused had lived on the farms and homesteads that dotted the road joining Salem to Ipswich. The prison in Ipswich had even welcomed some of the accused when Salem no longer had sufficient room to hold them. One such person who had found herself accused was a young woman from the tiny hamlet of Ipswich-by-the-Sea named Rachael Hathaway.

On a rainy afternoon not long after his arrival in the village, Gavin had ducked into the local bookshop to wait out the weather. While browsing the neat shelves of local-interest literature, he'd mentioned to the bookseller, Mrs. Evanson, that he was intrigued by the islands he'd spotted outside the summerhouse's bay window. She had recommended a book written by one of the local residents that told the story of Rachael Hathaway and how the islands had come to be named for her.

Rachael Hathaway was born sometime around 1670 and had been at various times, and by various individuals, branded a "spinster," a "widow," and even a "shameless wanton." It was rumored she had murdered her first husband when they'd had a particularly violent row, and that afterward she'd chopped him into tiny bits, scattering his remains over various parts of their farm. Many had retold this tale over the fire at the local tavern, yet no one could verify with any accuracy at all the actual existence of her husband. No one could recall his name, or confirm they ever actually met him. Still the rumor persisted.

Fanning the flames of these allegations had been the

"widow" Hathaway herself. Rachael hadn't dressed like other good Puritan women, choosing instead to wear brightly colored bodices of red and violet satin with laces and ribbon ties made more for decoration than utility. Her stockings had been red striped instead of proper white, and her favorite head covering hadn't been the prim linen skullcap worn by so many Puritan women in early American artwork. No, indeed. Rachael was always seen sporting a tall, wide-brimmed hat with a peacock feather tucked smartly in its band. Some even said that the eye of that feather was evil, that it would wink misfortune at anyone who happened to cross Rachael's path.

When the witchcraft fever took flame that summer in nearby Salem, Rachael's neighbors were more than eager to make their accusations against her known. Everything from crop failure to an infant's cleft lip was blamed on poor Rachael, and before long she found herself locked away in a sturdy Ipswich prison to await her day before the tribunal. The problem was, however, that no cell seemed capable of holding her. Each time they locked her up, she somehow vanished within two days' time, returning to her farm on the outskirts of the village to mind her own business, only to be brought back and locked up again. Finally, some forward-thinking village elder came up with the idea to incarcerate her on the island in the middle of Ipswich Bay, where she could never again harm the good, God-fearing people of Ipswich-by-the-Sea.

They rowed Rachael, in chains, out to the big island which according to maritime records from that time was the only island in the bay. It was claimed by the next day that three sister islands had suddenly appeared, pushing their rocky faces out of the sea—only further evidence of Rachael Hathaway's claimed witchcraft. But they weren't a cruel lot, the good people of the fledgling village. She was given a cow, a chicken, and a goat with which to sustain herself while she awaited her day in court. That day, however, never seemed to come, and soon the village folk forgot all about their resident witch.

"Out of sight, out of mind," or so the saying goes. Occasionally some calamity would befall the little village—flood, sickness, the fire that broke out in the church steeple—and the locals would simply shake their heads, casting their eyes to the sea and that distant hazy isle, making them all the more determined to keep the "Ipswitch" as far from them as possible.

Because of the shifting sands and rolling tides that collided and churned in the tiny bay, shipwrecks were commonplace, but after that time, any who were lost were said to have been caught in "Rachael Hathaway's cauldron." Hence the group of isles became known, changing over time to the Witch's Cauldron, and maps, even into the current day, marked them so. Though none of the townsfolk encountered Rachael again, occasionally someone would swear they'd seen her in a vision, walking through their gardens or lurking in their cowsheds, her striped stockings and tall, befeathered hat distinguishing her for all time.

Some sixty or seventy years later, after the witch frenzy had quieted down and Rachael Hathaway was long since thought dead, the village elders decided it was time to build a lighthouse to protect the ships coming into their tiny harbor. And what better place could there be than that isle? But who dared go out there to see what had become of Rachael Hathaway? They drew lots and the townsfolk formed a team of surveyors. Armed with rifles and pistols (because there was some lingering fear of what they might find), they sailed out to the forsaken island.

It was a damp, foggy morning when they made their landing on the isle's northern shore. None strayed too far from the group and more than one of the men nearly jumped out of his skin at any sudden, unexpected bird cry. After checking the area closest to the shore, they moved farther inland and were shocked to discover a modest cottage made of thatch and stone, stones far too heavy for a mere woman to have carried. Rachael Hathaway, they decided, must have used her witchcraft to build the cozy cottage. Even more surprising, however, was what they found inside.

They saw finely crafted furnishings, a mahogany table, and a bed draped in what had once been fine red velvet, now weathered with age and exposure to the elements beneath the by-then-collapsed roof. There were pewter dishes and cups, remnants of etched crystal wine goblets, and even a silver chocolate pot. Trunks revealed swaths of silk and carved boxes filled with exotic spices. They even found a cloak trimmed with ermine fur.

What they didn't find, however, was any evidence of Rachael Hathaway, dead or alive.

The story changed after that. Many claimed that the finery they'd found in that cottage could only have been the spoils of Rachael's pirate lover, whose crew had built her that cottage and who eventually had taken her away from her island prison. Of course no one could ever say they had actually seen a ship, pirate or otherwise, anchored anywhere near the isle. Yet some still believed she had become a pirate queen and had ended her days sailing the seas beneath the Jolly Roger with a cutlass at one side and her pirate lover at the other.

Those who'd claimed to have seen her as an apparition now swore that it had been Rachael Hathaway herself who had been skulking about in the shadows, come back to curse those who were responsible for her exile. It was a belief that became so commonplace, handed down generation to generation, that she had eventually become the resident Ipswich-by-the-Sea "spook." When an object fell from a shelf unexpectedly, or if a lightbulb suddenly flickered, Rachael Hathaway simply had to be responsible. At Halloween, Rachael Hathaway costumes were always the most popular for trick or treating. Parents still warned children that if they didn't behave, Rachael Hathaway would come for them.

After reading that book, Gavin had spent many a night sitting out in his lounge chair on the deck, peering at that cluster of islands through the telescope. What, he wondered, had really become of Rachael Hathaway? Had she truly been a witch, or just a poor unfortunate victim of the times in which she was born? Had she lived in modern times, her behavior would have been considered nothing more than notorious. In fact, it probably would have landed her a career as an actress or a pop star.

Oftentimes, he wondered what she must have looked like, this free spirit of a girl who had dared to defy Puritanical conventions. The only images of her were paintings created centuries later, which merely gave the artist's estimation of what she could have looked like. Some had painted her as fair-haired, others with wild, twisting locks as black as night. But Gavin had always imagined her standing bold and self-confident, with flaming hair tumbling from beneath that reckless tall hat, not at all unlike a certain young woman he'd found danglilng from a trellis.

Gavin stopped walking, only to find himself standing on the stretch of beach that lay beneath the blue sea captain's house.

He turned and peered up at it, watching as it loomed in

the shadow of the wakening day, and thought of the woman who lay sleeping inside.

For as long as he lived, Gavin doubted he would ever forget the sight of her perched up on that trellis with her skirt snagged on a nail, cursing as colorfully as any longshoreman. Nor would he forget the way she'd let that skirt fall and the vision of her long, white, seemingly endless legs.

Any comparison to a longshoreman had ended right there.

It had been a long, long time since Gavin had felt even the slightest stir of interest in a woman. Miranda had certainly done a number on him during the last year of their marriage and their subsequent separation. And then just when he was preparing to move on with his life, only days away from the final declaration of their divorce, she had made that fateful phone call to him from the airport, turning any life he'd had left completely upside down.

In fact, he'd begun to consider himself a candidate for monkhood. Flora MacCallum, however, had definitely sparked something in him.

Gavin started to turn, to head back to the beach house, where he planned to spend the better part of the morning trying to squeeze a few more notes onto the page, when he noticed something in the shadows, a light flickering faintly ahead of him.

He headed toward it.

As he drew nearer, Gavin saw that it was a lamp, the glass-and-kerosene sort that people usually kept more for decoration than anything else. But this lamp was just sitting there, alone in the sand, its flame dancing slowly in time to the soft rushing sound of the tide. Some floral cloth lay bunched on the ground beside it. When Gavin picked it up, he saw that it looked quite a bit like a woman's robe.

The wind lifted, sweeping along the shore, swirling around him, nearly putting the flickering lantern light out. Gavin lifted his head and looked toward the water. He couldn't see anything except the blackness of the morning, but somehow, he knew something was there.

He heard an echo of music, the same music he had heard in the café.

And then he saw her, her dark red hair now wet and plastered to her skin . . .

Her *naked* skin.

Sweet Mother Mary.

In the next moment he was sucking in and holding his breath as he watched her emerge from the shadowed surf.

The water glistened on her hair in the lantern light as it trickled down between her breasts—full breasts with nipples taut from the chilled morning air. Her waist was small, flaring to shapely hips, so incredibly feminine above those endlessly long white legs he'd appreciated earlier.

Gavin felt his his throat tighten, and then he felt a jolt that shot straight to his groin.

Monkhood be damned.

Flora froze when she noticed him, standing there holding her robe in the lantern light. Her hands rose instinctively to cover her breasts.

"What are you—?"

She stepped back, away from the glow of the lamp and into the shelter of the shadows. "May I have my dressing gown? Please?"

Gavin didn't know what to say, which was probably a good thing since he doubted his mouth could even form a word. He'd seen women naked before, countless times, but there was something about this time, and this woman, that simply left him stunned. He looked down at his feet as he held the robe out to her and waited while she wrapped it around her naked self.

"I was led to believe this was a private beach," he heard her say in the darkness.

Gavin blinked, cleared his throat, and then finally found his voice. "It is. But most of the residents sort of borrow each other's shore for walking. There's a pathway"—he pointed behind him—"just up there."

"I see," she said.

When she came back into the light, she had the robe belted around her waist, the floral silk wrapped tightly, covering her nearly to her chin. Her mouth was pressed in a frown. "I'll have to remember that if I'm ever of a mind for taking a morning swim again."

"Well, most of the people around here take their walks in the daylight." He glanced at her. "I, uh . . . had some trouble sleeping. You, too?"

She nodded. "I guess I'm not quite acclimated to the time here."

"Give it another day, maybe two."

There followed a pause, the two of them just standing there face-to-face, surrounded by the soft sound of the waves hitting the shore. He noticed her shiver slightly against the breeze, and knew an urge to cover her with his arms to warm her. He even took a step toward her, but she shifted away, as if sensing his thoughts.

"Well, then," she finally said. "I think I'll go and have some tea and see about getting a few more hours of sleep. Good-bye again, Mr. Matheson."

She took up the lantern to leave.

"Gavin."

"Excuse me?"

"You can call me Gavin."

She just looked at him, neither agreeing nor disagreeing, he noticed. Then she turned and Gavin watched her walk away, toward the house on the hill, vanishing into the twilight.

He wondered if she realized that the glow of the lamp she was carrying revealed a perfect silhouette of her beneath the silk of that robe.

Flora's heart was pounding. She had to force herself not to give in to the almost overpowering urge to run like a loon for the house. Even though she'd kept herself awake the night before until she absolutely couldn't keep her eyes from closing, she had fallen asleep right after she'd spoken with the kids, still sitting in the armchair in the front parlor, which meant the six or seven hours of sleep she was accustomed to left her awake well before the dawn.

Back home in Scotland, she always took a morning swim in the sea during the summer months. Some called her crazy, because it was a bracing sea, but it was something her mother had done, and her mother before her, a tradition purported to keep a woman in good health and her skin young and supple. Flora didn't know if this was true, but she'd swum with her mum ever since she was a child. The cold of it no longer bothered her. And now that her mum was gone, she did so with her own daughter Annie, partly for the tradition, but mostly because she found it cleared her head for the day, it brought her in touch with nature, and also because it gave her that special time alone with her only daughter as they splashed and danced in the waves, shivering from the cold, raising their arms above their heads and kicking at the tide.

So in that way, Flora supposed, it did indeed keep her young.

She'd woken early, the hour not quite two though nearly seven back home. As she sat alone in that chair, in that big empty stranger of a house, Flora had thought of her morning ritual with her daughter. She tried not to let it bother her that she had missed it that morning for the first time since Annie was an infant, back when Flora had taken her squirmy baby body up in her arms and danced with her in the surf, holding her tight to her breasts, skin to skin, mother to daughter. She was missing her kids and the longing for them had twisted her heart until tears were dampening her cheek. So, unable to sleep, she'd risen intent on keeping to that ritual despite the fact that thousands of miles stretched between them.

It was only an ocean, she told herself. Nothing more than a big, vast loch. Annie was on one side, and she was on the other. If she closed her eyes and thought about it, Flora could even visualize herself skipping a stone across the water's surface, skipping it all the way to Scotland. Annie would catch it in her little hands on the other side, jumping up and down and calling to her, "I caught it, Mummy. I caught it!"

As she dove into the water, sucking in her breath at the initial chill of it, Flora felt her skin tingle and her blood prickle. She was used to the cold, for the waters of the North Sea were a chilly lot, and a lifetime of swimming in it had long dulled the shock. She'd floated on her back, kicking her legs slowly as she felt the pull and ebb of the tide rock her as gently as a mother's arms. She imagined herself a mermaid visiting a faraway land. She pictured Annie doing the same, just as Flora had taught her. It had helped to ease the tension that was pinching at the back of her neck, that had throbbed just above her brow all that day before.

She'd expected nothing more than a simple, quick swim

to start what would be the first full day of her Amerian adventure. What she hadn't expected was to come out of the water to find Gavin Matheson standing on the shore, holding her dressing gown.

And staring at her in a way she'd never been stared at before.

Even now, as Flora nearly tripped over her feet in her haste to get back inside the house, she forced herself not to look back to see if he was still there, still watching her like that. Her breasts tingled beneath the thin covering of her robe, but it had nothing to do with the chill of the air on her wet skin.

It had everything to do with the heat of that man's stare.

In all the years she had been married, and despite having had a healthy physical relationship with her husband, Flora couldn't remember Seamus ever having looked at her with quite that much intensity.

Perhaps it was because Seamus had always known he would have Flora for his wife and that she would always be there to greet him whenever he came home after his weeks of working out to sea. The everydayness of life—the housework, the kids—meant Seamus had seen her at her very worst, be it covered in baby vomit when Robbie, at age six months, had caught a particularly violent flu, or up to her elbows in soot and ash when she took on the cleaning of the hearth. He'd seen her doubled over the loo with morning sickness and had watched her give birth not once but twice. While those times had only made the bond between them stronger, it had also taken away most of the mystery between them, and with it, admittedly, some of the excitement and the passion.

But that was marriage, wasn't it? What one lost in romance and spontaneity, one gained in the security, the trust, the deeper love of years spent building a life with each other.

So the sight of another man's eyes fixed so intently on her had certainly overwhelmed her.

Reaching the porch, Flora wrenched the door open and closed it tightly behind her. She sagged against it as she tried to calm her rapid pulse.

Damn bloody Angus!

Ever since his phone call the day before, when he had told her to . . .

Do that thing he'd told her to do . . .

She had found herself thinking about it. Almost constantly. Not that she was considering doing what he'd suggested, but still she couldn't help wondering what it would be like just once in her life to be so utterly reckless.

And what was worse was that she couldn't seem to avoid imagining what it would be like just once in her life to be so utterly reckless—

With Gavin Matheson.

Chapter Five

The next morning dawned bleak beneath a canopy of clouds that clung stubbornly to the whole of the North Shore. Rain threatened, and if the weather report Flora heard on the car radio was to be believed, was in fact likely. But she had far too much to do, and a little rain certainly wasn't about to stop her.

Flora had spent the better part of that morning compiling a list of the items she needed most, ordering them according to importance before she placed a call to Libby and Graeme to bring them up to speed on the situation with the house. They had both encouraged her idea of individualizing the guest rooms, and had even suggested she hire out for help with the cleaning and any necessary maintenance. Flora assured them she would keep in touch with them every step along the way.

Now, Flora circled the rented SUV in front of a massive red barn painted across one side in screaming white letters that read:

2ND CHANCE SHOP!

From the outside, it looked as if the building had just burst, spewing forth its contents from the wide mouth of its huge double doors into the parking area, over the tidy lawn, and all across the surrounding landscape. There were old wooden barrels in differing sizes stacked haphazardly against one wall. A bathtub planted with tulips docked alongside a fully pitched army tent. There were benches, baskets, buoys, and bottles. Weathered nautical ropes slung along one wall, and a regiment of old garden tools—rakes, shovels, and hoes among them—stood guard along the length of another wall.

The waitress at the coffee shop had recommended this place to Flora for finding furniture and any other second-hand sort of knickknacks. Jules had told Flora that the shop managed most of the estate sales in the area and that they were also one of a vast network of antique and secondhand shops. If she didn't see what she was looking for there, they could almost assuredly find it somewhere.

Flora's first priority was the dining table. After poking about in the chaos of the 2nd Chance Shop's makeshift "stalls," filled with every sort of collectible and knickknack imaginable, she climbed a set of rickety stairs to the barn's second floor, where she found a charming section called the "Hey! Loft." And there she found exactly what she was looking for.

It was a long trestle-style refectory table with a lovely warm, mellow color and a fine aged patina that could easily seat twelve. The tag attached to it read merely "Early Dining Table" but in looking closely at the joinings and the style of the turned legs, Flora guessed it was made of cherry, and dated back to the nineteenth century, if not earlier. It was covered in dust and had a few dings and scratches, but was in otherwise unspoiled condition. At the price they were asking, it was a true steal. The shop owner told Flora the table had been there for some time, unnoticed no doubt by most behind all the other pieces around it, and likely just too big for the average antique shopper. Flora quickly negotiated a price with him, then asked the shop owner to put her name on it.

Next, she had to find enough chairs to go around the table, and the shop had an entire floor of them to sort through. Flora chose a mixed assortment of Windsors, ladder-backs, and high-backs—some in cherry, some in mahogany—sixteen in all; twelve for placing around the table and four to keep against the walls for spares. Together, the table and chairs would be a lovely compliment to Matilde Hutchinson's mahogany sideboard and china hutch, much more in keeping with their theme of stepping back in time than the more modern café style tables there already.

With that task completed, and far more quickly than she'd expected, Flora was free to spend the rest of the day poking about at leisure in search of paintings and engravings to decorate the walls, candlesticks, decorative glassware and porcelain, and any other odd bits she might find.

And find she did.

She put together a set of early porcelain dishes for displaying on the wall by the staircase and found an old brass Victorian letterbox to hang near the front door for the guests' outgoing postcards. *Postcards,* she remembered, and quickly scribbled a reminder in her notebook. Libby had suggested Flora call a local photographer to have a few shots taken of the house for printing on postcards both for the guests to use and also for advertising purposes. Perhaps Jules—who seemed to know everyone in the town—could recommend someone for the job.

Flora gathered up old apothecary bottles and jars for arranging on windowsills, china vases for displaying fresh flowers, and ornate coat hooks for hanging near doors. She bought two dozen or more different teapots for serving morning and afternoon tea, and even found an assortment of old chamber pots that she thought would be a clever way to display rolled-up bath towels next to the bathtubs. *Bath towels,* she scribbled next in her notebook, remembering that she still needed to order them, preferably white and thick.

. As she turned to leave the shop, Flora spotted one last item, one that she couldn't resist adding to her already burgeoning pile of purchases. Libby had restored her mother's writing desk to use as the reception desk for greeting guests, and had outfitted the room with a computer, high-speed Internet, everything they could possibly need, except . . .

There, sitting on a shelf, nearly lost among the other items for sale, was a shiny brass hotel desk bell.

Flora stowed the smaller purchases in the back of the SUV, then made arrangements with the shop owner for the table and chairs to be delivered to the house the next afternoon. She knew she would return to the shop again as she thought of other things she would need before greeting their first guests.

By the time she started back for the house, it was approaching late afternoon. But instead of cutting straight back to town by way of the faster state route, she took a quieter road that wound its way along the coast, drinking in the views and breathing in the salty sea air through the open car window. She pulled over at a particularly picturesque spot and placed a quick call to the kids to check in with them about their day. They bombarded her with an endless list of questions about America, about Massachusetts, and about the house they would call home during the coming months. Before she hung up, Flora told Annie about her early-morning swim and made a date to meet her "across the pond" the following morning.

Once back in town, Flora stopped by the café to thank

Jules for having recommended the shop to her. She took home a freshly baked baguette and a small crock of Mrs. Capone's "chowdah" for her supper. She was on her way back to the car when she spotted a bookshop across the way, and decided to stop in for a quick poke about the shelves.

It wasn't often that Flora could afford the luxury of losing herself in a bookshop without kids tugging at her skirts, complaining that they were too "tired" or too "bored." Back before her days were filled with dirty nappies and sticky oatmeal fingers, Flora had been quite the bookworm, with a mind keen for knowledge beyond the primary education she had received in the village's small school. History, world cultures, and her own native Gaelic tongue were all subjects she had absorbed like a sponge, always thirsty for more. So what began as a quick peek inside the bookshop turned in to a two-hour browse that ended with her purchasing a stack of titles of local interest, both new and used, to familiarize herself with her surroundings and also to keep on the shelves in the front parlor for her guests' reading pleasure.

She would read the books—every one of them, she told herself—when she was alone at night, keeping her thoughts focused on sensible things. She reasoned that if she filled every waking moment with some preoccupation, it would prevent her mind from wandering to anything even remotely connected to Angus and his ridiculous suggestions.

As she pulled the SUV up the drive, she couldn't wait to start hanging pictures and finding places for all her purchases, so she headed off to fetch a hammer and nails from the toolshed while she still had the benefit of daylight, putting the crock of soup on the kitchen counter. As she worked—dusting, polishing, holding up paintings to see which would look best in each spot—Flora began to hum. Very soon, that humming turned to singing.

Flora was so lost in her decorating, she didn't notice the BMW convertible pull up the drive outside and roll to a stop just behind the SUV. Nor did she notice Gavin Matheson getting out of his car, wine bottle in hand.

Gavin had spent the better part of the day behind his keyboard, working on the new composition. Perhaps it had been their "meeting" on the beach that morning—God knows seeing her come out of the water as she had, naked, dripping and beautiful, had certainly been a sight to inspire—but he had managed to write two more bars of music that day.

It felt damn good.

Giving himself a well-deserved break, he'd gone out for a drive. He stopped at the local wine shop, bought a bottle of his favorite Australian sauvignon blanc, and soon had found himself heading over to the blue captain's house by the sea.

He was actually whistling as he started for the front porch steps. It was the last song he had heard on the radio, a catchy tune by the latest pop star reality show winner. He hesitated when he heard another kind of music coming from inside the house. He stopped, stood in the drive, and just let the sound wrap itself around him.

Throughout his career, Gavin had heard more singing voices than he could possibly count. Some were genuinely good; others, like the one he'd just heard on the radio, required the benefit of the studio mixers and equalizers. But this voice, the one coming from inside the house, was so musical, so clear, and so beautifully pure, it needed no accompaniment.

He spotted her inside through the screened storm door as

he approached the porch steps. She was perched on a ladder, wearing jeans and a soft green blouse, with that flaming red hair piled loosely on her head. He watched as she hammered a hook into the wall, still singing in that incredible voice.

Until she noticed him.

"Oh, hullo. Did you ring? I'm sorry if you did. I didn't hear it."

"No, I hadn't. I didn't want to interrupt the performance."

"Oh." She looked away, embarrassed. "Sorry. I guess I got a bit carried away while I was decorating. I do that sometimes."

"Please don't apologize. I enjoyed hearing you. Has anyone ever told you that you have an incredible singing voice?"

Flora came down from the ladder, approached him, and released the hook on the door to allow him in. "I've been told I can carry a decent enough tune."

A decent enough tune?

"That's a bit like calling Niagara Falls a leaky faucet. Listen, I know a bit about music. You have a voice that most singers would sign over their lives to the devil to have. Have you had much training?"

Cocking her head to the side, she sort of smiled. "Training? Well, I guess you could say I had training all my life. My mother sang. My father sang. My grandmother sang, too. Where I come from, everybody sings. 'Tis tradition, as much a part of us as . . . well, as breathing."

Gavin looked at her. "Well, you *breathe* very well."

They stood through a quiet moment. Then she looked away, motioned behind her to where the ladder still stood.

"I could certainly use an extra pair of hands, if you're willing. I'm afraid I don't have much to offer in return, other than half a crock of chowder that's long gone cold, and some bread."

Gavin held up the wine bottle. "And wine. If you have a corkscrew, that is . . ."

"Hmm. Good question. I'll go have a look in the kitchen."

Gavin stayed in the hall while he waited for her to return, looking through the pictures she was hanging. They were tasteful, pleasing to the eye—some landscape oils, another an antique map of the Massachusetts coast. All of them were in keeping with the sense of a sea captain's home.

Flora returned a few minutes later with a corkscrew and two wineglasses in her hands. "If you'd like to eat first, I can warm up the chowder in the microwave."

Gavin shook his head. "It can wait. I had a late lunch."

"Good. I was hoping I could get these hung before the daylight's completely gone."

"Well, then, we'd better get to it."

They spent the next hour going room to room, hanging the pictures and other wall decorations where Flora indicated she wanted them, and sharing the bottle of wine while they worked. By the time she finished the first glass, Flora felt herself beginning to unwind. Halfway into the second, she had a very pleasant warmth spreading from her belly to her toes. She realized she had been so busy earlier that day with shopping that she hadn't taken the time to eat anything since breakfast.

But it was probably a good thing. She was feeling relaxed, and was enjoying the company of a good-looking man for the first time in a long time. For once, she didn't have to feel like Flora MacCallum, the single mum, the widowed wife. She felt young and attractive, and she knew Gavin found her attractive, too, could see it in his eyes when lie spoke with her, the way his gaze held hers and his smile curved his mouth. And she could feel it in the frisson of awareness that sparked between them whenever his shoulder or his hand happened to brush hers.

So when he finally kissed her, it didn't come as a total surprise.

The way her body reacted, however, did.

It was as if a flame, long since gone out, suddenly burst to life. The cold and the darkness melted away beneath the smooth touch of his mouth on hers. Her heart pounded and her skin tingled beneath the touch of his hands. Tentative at first, Flora simply let herself give in to the physical indulgence of it. The taste of him. The scent of him. She didn't even stop to think, didn't second-guess it, just let the kiss take her wherever it would.

She felt Gavin press his hips forward just slightly against hers, and the awareness of his erection nearly buckled her knees, going straight to the emptiness that hollowed her insides. She felt his hands brush her arms and graze her breasts through the soft cotton of her blouse. She felt them swell beneath the heat of his touch. Good God, it had been so long since she'd been touched, caressed. She felt a desperate, almost overwhelming urgency. She sighed into his mouth, urging him on as her hands explored the contours of his neck, his shoulders, his arms. When he broke from the kiss and buried his face in her neck, Flora, swept along on the tide of a natural physical need, dropped her head and clung to him.

She felt Gavin lift his head and she opened her eyes to find him staring at her. His expression was one of hot, hazy confusion.

"Jesus, I knew I wanted you, but I didn't think . . ."

Don't think. She heard Angus's words echo through her

thoughts. She scarcely realized it when she repeated them aloud.

Gavin reclaimed her mouth, running his hands up under the hem of her shirt, gripping her waist, then cupping her breasts over the thin silk of her bra. Flora sucked in her breath, arched against his touch, and then raised her hands above her head as Gavin slipped off her shirt.

Flora opened her eyes to see Gavin staring at her with that same look of wanting he'd had when he saw her on the beach earlier that morning. It did something to her, that look, made her feel desirable, attractive, and fundamentally female. She reached up to undo the clip that held her hair, let it tumble down her shoulders and back. The heat in his eyes sparked, ignited. He pulled her to him, burying his face in her hair as he laid her back on the four-poster that obligingly waited behind them.

They were on the third floor, in the turreted room, where Flora had opened the windows to allow in the breeze coming off the water. The twilight cast the room in the soft shadows of a brilliant New England sunset. Flora rolled atop him on the bed, straddling him, her mouth still joined to his. Her pulse was pounding as the feelings of physical pleasure seized her and carried her along like a boat lost on a storm-thrashed sea.

Gavin's hands circled her waist while she quickly unfastened the buttons on his shirt. Then she pushed the fabric away, linking her hands with his and raising them up until they were pressed breast to chest. Their mouths continued exploring—tasting each another.

Gavin gave a low moan into her mouth and then flipped her onto the mattress beneath him, taking both wrists in one hand above her head. He covered her breast with his mouth, suckling her beneath the silk of her bra. Flora drew in a sharp breath, and arched against him, seeking more, yet more, of what he was giving her.

God, it felt so good.

She felt his hands on her belly, moving to the fastening on her jeans. Oh, *Dia,* she thought. It had been so long, so very long since she had felt this way—this *alive.* He loosened the button and slowly slid the zipper downward. Flora bit her bottom lip, clutching the hand that held her wrists above her head, and waited for him to touch her there.

Please, God, just let him touch her there.

And then she heard it, the ringing of her mobile on the table at the bottom of the stairs. Her eyes fluttered open and she instinctively tried to sit up, but Gavin still had her wrists pinned above her head.

"Let it ring," he breathed against her neck, kissing her.

She tried to free her hands. "I can't."

But he slid his hand inside the opening of her jeans, delving beneath the frilled waist of her panties. "Yes, you can . . ."

"No. I can't."

Flora jerked away, rolling off the bed.

"I have to answer it. It might be my kids."

Kids.

It took Gavin several seconds to recover from the weight of that one word.

Flora was already off the bed and out the door, pulling on her blouse and rushing down the stairs to the still ringing phone.

Had she really just said *kids*?

Gavin heard her answer the phone a few seconds later.

"Heya, m'cooshlin'. 'Tis late where you are. You should be abed."

Gone was the soft, singsong voice that had sent his blood

thrumming. Hers was suddenly a mother's voice speaking to her child.

"Oh, she has? Did you now? What were the boys about doing? Yeah, isn't that just grand? Okay, hinny, now 'tis time for bed for you. Aye. I miss you, too. Okay. Then let me talk to him."

A pause. Her voice changed again and Gavin knew she was no longer speaking to a child.

"Yeah. How's Libby doing, then?" A pause. "And Graeme?" She smiled audibly at whatever was the response on the other end. "You'll give them my love, yeah? And I expect pictures by morning, tell them. Aye. Give them all a kiss for me. Aye, everything's fine here. Nae, dinna worry. I'm fine. Okay, 'tis late for you, too. You should be abed. You've work in the morning and have to get the kids ready for school. Aye. 'Til then. Ta, Angus."

Standing at the bottom of the stairs, Flora pressed the button to disconnect the call. Then she stood for a moment, reflecting on the news she'd just received.

Libby had safely delivered an eight-pound, eight-ounce son at 11:19 p.m. UK time. She had apparently gone to Inverness for an appointment with her obstetrician, where they had planned to schedule an inducement for later that week. The baby must have overheard, however, and had other plans, because her waters broke right there, in the waiting room. Ten hours later, they welcomed Fraser Mackay John Calum Mackenzie into the world. Mother and baby were currently resting and doing well. Graeme's mother, the countess, and his uncle, the duke, had bought up every teddy bear they could find at Hamley's toy store on Regent Street in London and were currently en route to meet the new heir.

And the press were already camped outside the hospital, vying to see who could snap the first photo.

Flora would call her congratulations the next morning.

When she turned, she found Gavin sitting atop the steps on the landing above her. His shirt was rebuttoned and tucked into his jeans. The look on his face, however, was anything but warm.

"Sorry," she said. "I had to take that call. My friend just had a baby and—"

"You have kids."

"Yes, I do," she said, not much liking the way he'd said "kids," as if it were some incurable disease. She lifted her chin a little. "I have three of them."

"Why didn't you tell me?"

Flora crossed her arms, lifting her chin more. "Oh, was I obligated to? Hm. I wasna aware of that. I barely know you, and I don't generally introduce myself as 'Flora MacCallum, mother of three.' "

"No, but it might have been a good idea if you'd at least told me you were married before I had my hands down your pants. I know some guys wouldn't give a flip about it, would just take what was being offered, but I'm not one of those guys. I don't trespass on someone else's property, and I've a feeling *Angus* wouldn't take too kindly to knowing his wife had been for all intents and purposes straddling someone else's fence post when he called."

His crude words struck her like a slap. Flora took a deep breath, then let it go slowly. Few things really fanned the flames of her temper. This, however, was one of them.

"For your information, Mr. Matheson, Angus is my brother, not my husband. And aye, I have three kids, but I am no' married. And nae, afore you say it, I'm not divorced, nor did I have three children out of wedlock. I am a widow, if you must know. I lost my husband three years ago, and I havna been with a man since. In fact, you're the first, the only man I've ever kissed other than my husband, so no, I don't make it a habit of 'straddling fence posts' as you say. If it weren't for their schooling, my kids would have come with me, but as it is, they'll be arriving in a couple of weeks. 'Tis the first time I've ever been away from them. And as a matter of fact, it was Angus—my brother"—she reminded him—"who suggested I use this time away from my kids to do something other than be a widowed single mother."

Flora could see Gavin physically withdrawing. He stood, buttoning his shirt cuffs, and made to leave. And she knew the reason why even before he said it.

"Look. I can certainly appreciate your *situation,* but I have to tell you I've just come through a rather bad time myself, and to be honest, I don't know if I can handle a relationship right now, especially with someone who has a bunch of kids."

Flora's vision blurred. "Who said anything about a relationship, Mr. Matheson? Believe it or not, not all single mothers are desperate to find themselves another husband. How do you know I wasn't just after having you for a quick shag, aye?"

Gavin simply stared at her, looking dumbfounded. In fact, Flora was just as dumbfounded at what she'd just said.

"I don't quite know what to say," he said.

"There's nothing else to say, Mr. Matheson. Except goodbye. I appreciate your help today, and would appreciate it even more if you'd find your own way out."

And with that she turned away from him and walked toward the back of the house, slamming behind her the first door she came to.

Chapter Six

Flora had spent the past week ordering, arranging, stocking up, decorating, changing her mind, making lists, shopping, making appointments, keeping appointments, and otherwise doing everything that needed doing. But it seemed for every one task she managed to cross off her list, she ended up adding two more.

She looked at the calendar, noted the growing number of X's quickly filling in the days before the arrival of her first guests, and knew she'd never get it done on her own.

She needed help. A lot of it. She also knew just where to find it.

Flora ducked into Common Grounds shortly before nine that morning, when the café was at its busiest with fishermen coming in from the morning's trawl and pleasure sailors just getting ready to go out. The cozy café had become a regular stop on her morning walk each day.

Back home in Scotland, Flora usually walked from the cottage to her job at Castle Wrath each day. She'd never measured the distance, but she knew it was near three miles. She left as soon as the kids were off to school, and it gave her an hour of quiet time for reflection, organizing her thoughts, and for taking in the sounds and scents of nature uninterrupted by chattering children.

In Ipswich-by-the-Sea, Flora's route took her straight into the village, over the arched stone bridge that spanned Ipswich River, past the white church with its tall steeple. She sometimes paused to chat with the dog walkers, leashes in hand, she met on the village common, dropped her daily letter to the children at the post office, and then stopped in at the café for a cup of tea before heading back. Although she'd been in the village a little over a week, she was already getting to know a few of the locals.

"Good morning, dear," said Mrs. Evanson. The bookshop owner was just getting her breakfast muffin, always cranberry walnut, always warmed twenty seconds in the microwave, and not a second more. "I've set a few new acquisitions aside for you at the shop."

Flora thanked her and promised to stop by.

Jules's mother, Maria, called out *"Buon giorno"* to Flora as she ducked inside the café. Her husband, Sal, repeated the same, adding a *"bella Florina"* and a wink. Even Officer Faraday, who had nearly arrested her that first day, now waved to Flora as she slipped off her jacket and hung it by its hood on one of the hooks behind the café door.

As she scanned the open tables, a couple of the fishermen nodded to her over their coffee cups. Mac, the local garage mechanic, gave her a grin. She saw them all every morning, had enjoyed making their acquaintance but there was one local who had been conspicuously absent whenever Flora came in.

She hadn't seen Gavin again since asking him to leave the house that day. Not at the café. Not walking on the beach beneath the house. Not even at the local market. Not that she was looking for him, mind you. She was much too busy getting the house ready even to think about him, even to remember how her body had tingled when he'd kissed her, or how she'd nearly come undone with the need to lose herself in his arms. That might indicate it had mattered, that kiss, that crazy embrace, and hadn't Flora spent every day since then convincing herself it never would have come to anything between them? And after all, he'd all but told her that the very moment he'd learned about her children, hadn't he?

Yet, as much as she had proclaimed to him that it could have been nothing more than a physical thing, Flora knew deep in her heart she had only spoken in anger. Despite Angus's well-intentioned advice that she just have herself a crazy summer fling, Flora knew she was not the sort of woman who could ever be so irresponsible as to have sex with someone just for the pleasure of it. In the end, she knew she would have to look into her children's faces and see herself mirrored in their eyes.

Truth was, from the moment she'd first met Gavin Matheson, even when she'd been dangling from that trellis (which still needed to be repaired, she reminded herself), there had been something about him that had left her breath hitching in her throat. No, even before that. Because the first notice of him had come when she'd turned that day in this very café, spotted him sitting by that window, staring at her as if she had just walked out of a dream. There was a chemistry, immediate and undeniable, between them, a natural awareness that had only deepened each time she'd encountered him, stealing into her thoughts, making her consider for the first time the possibility of entering into a relationship with a man again.

And he'd seemed to feel it, too, that awareness, that chemistry. Or so Flora had thought. That is, until he'd learned about her kids.

"Good morning, Ms. MacCallum," Jules said to Flora, already bringing a steaming pot of Earl Grey. "How ya doin' today?"

Flora took up the lemon slice that accompanied the tea and squeezed it into the pot. "A bit overwhelmed, to be quite honest, Jules. I'm hoping I can hire someone to help with the garden as well as do some minor maintenance and repairs at the house. Do you think your da would mind if I posted a card on his notice board?"

"Better than that . . ." Jules turned toward the counter. "Hey, Pop! Ms. MacCallum needs someone to help her at the house with some yard work and repairs and stuff. Know anyone?"

The locals assured her that along with making a "wicked" good cup of coffee, Sal Capone was also a walking, talking telephone directory for the whole of the village.

"Jimmy O'Connell," he answered without batting an eye as he steamed a pitcher of milk for lattes.

"Thanks, Pop." Jules scribbled the name and number he gave her on a blank page from her order book. "There ya go. Anything else I can help ya with?"

"No. Thanks, Jules. This is grand. I think I'll just sit here for a spell and go over what else I have on my list of things to do."

"You know, why don't you take Table Seven today? Mr. Matheson hasn't been in for a while, and it really has the best view of the water. Here, let me help you move your things."

Jules followed Flora across the room to that table and set down her tea.

Since Jules had brought it up, Flora gave in to her curiosity and asked, "I hope nothing is wrong with Mr. Matheson. I, uh, haven't seen him around much."

"No. He's still in town, if that's what you mean. From what I hear down at the market, he's having his groceries sent to the house and Uncle Tino said he's been a regular customer for pizza delivery. Must be pretty deep into his work."

"Work?"

"Yeah. He's a songwriter, you know."

"No, actually, I didn't know that." Flora remembered that he had told her he knew a bit about music that day when he'd come upon her singing at the house—the day she'd ordered him out. But a songwriter?

"Is he very successful?"

"Oh, yeah. He's won a Grammy and everything. Not really a songwriter, but calls himself a *composer*." She snorted. "Like Mozart or something. He writes the music and his partner, Mr. Grayson, who owns that house he's staying at, he writes the words. I'm sure you must've heard some of their stuff. They've worked with some really famous names. Good to see he's finally getting back to it after what happened with his son and all."

Flora blinked. "Did you say 'his son?' "

"Yeah, you didn't know?" Jules dropped her tray onto the table and took the chair across from Flora, leaning toward her for a private chat. "It was in all the papers a few years back, but it probably didn't make it over to your part of the world. I remember reading about it, only back then, I didn't know the guy or anything. Apparently Gavin, uh, I mean Mr. Matheson, was in New York at the time and going through a wicked bad divorce. Seems his ex had been sneaking around behind his back, got into some trouble with her boyfriend and the police. I think it was drugs or something like that. They had this little boy, had to be about five or six years old at the time. The way I heard it, they were scheduled to appear in court and Mr. Matheson was almost certain to get custody because of what his wife had been up to. But then she calls him from the airport two days before the court date and says she's taking the kid and leaving the country. Can you believe it? He's been looking for them ever since, has to be a couple years now. I mean, can you imagine a mother kidnapping her own kid from his father?"

Flora, struggling to keep up with the story, could only shake her head. The police chief had said something about it, too, that first day. Only at the time, Flora had no idea what he'd been talking about. But she remembered how Gavin's whole mood had changed. And no wonder. She couldn't imagine the anguish of being separated from a child—her child—like that. How truly, truly awful.

"Jules!" Sal called from the counter. "What am I paying you for, to pour coffee or gossip all day, huh? Two lattes here to Table Four."

"Yeah, yeah . . ." Jules shrugged, taking up her tray as she vaulted from the chair. "I'm comin'."

God, it made such sense now. Gavin's reaction to her, the way he'd become so detached when he'd first learned about her children. Perhaps it hadn't been detachment. Perhaps it had been a response, a truly understandable response to his learning something so unexpected, and the feelings it must have brought up. Perhaps it wasn't so much that he didn't want children, or a relationship with a woman who came with three, but that he'd had one of his own, a son, who had been taken away from him. She could only imagine what Gavin must have gone through, what he must still be going through—wondering every day where his son could be and if he was safe and warm and fed.

Wondering if he was loved.

It tore at the very core of her mother's heart, so much so

that as soon as she left the café, Flora took out her mobile
and dialed the number for the widow MacNamara's cottage
back home in Scotland, just so she could hear wee Seamus's
voice on the other end. The older two were at school, but she
found comfort in hearing his tiny voice. She blinked away
tears as she listened to his heavy breathing when he pressed
the phone receiver close to his mouth so he could blow her
a kiss.

"Ta, Mumma!" he yelled as Flora thanked Mrs. Mac-
Namara and ended the call.

God, how she missed them. Even though there had been
times before when she'd longed for a quiet day alone, now
that she had it—two weeks of it—she found she couldn't
wait for them to arrive. It was a blessing that she had the luxury of knowing they would soon be with her.

A blessing that Gavin didn't have.

When she got back to the house, there was an overnight
package waiting by the door. Flora sat on the front steps
with the sunlight filtering down through the trees and
opened it. It contained photographs of Libby's new baby, a
beautiful bundle of dark hair and tiny eyes, tucked in Libby's
arms. Libby looked tired but incredibly content sitting beside a beaming Graeme. Along with the photos were a handful of crayon pictures that Annie and Seamus had colored
for her, pictures of rainbows above airplanes with the three
of them coming to meet her and hearts floating around them
like butterflies. Flora blinked away her tears and immediately papered the refrigerator door with them.

That afternoon Flora met Jimmy O'Connell, a salty Irish-
man of about fifty who was built like a giant. He took a look
at all she wanted him to do, made a list, offered her what
sounded like a fair price, and promised to start the very next
morning with the broken trellis. He assured her that with the

help of his three sons, all of it could be completed before the house was due to open.

While he was there walking the property with Flora, Jimmy also brought up the idea of converting the old boathouse down by the water into another cottage rental, suggesting that it would be the perfect retreat for an artist or a writer looking for a secluded place to stay. The view from there, poised as it was by the shore, was unparalleled and sure to inspire. Flora agreed it was a grand idea and sat to make some notes, then fired off an e-mail to Libby and Graeme asking for their thoughts.

Now that she'd delegated a big chunk of the work to the able hands of O'Connell and Sons, she was feeling a good deal less overwhelmed. Everything was coming together. After retrieving her messages from voice mail, she returned phone calls and booked reservations for two more guests in the upcoming weeks. Then she unpacked the new linens that had been delivered that day, piling them onto the washing machine to be laundered the next morning.

Before she knew it, daylight had faded once again.

It was past eight, and Flora was sitting in the parlor, reading one of the books she'd picked up from Mrs. Evanson, when she heard the mobile ringing in the hall.

It was Libby's voice on the other end of the line.

"And how's the new mama?"

Being away from her dearest friend at this special time in her life was nearly as difficult as being away from the kids.

"To be honest, I'm exhausted. Of course, the fact that I'm calling you at nearly two in the morning should tell you why."

"Aye. I ne'er could quite sort out why they called them 'midnight feedings' when they usually came about in the wee hours of the morning. How's that sweet bairn doing?"

Libby responded with what could only be described as the contented sigh of new motherhood. "He's perfect. Eating well, sleeping not so well. But I'm not complaining. I just can't stop looking at him, Flora. He's amazing. Even when I'm so exhausted I can't put two words together, I just want to stare at him, watch his mouth twitch and his lashes flutter against his little cheeks. And when he wraps his whole hand around my one finger, my heart swells and I just don't want to let go."

"You ne'er will let go." Flora knew exactly how Libby felt. It was unlike anything else in the world. "And Graeme? How's he adjusting to fatherhood?"

"He's been great, so supportive, even changing diapers."

"Now there's a photo the British press corps would kill for. The future Duke of Gransborough elbow deep in a dirty nappie."

"Oh, they've been just awful—the press, I mean, not the nappies. Although, hmm, there is something to be said for their similarities, now, isn't there? One of them even posed as an orderly to try to get a picture in the hospital nursery. But bless your brother. Angus called in a couple of colleagues from the nearby districts and they've been great about shooing the press away from the village. Told them we went to London, so they've camped outside His Grace's town house. Graeme's uncle even had a nappie delivery service stop by just to maintain the illusion. At least they aren't here. Oh, time for a burp. Let me just shift the phone . . ."

Flora waited while Libby positioned the baby on her shoulder, smiling when she heard the faint whimper of the babe's tiny voice.

"Where was I? Oh, right. Enough about the paparazzi. I've something I'd like to ask you. Something we, Graeme and I, would like to ask. We were wondering if you'd consider being the baby's godmother."

Flora blinked. "Consider it? I'd be honored to, of course. But winna you rather one of Graeme's relatives?"

"We talked about it, and you're the one we both chose to top our lists. There was never any question. You mean so much to us, and we cherish having you as a part of our lives. So it's decided. Keep the last weekend in June open. Don't accept any bookings. You haven't already, have you?"

Flora quickly double-checked the reservations calendar. "Nae. Right now, we're clear that weekend, but we've got three for the holiday weekend on July Fourth."

"Good. We'll fly you home for a few days, then have you back in time to get ready for the guests that next weekend. The kids won't want to miss the fireworks in Ipswich on the Fourth. They have them over the waterfront. Lights up the entire harbor. It's really something to see. And there's a parade down the main street with games and contests on the common. Tell the kids to wear their swimming clothes, too, because the firemen squirt water at the parade crowd from their truck as they drive by."

"Sounds like a lot of fun. They've never seen fireworks before, except on telly. I'm sure they'll love it."

The friends spent another fifteen minutes chatting about the progress on the house and Flora's thoughts and ideas for the upcoming season.

"Okay, well, this little one has nodded back off, so I'm going to put him in his cradle and head back to bed myself. Sounds like you're doing a fantastic job with the house, Flora. But then I'm not surprised. Graeme and I can't thank you enough. I don't know what we would have done without you."

"'Tis I who should be thanking you," Flora said. "You

were right. I needed this time to myself, if only to remind myself of . . ."

She felt her words become knotted in her throat as she thought of her kids, of the way she'd felt in Scotland—almost suffocating in her attempt to avoid dealing with her grief for Seamus. In the past week, and particularly in the quiet hours of evening, she'd spent a lot of time facing her loss, thinking about Seamus and crying quite a bit, but also planning for her future and the kids' futures as well. It was almost as if the past three years had been one long sleep. She'd awoken and found that the daylight wasn't quite as frightening as she'd feared—because each new day offered promise . . .

And hope.

"Flora?" Libby's voice summoned her from her thoughts. "Is everything okay? Did something happen?"

Flora closed her eyes, took a breath. "Nae, not at all. Everything's grand. To bed with you now, aye? I'll check in with you tomorrow, then."

She ended the call and then headed off to bed, wondering as she put out the lights and checked the doors what the next day might bring.

Hope.

"Well, look who's decided to come out of his cave," Jules said, cocking her tray on one hip as Gavin ducked into the café.

"Hey, Jules." He nodded. "Sorry. I've been a little busy."

"So I gather. Tell me, when do we get to hear it?"

"Hear what?"

"Your new song. That is what you've been doing, locking yourself away in that house all this time, surviving on nothing but my uncle's pizza, isn't it?"

Gavin smiled. Word sure got around in a small town. "It'll be a while yet. Progress has been slow. There's still something that isn't quite right with it. I'm beginning to think my composing skills have gone rusty from neglect these past two years."

She served him his coffee—black and strong like he preferred—and added one of Maria's fresh *sfogliatelle* on the side. "Here. You look like you haven't eaten in days. Or shaved. You've got that beach bum thing working overtime."

Gavin scratched his chin, where there was indeed a short scruff of a beard. Only when the sun came out that morning, and the refrigerator revealed nothing more than a wedge of cheese and some leftover pizza, had Gavin decided it was time he got out for a breath of fresh air and some decent food.

The morning was perfect for it. The sun was high and bright, sparkling on the harbor like a million tiny camera flashes. The gulls were soaring, circling above the fishing boats as they came in with that morning's catch. All along Main Street, residents were putting up screens, throwing open the windows, and letting in the summer air.

Gavin was hunched over the morning sports page, catching up on the Red Sox stats and sipping his second cup of coffee when Flora came into the café.

He glanced up briefly, then glanced down again. He picked up his sports page, telling himself he wasn't hiding from her. He just wanted a few minutes of camouflaged observation.

She was wearing a pair of sport pants, black with a white stripe down each side, and a white T-shirt that fit her well. *Very* well. Her hair was pulled up in a springy ponytail, bouncing behind the curved brim of a blue baseball cap. On her feet she wore a pair of new-looking Nikes.

"How do you like the shoes?" he heard Jules ask her as she poured Flora a pot of tea.

"You know, you were right," she answered. "They are like walking on air." Then she said, "I think I'll have that tea takeaway today. I should get back to the house. There's still so much work to do, and I'm getting close to naught but a week afore we open."

"Sure thing." Jules poured the tea into a tall paper cup, from which the tea bag tag fluttered like a kite's tail under the plastic lid.

Gavin watched her go as she passed by the front window. He quickly folded his newspaper and took up the pastry, wrapping it in a napkin as he tossed a five on the counter. "See ya later, Jules."

"Thanks, Mr. Matheson," she said. Then she added with a grin, "Uh, she usually takes the bridge and goes down Church Street."

Everyone in the café turned to watch as Gavin rushed out the door.

Sal chuckled. "I've got a ten on it says he catches up to her before she reaches the post office."

Mac the mechanic took the bet and even doubled it to twenty.

They all crowded the café's front window and watched Gavin jog down the street after Flora, trying not to look like he was chasing after her as he tossed his paper in the trash bin and even paused a second to greet old Mrs. Wilkins and her shih tzu. He strolled down Main Street then, peering in the bookshop window before cutting a path across the common. He reached Flora just as she dropped her morning letter in the outgoing mailbox—earning a smiling Sal that twenty.

"Flora!"

She turned, green eyes peering at him from beneath the brim of her cap. "Oh, Gavin. Hello. How've you been?"

"Listen. I wanted to talk to you. About that night last week . . . I owe you an explanation for the way I reacted."

"Nae, you dinna."

"I do. I don't want you to go around thinking this is about you, or your kids. Because it's not. It's about me."

Gavin had spent the past several days doing nothing but thinking of her, replaying that day over and over in his mind each time he sat at the piano working on her song. Now, days later, he had so much he wanted to tell her, and he wanted to get it right. He hesitated, choosing his words. "I think you should know I—"

"I know, Gavin. It's about your son."

What he had intended to say got stuck in the back of his throat. He just looked at her, and the compassion in her eyes for the misery that was his life since he'd lost Gabriel left him speechless.

"I'm so sorry," she said. "If I had known about it that night, I winna have admonished you the way I did. I just assumed that you were painting me as one of those desperate single mums whose only aim is to find a man to take the place of the one who was there afore. That's not me. The truth is, I dinna know what I want. I'm trying to work that out. 'Tis part of the reason I'm here, in the States. But this is all very new to me and I'm not quite sure where I'm headed. I know only that the past three years have been the most difficult of my life, and I dinna want to spend the rest of my life living that same way."

"What same way?"

"Afraid. Terrified really to the point of wanting to lock myself away in a closet every minute of every day."

Gavin watched as tears swelled in her eyes and she

quickly glanced at her feet to stem them. Giving her a moment, he looked up the street, and that was when he saw that they had drawn a bit of an audience in the café window.

"Take a walk with me?"

"Sure."

They followed the walkway in silence, both lost to their own thoughts, until they got to the other side of the old stone bridge. There was a small bench there, with bright yellow pansies planted around it, dedicated to the memory of one of the village's past notables. Gavin motioned to it, and they sat together just looking out at the boats in the harbor while the breeze came in off the water, stirring wind chimes in a nearby garden.

"What's his name?" Flora finally said. Gavin looked at her, but she kept her eyes fixed on the horizon. "Your son," she asked again. "What's his name?"

"Gabriel. Gabriel William Matheson."

"How old was"—she quickly corrected herself—"how old *is* he?"

"He's eight years old now. He was just six when he—when his mother took him." His voice broke a little, and he coughed to hide it.

"Robbie, he's my oldest. He's eleven—eleven going on twenty-five for as fast as he wants to grow up. My daughter is Fiona, but we call her Annie. She's seven. And then there's wee Seamus, my youngest. He'll be turning three this summer."

"You said you lost your husband three years ago, so Seamus . . ."

"Never knew his father," Flora finished for him. "I found out I was expecting him after Seamus, my husband, died."

"How did he? . . ."

Back home in Wrath Village, everyone had known Flora

and Seamus, and so everyone knew about the accident that took his life. While it spared her from some of the burden of confronting it, it had also robbed Flora of the opportunity to really talk about what had happened to someone who hadn't been there to watch it all unfold. Speaking about it now, in terms of telling the events, was in its own way cathartic.

"Seamus worked on an oil rig in the North Sea. It was the sort of job where he would be gone for four, sometimes six, weeks at a time, and then home for a month afore going back again. He had just been home. We'd celebrated Robbie's birthday the day afore he left. But there was an accident. The helicopter that was taking him back to the rig went down shortly after taking off. They were ne'er really able to determine the reason why."

"God, Flora. I'm sorry."

She swallowed back the lump in her throat and nodded once. "I was numb for days after they told me." She smiled regretfully. "I suppose in some ways I've been numb ever since. Thank God for my brother. Angus was actually here in the States when it happened, working in New York, but he came back home and immediately took care of everything for me. The worst of it was having to tell the kids. Robbie, especially, took it hard. He'd been very close to his father, idolized him. I dinna think a birthday will ever go by again that he winna be haunted by it. Then I found out I was pregnant. I was a mess. I thought sure I'd lose the baby from the stress and constant emotional upheaval. But wee Seamus was born healthy and strong. Somehow, strangely, life works that way. We lose someone. Another comes along. I ne'er believed that, not really, until the day wee Seamus came and I saw he had a dimple in his cheek, same as his da. 'Tis amazing, it is."

They sat for a few quiet minutes. A parade of kindergartners wearing newspaper hats and paired off in twos marched by with their teacher on the way to the village common.

"Gabriel was their same age when he was . . ." Gavin swallowed. "The last time I saw him, he was waving at me through the front window of our house." He shook his head. "I mean what had been our house before I moved out. I had just dropped him off after our last visit. We'd gone to the zoo. He loved the zoo, especially the monkeys. I can still see him, face pressed to the glass, as he looked when I walked away. He had a chocolate ice cream mustache from the cone I'd gotten him."

Flora looked at Gavin, saw the raw emotion he struggled to contain. "He will remember you, you know. The things you did together, the places you went. Annie was only four when her father died, but she remembers how he used to bring her a bunch of heather whenever he came home. White heather, for luck. Every time we see some, even now, she picks it, looks up at the clouds, and says thank you to her da."

Gavin sucked in a breath, measuring it out slowly. "You have no idea how much I cling to that hope. It's all I have sometimes. But at this point, I don't know if I'll ever see him again. I mean, maybe as an adult he'll look me up, but then, I've no idea what she's told him. I've heard stories of other parents telling their kids that the parent they left didn't want them anymore, or worse, that they're dead. Miranda's cruel that way. I don't think she'd ever hurt Gabriel knowingly. She'd just convince herself she was doing what was best. For him. For her."

"You've no idea where she's taken him?"

"Actually, the question should be where *hasn't* she taken him. I hired a private investigator who has practically spanned the globe following their trail. Rome. Paris.

Switzerland. Greece. Singapore. Every time we get close, she runs again and it takes us months to track her down. Her parents live in London and I know they've been in contact with her. They have to be helping her financially, but they refuse to tell us anything. They didn't want her to marry me and move here to begin with. So unless she returns to the States, there isn't much else I can do. International child abduction is a diplomatic nightmare. Most governments don't want to get involved in what they consider nothing more than a domestic dispute, even though I have a court order granting me full custody and despite the fact that there's a warrant out for her arrest. When we found out she was in Paris, the French officials even told her we were coming. She left her apartment in such a hurry, she didn't take her things. That's where I found this."

He took his wallet from his back pocket and opened it to a photograph of a boy with blond hair and the biggest pair of eyes Flora had ever seen. He was holding a toy airplane, but was not smiling. He looked completely lost.

How could he look anything but lost? He had no place that he could really call home, just an ever-changing string of addresses, none of them with a solid foundation beneath them.

Flora took Gavin's hand and squeezed it. "You'll get him back. You have to believe that. You just have to keep trying to find him."

"I know that." He nodded. Then he looked at her with those same lost eyes that she'd seen in Gabriel's photograph. "It's the only thing that keeps me going."

Chapter Seven

Five days.

In just five days' time, Ipswich-by-the-Sea's first bed-and-breakfast would officially open for business, welcoming a Mr. and Mrs. George Squires from Dallas, Texas.

And Flora would be ready for them.

She had worked herself to within an inch of exhaustion making sure each detail—everything from the thread count of the bed linens to the blend of teas she would serve at breakfast—had been seen to. Even the toiletries she had set out on the sinks in each bathroom had been chosen with care, sent all the way from Scotland—more precisely, the Scottish kitchen of her friend Hattie Macleod.

The two young women shared a sad bond, for Hattie's husband, Archibald, had worked on the oil rig with Seamus, and they had been traveling together on the same helicopter. In those early days after the accident, Flora and Hattie had grown close to one another, realizing they would have to leave their roles as housewives and mothers and find a way to make their own living. Flora had found a position at Castle Wrath, first starting as housekeeper and then, after Libby's arrival, moving on to estate manager. Hattie had turned her talent for growing herbs and gardening into a true cottage industry, making all-natural soaps and lotions in her tiny kitchen as a means of supporting herself and her baby daughter.

Hoping to convince the tourist shops to offer her goods for sale, Hattie spent much of her time driving from village to village across the Highlands. The sad truth was that most of the time she barely managed to eke out a living, and there were days when Hattie despaired of being able to put bread on the table at all. She'd recently begun to consider leaving the village altogether to move nearer to her husband's family in Glasgow. She hadn't wanted to leave Wrath—it was her home—but in a village so small and so remote, opportunities for extra income were hard to come by.

So Flora had rung her up and placed an order for six dozen of her soaps, convincing her to produce smaller, convenient-sized bottles of her hand lotions and shampoos for Flora to supply in each of the guests' bathrooms.

Hattie had been thrilled.

And Flora had been delighted to help her.

Flora had done much the same in stocking up on jams and marmalades for Thar Muir's breakfast table by calling on Janet MacNeish for her prized black-currant and gooseberry preserves. Colin MacDonald had sent over two of his hand-carved chess sets for the parlor. Even the wool blankets that Flora had draped at the foot of each guest's bed had been woven on the looms of the Wrath Village Ladies' Auxiliary. It did Flora's heart good to help boost her local economy while at the same time providing Thar Muir with that unique touch, that "bit o' Scotland" on this side of the Atlantic.

Flora now sat taking tea and a breakfast scone, giving a watchful eye to the storm clouds that had begun to gather on the horizon over the sea. Bad weather or not, it felt good to have a quiet morning to herself after two weeks of nearly endless activity. She had thought the time alone without the kids would go slowly, but the truth was the days had flown by in a flurry of plans, arrangements, and plain old hard work. When she arrived, the house had seemed like an artist's canvas, nearly but not quite finished. She had carefully brushed in the details, adding color and texture, to create something that was uniquely and distinctly *hers*. The resulting sense of accomplishment was truly a heady thing. And she'd finished just in time for the kids and Angus to join her.

They would be coming in three days, and Flora couldn't wait to see them. The time away from them had been a healing time for her, but she longed so much to see their little faces, to hear their nonstop chatter, and to feel the softness of their hair against her cheek when she hugged them tightly to her. She felt as if she had finally come to terms with the loss of Seamus and could now live her life *with* her children, and not just *for* them.

But for now she had the next couple of days to spend any way she wanted. As much as she had come to love the house—she beamed with pride whenever she looked around and saw the results of her hard work—Flora knew she was in sorry need of a day away.

But what should she do?

She hadn't had a full day all to herself since before she'd had Robbie. Back in Scotland whenever she had time off from her job, she spent it catching up on housework—repairing leaky faucets or patching up the knees on the kids' trousers. Occasionally she would forego the chores and treat the kids to a picnic or the cinema in Inverness. But the treats she arranged were always for someone else.

This time, she had the opportunity to do something solely for herself, and the possibilities were endless. Given the weather, a day at the beach was not a likelihood, but she could drive to Boston and visit a museum or take in some of the tourist sights. Or she could put on her best dress and treat herself to lunch at a gourmet restaurant. But in the end, Flora decided to leave those for another time and opted to do something completely frivolous and ultimately feminine.

What better way than an afternoon at the local salon?

Back home in Wrath, they didn't have a salon or even a barber for that matter. Most people had to go to the larger towns or enlist the help of a friend. Flora usually just trimmed the ends of her hair herself. As such, her style was rather simple. It was basically all one length, perhaps a little uneven, falling to midback, and the same dark red she was born with. Most of the time she just kept it pulled back with an elastic or a clip.

The suggestion that Flora take a day for the salon had come from Jules, actually, who had even recommended a stylist named Jen, the salon's owner.

"You must be Flora," said a petite young woman with a chin-length bob of straight, jet-black hair. She had eyes the color of platinum that smiled behind a pair of old-fashioned-looking eyeglasses. Silver bangles jingled from her wrist as she stuck out her hand in greeting. "I'm Jen. Jules told me she'd sent you in. Come on to the back of the shop and let's get you comfortable."

The salon, called Ipsnips, was housed in an old saltbox colonial within walking distance of the common just off the main village street. Even though the shop was busy and nearly every stylist's chair was filled, Jen spent the first half hour with Flora just going over style books and chatting in a cozy reception parlor.

As they got to know each other, they discovered they shared a fondness for Earl Grey tea and lavender-scented candles. Jen also had two children, Sam and Cassie, both close in age to Robbie and Annie. Once Flora's family arrived, she offered to have Jen and company come to the house so the kids could spend a day on the beach while their mothers had tea and got better acquainted.

"Okay, now onto business. Your hair is in great shape," Jen said as she loosened the clip that Flora had used to pull it back. She fluffed out the curls with her manicured fingers. "What do you use on it?"

" 'Tis a botanical shampoo made with heather and oats. My friend back home in Scotland makes it herself."

"And it leaves it this soft and healthy?"

Within fifteen minutes, Jen had asked Flora to place an order for her so that she could sell Hattie's shampoos and lotions at the salon exclusively.

Jen regarded Flora's reflection in her salon mirror. "You don't seem quite sure of what you'd like to do with your hair, and I sense you're a little intimidated to do anything too radical. I completely understand. Women are very connected to their hair. After all, it's a big part of their identities, and changing that identity too much, too suddenly, can be, well, frightening."

Flora marveled at her insight. "I'm just not quite sure my kids are ready for their mum to go platinum blond or anything like that."

"Well, I know women who would kill to have hair this color, so I wouldn't let you near a dye bottle even if you tried. But can I make a suggestion? I think the style you have it in now is really well suited to your face. It complements the shape of your eyes and your delicate bone structure." She tipped Flora's chin up a little to demonstrate her point. "So how about this first visit we just clean up the ends a bit, take off an inch or two of length, and maybe layer it just a little to give it some extra bounce, and we'll see how you like it. Nothing too radical, just an enhancement to what you already have."

Flora agreed and surrendered herself to Jen's comfy salon chair.

An hour later, Jen turned that same chair back toward the mirror, and Flora saw a new woman reflected there. Jen might not have considered what she'd done radical, but Flora was amazed at how just a few snips of the styling shears and some curl-enhancing balm had made her hair come alive. It bounced around her shoulders, softly framing her face. But it was only the first step of Jen's makeover plan.

"Okay, now I'm going to send you upstairs to Maureen. She's our masseuse, and she's going to make those achy muscles you've been working so hard feel just like warm honey. I promise you, she's amazing."

Flora had never had a professional massage and she wasn't quite sure what to expect. Maureen showed her to a small room upstairs where there was a table draped with a sheet under soft recessed lighting. Relaxing music breezed in by way of a pair of speakers set into the ceiling, and candles filled the room with the mingling scents of lavender and vanilla. Maureen, who looked more like a schoolteacher than anything as exotic as a masseuse, left Flora with a warm sheet to wrap around herself before she ducked out the door.

When she returned a few minutes later, she asked Flora to lay facedown on the table and spent the next hour working every knot from Flora's neck, back, and shoulders with oil that smelled of almonds and melted warmly into her skin. Maureen even kneaded Flora's fingers and the palms of her overworked hands, and then smoothed a peppermint-scented lotion into the soles of her feet, showing her the different reflexology points and how they related to various parts of the body. Jen had been right. By the time their hour was over, Flora felt as if her entire body had melted into a honey pot.

It didn't end there.

She had a manicure to shape her sadly overworked nails, a pedicure complete with a bright pink polish, and then finally a facial treatment made with seaweed and avocado that left her skin feeling soft and utterly revitalized. Four hours later, as she gathered her things to leave, Flora knew firsthand what it meant to "feel like a new woman."

She met Jen at the front counter to settle up.

"For you," Jen said as she handed her an envelope.

Flora took it and opened the seal. "What is this?"

Jen merely smiled, revealing nothing.

Inside was a pretty printed card. Flora recognized Libby's e-mail address on the note inside.

I hope you enjoyed your day. This is our gift to you for all the hard work you've done for us these past two weeks. We can't thank you enough. Love, Libby and Graeme

She looked up at the smiling Jen. "And that includes my tip, so put your wallet back in your bag. Libby said I wasn't to take a cent from you."

"But how . . . how did Libby know?"

"As it happens, my mother was good friends with Libby's mother, Matilde. She put in a call to Libby this morning to congratulate her on the baby and happened to mention you were coming in. Don't you just love the small-town grapevine?"

Flora stared at her, stunned. "I don't quite know what to say."

Jen handed her a card with the salon's name and phone number after scribbling her home number on the back.

"Whenever you want to come back, just give me a call. And be sure to let me know when the kids are in and settled. My two will be chomping at the bit to get to that beach. It's the best stretch of shore in the whole village."

After she left the salon, Flora decided to take advantage of whatever remained of the day's fair weather and walked the length of Main Street, peering in the shop windows and popping in every so often for a browse.

She'd overheard one of the ladies in the salon earlier saying that the storm that was heading their way was reported to be a particularly nasty one. So Flora stopped in at the market and bought some chicken to broil and a salad mix for a quick supper over the handful of DVDs she'd rented from the local video store. It had been ages since she'd watched any film over the rating of G, and she couldn't think of a better way to spend a surly, stormy evening than to curl up in a comfortable corner of the couch and treat herself to a helping of Hugh Grant and Colin Firth.

By the time she slipped out of Mrs. Evanson's bookshop, the sky had turned an ugly shade of gray with a front of glowering clouds that seemed to be waiting just off the shore like a bully daring the daylight to a fight.

Flora's last stop before heading back to the house was to Common Grounds to thank Jules for recommending Jen's salon and to let her see the finished result.

"You look fabulous!" Jules crossed the café, circling Flora to get a full view. "I don't know what Jen did with your hair. I mean it's still basically the same style, but it looks so vibrant, so alive, and your face . . . you're simply beaming. Too bad Gavin Matheson isn't here. One look at you and he'd have his eyes popping clear out of his head."

Flora shook her head. "Oh, no, Jules. It's not like that. We're just friends."

"Ah, yeah . . ." Jules said on a slow nod. "Right."

In fact, since that day they'd talked together by the stone bridge, Flora and Gavin had met nearly every morning at the café. They would share a cup of coffee and sometimes a stroll along the common. They talked about her kids and about her life in Wrath Village. He told her about his career as a composer, and Flora was astounded to realize that he had written several of her favorite songs. They discussed politics and world events; they even chatted about sports, with Gavin educating Flora on the basics of the American game of baseball and especially its century-old rivalry between the New York Yankees and the Boston Red Sox. He warned her that continuing to wear the ball cap with the distinctive NY logo that Angus had brought back for her from the States while anywhere within the region of New England was akin to taking her life into her own hands.

Flora enjoyed being with Gavin. Even while she was married to Seamus, he'd been away much of the time. When he was home, he'd spent most of his time catching up on the everydayness of their life—working around the cottage, making up for lost time being a da to the kids. Opportunities for thought-provoking adult conversation had been seldom, and much as she'd loved Seamus, their interests had been varied. Flora loved poetry and quiet nights by the fire. Seamus had preferred taking a pint down at the pub. Yet even the pub was preferable to the utter aloneness of the past three years. These times she'd spent with Gavin had given her back some of that companionship. But with his past and her kids to remind him of the loss of his own . . .

"No, 'tis true," Flora insisted to Jules. "We *are* just friends."

"Well, you'd better clue him in on that fact, then, because I've seen the way he looks at you and how he looks *for* you every morning. He sits by that window, just waiting for you to stroll up. Let me tell you, that is not the way a man looks at a woman he considers only a *friend*."

Jules's mother, the tiny rotund Maria, who was wiping the café counter beside them, nodded in silent agreement.

Flora was in the kitchen chopping cucumbers and carrots into her salad, swinging her hips, and singing out loud while Aretha Franklin boomed from the hi-fi. Gavin had rung the bell, but the music was so loud she hadn't heard it. He stopped just inside the kitchen doorway. Her faded jeans hugged her curves in all the right places as she moved in time to the Motown beat, and the dark color of her sweater set her hair afire. She was definitely a vision to get a man's blood pumping. It was no wonder she'd inspired music in him again with just the sight of her.

He knew she had worked night and day to get the house ready in time for her guests, and she'd certainly done an incredible job. The house had been fine the first time he'd come there. Adequate. Serviceable. But after nearly two weeks of Flora's attention to the smallest details, what had been planned as a guest house now welcomed anyone who walked through its door more as a home away from home.

"Oh," she said suddenly when she turned and noticed him standing there. She quickly lowered the volume on the stereo. "I didn't . . . Did you ring the bell and I didn't hear?"

He nodded. "I hope you don't mind that I showed myself in."

"Not at all." She looked around at the kitchen. "I was just making some chicken and a salad for supper. There's plenty for two. Would you"—she looked at him—"care to join me?"

He'd come over only to bring her the newspaper after

he'd spotted the advertisement for Thar Muir in that morning's edition. Or so he told himself. But he knew that was just the best excuse he'd come up with to see her again. In the past two weeks, Gavin had seen quite a lot of Flora, and his work had thrived as a result. And like anyone obsessed with his work, he was hungry for more.

He had come to look forward to every morning when he'd sit in the café watching for her to appear at that turn on Main Street, with an incredible smile lighting up her face as she paused to greet the older ladies feeding the squirrels on the common. She was a woman of intelligence, with a playful sense of humor and a razor-sharp mind. He'd started to seek out her opinion and relished engaging her in conversation. Flora felt things deeply; she saw the world through the eyes of a mother who wanted the very best for her children.

She was the woman he was falling in love with.

But she was also a woman who had three children, and Gavin had spent the past two years purposely avoiding such a stark reminder of his own loss. It was a natural means of protection against the pain that each day brought with Gabriel still missing. What would happen, he wondered, when her kids arrived? He had no idea how he would feel until the very moment they were standing there before him. While his every impulse made him want to know more about her, a part of him still wondered whether he should just leave the newspaper, turn, and go back to Alec's summerhouse.

Mother Nature stepped in to make up his mind for him as a deep rumble of thunder suddenly shuddered across the yard and over the house, rattling the teacups in their saucers. Gavin stood looking at Flora. A moment later, rain began to pebble the windowpanes.

"Well, I guess that decides it. I walked over, so it looks

like I'll be staying at least for a little while," he said. "Can I do anything to help?"

She handed him the chopping knife. "If you wouldn't mind finishing the veggies, I can brown up the bannocks."

They worked alongside each other with the muted sounds of "You Make Me Feel Like a Natural Woman" murmuring in the background. More than once Gavin's gaze wandered over to where she stood with her hair drawn up off her face and one twisting tendril falling against her cheek. He marveled at the way her slender fingers kneaded the bread dough, deftly flipping it onto the butcher block where she rolled it out and cut it into neat circles.

A natural woman indeed.

While the bannocks browned in a frying pan on the stove, she seasoned the chicken and placed it under the broiler.

Gavin finished the salad and wiped his hands on a dish towel. "Have any wine?"

She nodded and motioned toward the cellar door. "Wine cellar's fully stocked now."

It was an impressive selection, and Gavin chose a California Chardonnay, pouring them each a glass. The CD changed from breathy Aretha to the bluesy sounds of Van Morrison.

Flora lit a couple of candles in the dining room, setting places at one end of the dining table. The music filtered in softly from the kitchen by way of speakers cleverly hidden in the potted topiary that decorated the corners of the room.

Outside, a true nor'easter surged, wind howling through the trees while the rain poured down the windows in sheets. A flash of lightning splintered the night sky; thunder cracked its whiplash over the rooftop.

It was a good thing Flora had lit the candles, because they lost power only moments after they sat down to dinner.

They had their meal by candlelight, chatting to fill the silence. Flora asked Gavin what he was currently working on, but he kept his answers purposely vague. He didn't know how she'd feel if she knew he was writing a song that had her name written across the top of every sheet of music.

He asked her about her children, when they were arriving from Scotland. He suspected once they came, and once the house opened to its guests, he wouldn't be seeing her as often. He silently thanked the storm for giving him these quiet few hours alone with her.

They finished eating and cleared the table, even washing the dishes together. Gavin was reluctant to leave, looking for an excuse, any excuse, to stay longer. Flora, too, seemed unwilling to call it a night. She refilled his wine and showed him into the front parlor, taking up the candles to light their way.

Once there, she lit several more candles, then curled into the corner of the overstuffed couch with the polished toes on her bare feet peeking out from under the cuffs of her jeans.

The storm raged on outside. Flora scarcely noticed. Perhaps it was the candlelight. Perhaps it was the wine and the pleasant warmth it was spreading through her body. Perhaps it was the fact that she'd spent the day at the salon and felt, for the first time in a long, long time, like a woman and not a tired, stressed-out single mum. But when Gavin finished his wine and glanced at his watch as if he should leave, she found herself reaching for his hand, and covering it with hers.

"Stay."

With that one word, the nearly electric tension that had been subtly building between them throughout that night seemed to splinter and spark. Gavin reached for Flora and she melted into him, sharing a kiss that was somewhat tentative at first, but became more heated with the invitation of her response.

Dia, Flora thought, and ran her hands over Gavin's arms, tracing the contours of his neck, running a thumb over the curve of his ear. When she felt him moan into her mouth, she smiled against his mouth and took more.

Gavin pulled away, looking deeply into her eyes.

"I've been wanting to do that since the moment I saw you dancing in the kitchen."

She smiled. Suddenly she couldn't remember any of the reasons why she had convinced herself they were "just friends."

"Gavin, we both had things happen to us in the past that made us reluctant to risk our hearts another time. But I've spent the past three years living by *not* living. I've had a lot of time to think during the past two weeks, and I've decided I'm too young to spend the rest of my life alone."

Gavin looked at her. "So what are you saying?"

"What I'm *not* saying is that I expect us to get married tomorrow. No relationship comes with a guarantee, but that doesn't mean I dinna ever want to try. I dinna want to go on assuming what I had with Seamus was all I am meant to have for the rest of my life. I want to believe I deserve a second chance to be happy, to be loved." She looked down at her wineglass, fearing she'd said too much, too soon. "Perhaps I'm wrong. Perhaps you dinna feel the way I do."

Gavin opened his mouth to answer when there came a sudden and insistent pounding on the front door. Flora sat up, looked at Gavin, then went to answer it.

A man of no more than twenty-five stood on the other side, soaked to the skin, his teeth chattering from the storm's chill. A car stood on the drive, engine idling, headlights shining on the back of Flora's SUV. A woman's face peered out from the foggy window.

"Hi," the man said breathlessly. "Thank God you're home. We're desperate. We seem to have lost our way and the weather just keeps growing worse." The thunder grumbled as if to confirm his words. "My wife and I, we're on our way up to Maine to visit my parents. But I don't think we should risk staying on the road. I spotted your sign. I was wondering . . . hoping . . . Do you have any rooms available for the night?"

Flora looked at him. "We dinna actually open for another five days . . ."

"Damn!" He ran a hand back through his dripping hair. The gold of his wedding ring glimmered in the candlelight. "Would you know of anyplace else close by where we can stop for the night? You see, we have a new baby. She's just three weeks old and we had planned to drive through the night, thinking she would sleep for most of the trip. But she's been crying nonstop ever since we left Boston. My wife is so upset and . . ."

Flora peered over his shoulder at the woman who was sitting in the backseat of the car. The expression on her face was one of clear desperation. She couldn't possibly refuse them.

She nodded. "Of course you can stay here."

"We can? But . . ."

Flora grabbed an umbrella from the stand by the door and handed it to him. "Please. Bring in your wife and daughter. I'm afraid we've lost power, but we've candles aplenty, and I can probably find something to fix you to eat. Leave the car there till morning."

Having come up behind her to hear the whole thing, Gavin took another umbrella. "Here. I'll help you with your things."

Flora stood at the door, holding a lantern to light their

way, and waited while the man trotted back to the car. Moments later, he was helping his wife from inside the car. She had a small blanket-wrapped bundle clutched to her breast as they walked through the pouring rain to the porch.

"Hullo," Flora greeted her with a smile. She could hear the desperate crying of an infant over the sound of the rain. "Come in. Come in where 'tis warm and dry."

The woman looked as if she might burst into tears at any moment. Her eyes were hollowed and shadowed from lack of sleep. She'd been crying, no doubt over her inability to soothe her infant daughter. She looked like she could really use a friend.

"Here. Would you like me to hold her whilst you take off your coat?"

She could see the woman hesitate, instinctively seeking to protect her child. It was a completely natural, truly expected response.

"I'm Flora MacCallum," Flora said, hoping to put her at ease. "Really, 'tis all right. I have three children of my own. My youngest isn't yet three."

Flora waited, allowing the woman to consider her offer. She remembered when her Robbie was just a babe, how she had refused to allow anyone to touch him, much less take him from her arms. Seamus used to tease her that they would never be able to have any other children with Robbie glued to her breast the way she'd kept him. There were few things on earth more fierce than a new mother's protective instincts.

This woman, however, must have sensed she had nothing to fear from Flora, because she slowly eased the wailing bundle into Flora's arms.

"May I?" Flora asked before unwrapping the blanket to see the babe inside.

The woman nodded. Her teeth were chattering too much for her to speak.

Gavin and the other man quickly brought the couple's things inside. Realizing they were chilled both from the storm and their anxiety, Gavin crossed the parlor and knelt to light a fire.

"Well, hullo there, wee one," Flora said softly as she eased open the soft pink flannel covering of blanket. A tiny red face blinked back at her with dark eyes. Flora smiled at her. A moment later, the baby screwed up her face again and began to wail anew.

Flora looked at the mother, who was removing her soaked shoes. "What's her name?"

"It's Catherine. Catherine Anne. I just don't know what's wrong with her. I've fed her. I've changed her. I've burped her. She's not too cold or too hot. I even held her after we stopped driving, but she won't stop crying."

"Shh . . . " Flora soothed, more to the mother, who was now fighting her own tears. She tucked Baby Catherine tightly in her arms and started rocking her, swaying her gently as she softly *shh*'d close to the infant's ear. She walked the length of the floor. She fell into a natural rhythm, a timeless dance of rocking and singing that she had performed with her own children. Her mother had done the same with her, too. After a few minutes, the baby's cries began to ease. Flora started a quiet lullaby, singing to her in Gaelic until after a time the baby's cries went silent.

When Flora looked up, Catherine's parents were staring at her as if she were an angel sent from heaven.

Standing in the doorway, Gavin, too, could simply stare.

Chapter Eight

Flora settled the young family, who later introduced themselves as Matt and Christy Shore from New York, in the Heather Room.

It was the first room off the stairway landing, so they didn't have to haul their baggage too far. It had a small reading nook that provided the perfect spot for the baby's portable crib, near the windows where the sound of the rain that was still falling outside, pattering softly now, would provide the perfect soothing lullaby.

Once the sleeping Catherine was safely tucked away, Flora turned her attention to the fatigued and obviously overstressed Christy.

"I just don't understand it," the petite blonde said over the pot of Darjeeling Flora had fixed for her. Thankfully, the gas stove hadn't been knocked out by the power loss.

"Catherine was fine the first couple of weeks. She slept and ate well, but in the past few days, she has had these bouts of incessant crying. She doesn't sleep like they say a newborn is supposed to sleep. I know she's so tired, but I don't know what to do to help her sleep. The pediatrician wasn't any help. He simply called it colic and said she'd outgrow it by three or four months. Three months! I cannot imagine living through this that long. It's been only three days and already I'm at my wit's end. And this lack of sleep can't be good for her."

Flora sensed in Christy a need to talk, and so she let her, responding with a reassuring nod when needed.

"I've read every book there is from all the 'experts' and nothing seems to work. I've tried everything I can think of. Then we arrive here, and you just pick her up and she quiets down in seconds and is sleeping now for"—she glanced at her watch in the light of the candle flickering on the table between them—"over an hour, which is just incredible. She hasn't slept for more than a half hour at a time in the past four days. Don't misunderstand me. I'm so happy she's finally sleeping because I know she needs it, and I'm grateful to you for whatever it was you did to help her, but I just wish I knew what I'm doing wrong."

She closed her eyes with a shaking hand, fighting tears.

Flora took her hand. "Christy, you're not doing anything wrong. I went through a similar time with my Annie. She's my second child. My eldest, Robbie, was a perfect bairn. He was quiet. He slept for hours at a time. I ne'er had a day of trouble from him. Annie, however, was the complete opposite. She cried all the time, from the moment she was born, it seemed, and so did I. I heard the same explanations from the doctor about colic, but when I asked him what exactly colic was, he couldna tell me. All he gave me was a bunch of could be's. It could be food allergies, or it could be gas. I was at the end of my tether, quite like you, and my husband was away working at the time, so I was completely alone with a screaming newborn and a three-year-old who wasna much liking his new baby sister."

Christy blinked. "What did you do?"

"I listened to Effie MacDougal."

"MacDougal," Christy repeated. "What's the title of her book?"

Flora smiled. "Mrs. MacDougal doesna have any book. She's a woman who lives back home in my village in Scotland. She'd had eight children, and had been a help to me after Robbie was born. So she seemed the best person to ask for help. She gave me the explanation that seemed to make the most sense."

Christy's tired eyes sparked with hope as Flora went on.

"The way she explained it to me was that some babies, even if they go all the way to term, are just born too early. They need a little extra time in the womb because their wee senses aren't yet ready to sort out all the noise and light of the outside world."

Christy nodded. "I do notice that Catherine seems overly sensitive to some things, especially by the end of the day."

"Well, if you think about it, bairns are safe and protected inside their mums' bellies for nine months, always warm and comfortable, always sheltered from the glare and blare of this modern world. Then suddenly they are thrust into a loud, frightening place where doctors and nurses poke and prod them, where they canna even hear the comforting sound of their mother's heartbeat. 'Tis no wonder some of them are overwhelmed. What wise dear Mrs. MacDougal suggested was that I do everything I could to keep Annie in an environment that mimicked the womb as much as possible. So I kept the lighting dim and turned the telephone ringer down. I kept the noise level low—that is, as low as I could keep it with my three-year-old running about. And when Annie's poor nervous system was on overdrive, Mrs. MacDougal showed me how to wrap her tightly in her blanket and move with her, swinging her back and forth, similar to the movement in the womb while *shh*ing softly and rhythmically into her ear like the pulse beat of my heart."

Christy blinked at her. "What you've just said makes the most sense over everything else I've read or heard."

"Trust your mother's instinct, Christy. 'Tis a strong sense of what's best for your baby. But the most important thing to remember is to try to keep yourself from getting upset. Sometimes, when babies become overstimulated, they just need to blow off steam. You and I can yell or slam a door or pound piano keys if we have to in order to rid ourselves of that anxiety. The only way babies know how is by crying. But babies are very intuitive. After spending nine months literally connected to their mums, they feel much of what she feels. So the more anxious you get over her crying, the more anxious she'll feel and the more she'll continue to cry."

Christy nodded. She squeezed her fingers around Flora's hand. "Thank you. Thank you for everything. For letting us stay tonight. Matt told me you aren't even open for business yet. For helping me with Catherine. For just listening to me. Matt tries, but he's not a mother, so he doesn't really understand the feelings and the fears. He thinks I'm just being hormonal."

"Men." Flora smiled at her. "Being a mum is one of the most difficult jobs on earth. But 'tis also the most wonderful, and the most worthwhile. Dinna ever lose sight of that, and you'll do just grand. Now, I'd like to do something for you, but I dinna want you to feel as if you canna refuse. I will completely understand. But I think you are in desperate need of a good night's sleep. I'd like to allow you to do that by watching over Catherine for you tonight."

Christy blinked. "But how?"

"Since Catherine is already tucked away in the Heather Room, you and Matt can take one of the other rooms tonight. My personal suggestion would be the Turret Room, but 'tis completely your choice. I'd be happy to stay with Catherine and tend to her when she wakes. You've already stored some of her bottles in the refrigerator, so 'twill be no trouble for me to feed her for you."

Flora watched the play of emotions cross Christy's face, her nearly overwhelming fatigue doing battle with her mother's sense of duty to her baby daughter. "Talk it over with Matt. But I really do hope you'll consider it. You'll be in a much better frame of mind after a good night's sleep, and if anything comes up other than the usual changing, feeding, burping and rocking, I promise I will wake you."

Matt was in complete agreement with the idea. "I wanted to hire a nanny, but Christy was determined to do everything herself." He wrapped a loving arm around his wife's shoulders. "And she's done an incredible job with Catherine, but even Supermoms need a break now and then. And I haven't been much help to her. My job is so demanding with deadlines and a boss who doesn't believe families are any excuse for time off. This week is the first break I've had since Catherine was born."

He looked at his wife with his love and admiration for her shining in his eyes. "Please, Christy. I'm worried about you. You're not eating. You're not sleeping. You can't continue on this way. It's obvious Ms. MacCallum knows what to do. Give yourself this rest. Please. Just once. Just till morning."

A half hour later, Matt and Christy were tucked away in the Turret Room, and Flora was in the kitchen making up a tray with a fresh pot of tea before she headed off for baby duty.

Gavin watched her from the kitchen doorway, not quite sure what part he played in it all.

Flora soon made up his mind for him. "Come. You can keep me company."

And so they spent the night together, not as they could have, lost among the sheets probably in the very Turret Room where Matt and Christy were now sleeping, but sitting on the settee in the Heather Room, talking quietly to each other while Baby Catherine slept nearby. The baby woke after a couple of hours and Flora changed her, fed her, and then soothed her back to sleep by singing to her softly.

Gavin smiled to himself when he heard Flora sing the haunting lilt of a Gaelic lullaby.

There was something about her voice that wrapped itself around whoever heard it, making all tension and stress simply disappear. She could sing a lullaby, or even Aerosmith, and make it sound soothing.

And it was that which first gave Gavin an idea.

"Have you ever considered pursuing a singing career?" he asked Flora after she had laid the baby back down and rejoined him on the settee.

She looked at him, her expression a mixture of amusement and incredulity. "Nae, Gavin. I couldna possibly do something like that."

"Why not?"

"Well, for starters, I'm a single mum to three young children."

"And . . . ?"

"And I've had no formal training."

"Believe me," Gavin said, "your voice needs no formal training. I've heard singers who studied for years at Julliard who don't even come close to your clarity."

She shook her head. "Nae, my singing is suited more for soothing cranky bairns than a recording studio."

"Actually, that's sort of what I was thinking."

She looked at him.

"Traditional lullaby tracks are a dime a dozen. There's nothing to distinguish them from one another. What I'm thinking of is more an album of nontraditional songs, something frazzled parents can put on to soothe their children at night, but with songs that won't leave them humming 'Twinkle Twinkle Little Star' all the way to work the next morning. It would be an eclectic collection and to make it truly unique, I think we should include your Gaelic songs as well. We could also look at the Beatles, Zeppelin, even Aretha if you like. I'll make a few calls."

She shook her head. "I don't know, Gavin. I mean, I have the house to manage this summer and—"

"That's perfect, really. We can spend the next few months deciding which songs we want to include, and I can look into getting the necessary song permissions. Then we can plan to hit the studio this winter, once the tourist season is over and the house is closed for the season."

"But my kids . . . they'll be going back to school. In Scotland. And wee Seamus, he'll have to be tended to. And I still have my other job back in Scotland . . ."

"Details." Gavin put a finger over her lips to quiet any further objections. "Just answer me one thing. Tell me you've never thought about it. Tell me you've never dreamed just once of singing professionally."

"Well, of course I have. Since I was a little girl singing at the village hall, people would remark that they enjoyed hearing me. But to think I could be a recording artist, 'tis just a flight of fancy—"

"It doesn't have to be, Flora. There's always a way to make it work. Always. If you really want it to. Promise me you'll at least think about it."

Flora looked at Gavin and he could see she wondered

whether she even dared to consider it. Finally, she nodded. "All right. I will. I'll think about it. But 'tis all I can promise you now."

Gavin nodded, satisfied.

It was a start.

"Well, good morning to you both," Flora said when Christy and Matt Shore appeared in the kitchen doorway around nine the following morning.

Well rested and freshly showered, Christy looked one hundred percent improved from her frazzled self the night before. Her blond hair was neatly brushed, pulled back beneath a headband, and flipping softly about her shoulders, and her eyes were bright blue and alert.

Christy looked around. "Where's Catherine? I haven't heard her cry all morning. Is she all right?"

"Oh, aye," Flora said and showed Christy to the sun porch where they'd moved the portable crib earlier that morning. After the fury of the storm the night before, the morning had dawned with peace, bathed in the summer's glorious sunlight. Flora had draped a blanket bonnetlike over the top and one side of the crib to shield the baby while the soft sound of the ocean drifted through the open windows across the room.

"When my Annie was a wee babe," Flora whispered, "the sea's song always did the trick to calm her. Even now, she'd rather be running around the sand and surf than playing with her dollies. I swear you'd think the child was half fish."

"Where are your children?" Christy asked. "I'd love to meet them."

"Oh, they're not with me just yet. They'll be arriving here from Scotland in just a couple of days. My brother is bringing them. They had to finish their studies back home afore they could come here to join me. But I canna wait till they get here."

"You and your husband must miss them very much."

Flora blinked, realizing that Christy had assumed she and Gavin were married. She decided to just leave it at that, rather than launch into a lengthy explanation about having lost Seamus and especially to avoid having to define what exactly her relationship with Gavin might be. Truth was, she really didn't know. They weren't lovers, but they were more than just friends. So she simply smiled and said, "Now, why don't you tell me what I can fix you for breakfast?"

Matt and Christy, seemingly in no hurry to leave, stayed on at Thar Muir until later that afternoon. They took Catherine for a stroll down to the shore and spread out a blanket, where they sat together beneath a beach umbrella, enjoying the fine weather. Flora smiled as she watched the two young parents embrace and kiss while their baby daughter suckled at her mother's breast, thinking back to her own days as a new mother and how she, too, had shared the wonder of their son and then their daughter with Seamus.

When they did leave later that day, Christy hugged Flora tightly and promised to keep in touch about Catherine's progress by e-mail. They were halfway down the porch stairs when Flora went running after them.

"Wait! One more thing afore you leave, if you winna mind . . ."

She handed them a pen and a red leather-bound book. "You're our first official guests here at Thar Muir. I would hate for you to miss signing the first place in the guests' register."

Afterward Flora stood in the drive and watched them go, waving until they vanished around the lilac hedge. When she went inside, she set the guest book on the reception desk, and quickly read what they'd written.

Matthew and Christine Shore, New York, New York. We came as strangers lost in a storm and left with a friendship we'll always cherish.

Flora smiled to herself. She could think of no finer way to begin Thar Muir's new life as a guesthouse.

Gavin had left earlier in the day to see to some things at his place, so Flora decided to have a quick shower and then curled up in a chaise on the sun porch with the paperback romance Mrs. Evanson had recommended during her last visit to the bookshop. Baby duty from the night before, however, and the soft, lulling sounds of the ocean quickly overtook her. Even before she could lose herself in the characters' lives playing out on the book's pages, Flora's eyes were drifting closed.

It was there Gavin found her a couple of hours later.

When he'd received no answer at the front door, he'd come around to the back of the house, thinking Flora might be in the garden. He glimpsed her lying inside the screened sun porch, wrapped in her robe with her hair twisted in a towel. He stood there, just drinking in the sight of her.

He had never met a woman like her.

All it had taken was one night, watching as she rocked and loved that baby as if she were her own, and he'd completely lost his heart to her. This was a woman who had been made to be a mother, a woman with an incredible capacity to love, yet with a vulnerability, a need to be loved in return.

Miranda had never had that. Whenever they'd been out at a restaurant and another diner's child started to cry, Miranda had rolled her eyes and made comments not quite under her breath about how if someone couldn't "handle" their child, they should not go out among the public. Ironic, considering Miranda had done so very little "handling" of Gabriel herself, doling it out instead to a procession of different nannies, all of whom she'd eventually dismissed when they hadn't lived up to her unrealistic expectations.

But Gavin couldn't blame Miranda entirely. He was Gabriel's father. He should have been more involved, and would do nearly anything to turn back time, go back, and make it right. He'd known shortly after Gabriel's second birthday that his marriage was not going to succeed. Miranda was too spoiled, too self-involved. In order to avoid the tension that festered between them, he'd spent more and more time at the studio. In doing so, he'd neglected to be the father he should have been. It was something he would regret for the rest of his life.

As he stood there, watching Flora sleep, Gavin doubted she had taken the time to eat much of anything since breakfast. He'd already suspected as much, so he'd spent the afternoon preparing his specialty—actually the only thing in his cooking repertoire—spaghetti with meatballs Matheson style: sauce heavy on the spices, with a generous splash of Chianti.

Moving quietly to the kitchen so as not to wake her, Gavin prepared two plates, uncorked a new Chianti, and lit the candles in the dining room. He looked through Flora's CDs and slid Norah Jones into the stereo, then warmed the baguette he'd picked up at the café in the oven. The sun was just setting when he went to wake Flora from her nap.

Gavin did so by way of a long, slow, very wet kiss that left her sighing out loud. He lifted his head to look at her in the twilight.

"Hello there, sleepyhead."

She smiled a lazy smile, stretching on the chaise. Gavin allowed himself the fantasy of waking beside her, having her stretch that same way, naked beneath him. He felt a surge of awareness streak straight to his groin when he noticed her robe gapping slightly to reveal her pale, smooth breasts.

"Goodness," she said, " 'tis already dark outside. What time is it?"

"Time for you to let me take care of you for once."

He took her hand and helped her up from the chaise. The towel that she'd wrapped around her head had fallen and her hair, still damp, fell in a mass of red curls about her face.

Flora tried to tame it with a quick finger comb. "I'm a mess, Gavin. Let me just go inside and get dressed and try to do something with this hair."

"Oh, no, you don't." He grabbed her hand. "You look beautiful. And that robe is more than adequate for my dinner party."

Refusing any further protest, Gavin led Flora to the dining room, where candlelight and low, honeyed music awaited them.

"Now, I don't claim to be a gourmet, but I've been told I make a decent enough pasta sauce. I hope you like spaghetti."

Flora grinned. "I love it."

They shared an intimate meal and pleasant conversation, mostly about the Shores' arrival the previous night and curiosity about how the family was faring on the rest of their journey. Although neither mentioned it, they both realized it was probably the last opportunity they would have for time alone together before Flora's children arrived from Scotland. That shared realization charged the air with a sense of unspoken anticipation.

After cleaning and washing the dishes, Gavin suggested

a walk down by the shore. The night was warm and the sky was lit only by a sliver of a moon. They could hear the rush of the water echoing around them and smell air filled with the heady salt scent of the sea.

They walked barefoot on the sand with hands linked and the water swirling over their toes. Neither really spoke as both were lost to their own thoughts. There wasn't any need for words. They knew without saying it aloud where this night would take them.

It was Flora who broke away first. She turned to look at Gavin with a knowing smile and a spark of mischief in her alluring green eyes. Without saying a word, she loosened the belt of her robe, hooked her finger in a "follow me" gesture, and then turned and started walking toward the water. As she faded into the shadows, Gavin saw the robe drop to the sand and a flash of her naked backside before she vanished into the night.

Then he heard a splash.

"Flora? Are you crazy? You'll freeze out there. . . ."

Her voice, a siren's song, called to him. "Och, a fine braw mon like yerself's not afraid of a wee bit o' water, are you?"

She gave herself over to the brogue of her roots, a magical singsong voice that whispered on the breeze. Just the sound of her voice coming from somewhere in the darkness sent a shiver running through him. Gavin thought back to that early morning when he'd first come to that same stretch of beach, when she'd emerged from the sea, all wet, all skin. Apparently the cold didn't bother her. But it had been a long, long time since he'd taken a swim in the ocean, especially in the North Atlantic . . .

Was he really going to let a little cold water keep him from a beautiful naked woman?

Gavin shed his clothes and headed for the water. It cov-

ered his feet and sent gooseflesh racing over the length of
his body. At first, the cold was a shock, numbing his skin.
But he went on, wading in, trying to accustom himself to the
chill until the water was waist deep. He couldn't see Flora
anywhere.

"Flora?"

But then he felt her.

Her feather-light hands encircled his waist from behind
and splayed across his chest. The clouds had moved to cover
what little light the moon provided, cloaking them in darkness. It was a heady, sensual combination: the thick of the
night, the cold, cold water, and the heat of her hands on his
tingling skin.

Flora didn't say a word. She just pressed her body against
the length of his, kissing his shoulder, nibbling softly. He
could feel the fullness of her breasts against his back, her
hips against his buttocks. The cold water was little deterrent
against the pleasure of her touch, and his body responded,
hardening. And then softly, he heard her, that voice, smoky
and swirling, wrapping over him.

"There once was a mermaid, a princess of the sea. She
was happy in her home with only the dark cold water and
the fish for company, until the day she swam too close to
the shore. She caught a glimpse of a man standing there,
she did, and he was beautiful to her. So different. So pow-
erful. As if carved from stone. She was mesmerized by
him"—he felt her hands slip down over his arms—"by his
strong arms, and his fine, trim legs so unlike her fish's tail."

Gavin closed his eyes, giving himself over to the fantasy.
He felt her rub her leg against his as she moved next to him.
If he hadn't known better, the way she'd moved and the
smoothness of her skin against his, he would have sworn she
had indeed transformed into a mermaid.

Her voice went on, breathy against his neck. "She knew she had to have him, this beautiful man, but she knew she could not leave the sea to join him. She was a mermaid after all. She had no legs to walk to him. The only way she could get to him would be to tempt him to come to her, to lure him into the water. And so she waited, day by day, night by night, until she saw him again. She swam as close as she dared, shielded by the rocks. Then, softly she began to sing him her siren's song."

Flora began to sing then, in her rich, seductive voice, singing in the Gaelic of her ancestors. Gavin had no idea what she sang, or the words she used. It didn't matter. Just the sound of her voice, the exotic language, had his blood rushing through him, banishing the water's chill, with his body tightening and hardening even more in response.

What had she said to him the night before? A voice suited only for soothing cranky babies?

Yeah, right.

Gavin reached for her, anxious to taste her mouth, but she skirted away, the music of her voice drifting on the hush of the sea.

"The mermaid enticed him farther out into the water and he followed the soft sound of her voice, seeking the promise of her charms."

Gavin did the same, following her lilting voice.

"Every time he drew near enough to touch her"—Gavin felt her hands brush his naked hip. He sucked in his breath, reached for her—"she only slipped away again."

He heard a splash, and she was gone.

His body jolted.

The water was higher now, up to Gavin's belly, and he could feel the surge and pull of the tide against his legs. He should have been shivering from the cold, but the heat of her voice kept him warm.

She spoke again, and her voice was deeper now, wrapping around him like smooth velvet.

"And when she finally felt she had drawn him out far enough from the shore that he winna be able to escape her, the mermaid allowed the man to catch her."

Suddenly Flora was standing right before him.

Gavin could see her shadowy silhouette in the muted moonlight. She raised her hands slowly above her head, reaching for the stars. The outline of her breasts beckoned to him.

This time when he reached for her, she did not shy away.

Gavin was nearly out of his mind with need for her. She came closer to him, pressed her body to his, and he could feel the warmth and pressure of her sliding up against his hardness. He nearly came undone. He locked his arms around her so that she couldn't skirt away. And he ground his mouth over hers as his hands rubbed down her body, cupping her bottom, lifting her, and pulling her hard against him.

The heat of her touch pounded through his veins. When he broke away from the kiss moments later, they were both breathing hard. He could feel the rapid rise and fall of her breasts against his chest.

"And what did the man do when he caught the mermaid?" he rasped against her wet hair, nuzzling the damp curve of her neck, tasting the salt of the sea on her skin.

She bit lightly at his shoulder, causing him to draw in his breath sharply. "Why . . . he made love to her, of course, like no mortal man has ever made love to a woman afore."

Gavin nearly exploded, his need for her was so great. He growled and captured her mouth while his hands kneaded her bottom, pulling her up so that he could taste her neck, bite her shoulder, bury his face in her full, warm breasts. Flora splayed her hands over his shoulders and wrapped her legs around his waist. Slowly, he lowered her, guiding her hips, easing her over him until he was filling her completely.

He heard her breath sigh past her lips, then felt it brush his forehead. It was a sigh of pure sexual satisfaction. She locked her legs around him, tightening around the rigid length of his sex, and he nearly lost all control over himself.

His breathing was ragged against her mouth as she held him there. He filled her so completely. When she moved her hips and rocked with the smooth motion of the water, Gavin groaned, squeezing his hands on her bottom. She moved again, tightened her legs.

Moved.

Tightened.

She took him fully and deeply into herself, and he suckled her, clinging to her as she continued to rock against him.

It had been so long, so very long for them both. So very long since he had felt the ultimate completion of man joining woman. What she had begun as a playful midnight seduction had suddenly changed in the rush of their mingled breaths. It had grown desperate. It had become vital.

It was as if a part of him that had died suddenly came alive. Gavin seized that feeling, clung to it, and refused to let go. All thought, all reason, left them as Flora and Gavin clung to each other with both body and soul. They rocked and writhed to the motion of the water, following nature's dance. Flora reached her climax first, gasping against Gavin's hair as she strained her body, threw back her head, and let the power of her orgasm sweep through her. When Gavin found his own release he nearly shouted out loud as he gripped her hips and buried himself inside her, locked with her in a lover's embrace and wrapped in the blanket of the moon and the sea and the night.

Flora started from the warm, dreamy haze of her sleep, opened her eyes and listened.

Had that been a car door she'd just heard outside?

She waited, blinking against the daylight, then decided she must have been mistaken. Until a moment later when she heard footsteps pounding on the porch stairs followed by a high-pitched voice calling from below.

"Mummy! Surprise! We're here!"

For a split second, she actually saw her consciousness blur. "Oh, sweet *Dia*. It's the kids."

That sent Gavin jerking awake. "What? *Your* kids? But I thought they weren't coming until tomorrow."

"They weren't."

Flora sprung up. She began searching frantically for her robe. Neither of them wore a stitch of clothing and she prayed they hadn't been so caught up in their lovemaking the night before that they'd left their clothes down on the beach. She rather doubted Gavin would pass muster wearing anything of hers.

"Mummy!" They were ringing the front bell. "Where are you?"

Please, God, let her have remembered to lock the front door.

She hadn't.

Seconds later, she could hear them filing in, calling to her.

"Mumma!"

"Flor? You here?"

"Mummmmm!"

Flora looked at Gavin. "You can't be here. *We* can't be

here. Together. I can't let them find us like this the very moment they arrive."

Already she could hear them bounding up the stairs. She belted her robe and uttered that same curse word she'd shouted the day she'd been stuck on the trellis.

"Just stay here," she said, trying to think. "And don't open this door for any reason."

Flora made it out of the room just as Annie reached the landing.

"Mumma!"

"Hi, my baby girl." She closed the door quickly behind her. "What are you doing here? You weren't supposed to come till tomorrow."

"We finished school a day early and Uncle Angus got us on an earlier flight so we could surprise you. Are you surprised, Mumma?"

"More than you can possibly know."

Robbie appeared next on the stairs, followed after by Angus carrying wee Seamus, whose arms were already open and waiting for her to take him.

They surrounded her, demanding hugs and kisses. Flora wrapped them in her arms and moved them gently toward the stairs, away from the door behind her.

"All right, let's get your mum something to wear from her closet and—"

Flora looked at Angus, eyes wide, and quickly shook her head.

Thank God he had the perception and quick wits of a police constable.

"Or I've an even better idea. Let's go down to the kitchen and make your mum some breakfast, aye?" Angus glanced at her with a half grin. "I'm sure she's starving. What do you think, Annie? Do you suppose you and Robbie can scramble some eggs?"

"Can we? Come on, Robbie," Annie squealed, grabbing her older brother by the arm and dragging him toward the stairs.

"Wanna go, too!" Seamus whined, and Angus set him down so he could race after his siblings.

"Take the baby's hand on the stairs!" Flora called to Annie.

When the kids had gone, she let go of the petrified breath she'd been holding.

Angus grinned at her. "Well, am I to guess from the fact that it would take a herd of elephants to move you from that door that you took my advice, then?"

Flora looked down, embarrassed. Then she told herself she had nothing to be embarrassed about. She was a woman. A healthy adult woman with physical and emotional needs. She lifted her chin, stared her brother square in the eye, and said with conviction, "Yes, Angus, I had sex, a'right? And afore you ask, aye! It was good, too!"

Standing on the other side of the door, stuffing his shirt-tails into his jeans with a smile curling his mouth, Gavin couldn't have agreed more.

Chapter Nine

Gavin looked at his watch.

This was ridiculous.

He'd been hiding up in that bedroom for the past fifteen minutes, listening to the muffled voices of Flora and her children and feeling more like a seventeen-year-old who'd shimmied up to his girlfriend's bedroom window than a thirty-six-year-old award-winning composer.

He'd stayed because Flora had asked him to, and he'd sat on the bed they'd shared the night before. The bed where they'd made love through the night and into the morning. Where he'd taken his time, running his hands over every soft inch of her body. Where he'd touched her, learned her, memorized her until she was trembling and gasping beneath him.

But as he sat there listening to them below, he found himself not wanting to hide but wanting to see them—Flora's children—the very ones he'd told himself he needed to do everything to avoid.

And he wanted to see them for *her*.

The night he had spent with her had changed everything. He could no longer tiptoe around the fact that this woman—the only woman who had sparked a fire in him in the past two years—was also the mother of three kids. He could no longer watch the sun set, day after day, asking himself if he could or could not put himself in a situation with the potential to cause him heartache. Because he'd been watching that sunset alone too long, without anyone to watch with him. Alone was something he no longer wanted to be.

He stood atop the steps, looking down on the entryway, and knew that just beyond it was the front door. He could easily slip out, return to the life he knew, but he would only be left wondering what might have awaited him if he had turned at the bottom of the stairs and followed the voices.

Three pairs of eyes turned to stare at Gavin when he walked into the kitchen moments later. Three pairs of very curious eyes. Four, when you added Flora's brother, who'd just looked up from where he'd been standing by the sink. Only his eyes weren't curious at all.

His were assessing.

A brother's eyes.

"Hullo," said a sweet-faced little girl with a strawberry-blond lopsided ponytail. "Who are you?"

Gavin was just about to answer her when Flora, coming from the back of the house where she'd gone to get dressed, walked into the room. She wore jeans and a T-shirt, her hair hastily clipped back. She looked at Gavin, and for a moment she seemed stunned, as if she'd expected him to be somewhere a million miles away—as if she wanted him anywhere but there.

And then she quickly recovered herself, saying to her daughter, "Annie, that's not a very polite way to introduce yourself to someone."

"Sorry, Mummy . . ." The little girl thought a moment, then tried again. "Hullo. I'm Fiona Margaret Jean MacCallum. Everyone just calls me Annie. Who are you?"

Gavin smiled at her. "I'm Gavin Matheson, Annie Mac-Callum. It's a pleasure to meet you."

Her cheek smudged with strawberry jam, she nodded over a bite of toast. "And you, sir. Mr. Matheson."

"You can call me Gavin."

Annie looked at her mother as if to ask if that would be all right. Flora nodded.

"Gavin, did you sleep here last night?"

The cough that came from Flora's brother wasn't lost on Gavin. Nor was the dangerous look Flora gave him in response.

"Well, actually—" Gavin felt his throat tighten around his answer.

"This is a guesthouse, Annie," Flora cut in. "You're going to have to get used to the idea that people other than us will be staying here."

"Yes, but I thought the guests weren't coming until Friday, Mummy."

"Well, we've already had a few come to stay. In fact, we had another family yesterday with a new baby. They were caught in a storm. I couldna turn them away."

While Annie quizzed her mother about the baby she had missed seeing, which was tantamount to a calamity in her eyes, Gavin offered a handshake to Flora's brother. "Gavin Matheson."

"Angus MacLeith," he answered and stood his full two inches over six feet, looking Gavin square in the eye. He was a burly Scot with reddish brown hair who looked quite capable of handling pretty much any situation, a good quality for a police constable. Gavin was glad Flora had had such a solid brother to lean on.

The hand Angus extended gripped Gavin's firmly. They

exchanged a glance. An air of understanding passed between them.

Two down. Two to go, Gavin thought. And they would be the hardest two, the two who would most call to mind thoughts of Gabriel.

Gavin steeled himself and went to the elder of the boys, who had a mop of chestnut-colored hair that fell over his eyes. He was eleven, Gavin remembered Flora telling him. And to an eleven year old, that meant having one foot firmly in the door of manhood.

Don't speak to him like he's a kid, Gavin told himself.

"You're Robbie?"

"Robert Angus MacCallum, sir."

Though he'd obviously been taught to address adults with respect, Gavin could see from the guarded look in his eyes that he wasn't quite sure whether this strange man they'd found alone in a house with their mother represented friend or foe.

"Nice to meet you, Robbie."

He had a flash then of Gabriel standing much the same way, meeting one of his mother's "friends," and the thought of it knifed through him like a shard of glass.

Gavin felt a tug on his shirtsleeve. Pushing the thought away, he looked down into a pair of mischievous eyes the same green as his mother's.

"'m Seamu*sh*," the boy said around the thumb he was casually sucking.

Gavin waited for the feeling to come, that knee-jerk flinch that burned in his gut, threatening to double him over. He waited because he fully expected it would come. It had to. It always did.

But something about Seamus, the light in his eyes—a

light that seemed to touch his soul—reached through the darkness to Gavin. He reached out and took Seamus's hand.

It was the oddest, most incredible thing.

"Nice to meet you, Seamus. I'm Gavin."

Seamus smiled around his thumb, a dimple deepening one pudgy cheek as he repeated, *"Gaaa-vinnn."*

Annie piped in then. "Are you going to have some of my omelet, Gavin? I cooked it m'self."

Gavin looked to a frying pan that contained something that probably could have been eggs, before it had been mixed with pieces of carrot, celery, and—what was that red stuff?

"Red Hots," Angus said in answer to his look of confusion.

"Red Hots," Gavin repeated. "As in the candy?"

Angus nodded. "That would be correct. Straight from Scotland, delivered by way of Annie's jacket pocket."

"Well." Gavin looked at Annie. "Now, how did you know that was my favorite kind of omelet?"

Annie beamed.

While the children quizzed their mother about the house, the town, and anything else they could think of, Gavin ate the whole thing, washing it down with a glass of Annie's "special," cocoa that tasted as if it was made more from chocolate syrup than milk.

Afterward, as the kids went off with Angus to explore the guest rooms—*without touching anything,* Flora warned—Gavin poured himself a cup of fresh coffee.

Flora, he noticed, had fallen quiet. She was standing at the kitchen sink, contemplating, it seemed, the tea leaves in the bottom of her cup.

"I had planned to make you breakfast in bed," he said as he came up behind her.

He'd met Flora's children, had faced his angst instead of hiding from it as he had for so long. It had sparked a feeling in him—a feeling of hope he'd previously refused to consider possible. That wasn't to say it would be an easy road, but walking that road with Flora would certainly make it more bearable.

Yet when he moved her hair aside to brush her neck with a kiss, Flora sidestepped away from him.

"The kids . . ." she mumbled.

"Are upstairs with your brother."

She spun on him. "And they could come down at any moment. Then what am I supposed to tell them? That their mother—their father's wife—just spent the night in bed with a strange man?"

Gavin drew himself up and took two steps back as he looked at her. "You have nothing to feel guilty about, Flora."

"I have *everything* to feel guilty about." She lifted her gaze to stare at him. "I should have been at the door, ready to meet them with open arms and kisses when they arrived this morning, not lying about naked in bed like some sort of . . ."

She didn't finish the thought, but Gavin knew he wouldn't have liked anything she might have said.

"I married Seamus, had my children with him . . ."

So that's what this was about. She'd suddenly reverted from the role of woman to mom. Her kids had arrived and apparently with them came their father's ghost.

"Last night was incredible, Flora. It was beautiful, and I am not going to regret it. You shouldn't regret it either. Why should you punish yourself for wanting to feel alive? Seamus is gone. He's not coming back. You can't be unfaithful to a memory any more than you can remain married to it."

"That's for me to decide." She looked at him, her eyes flinty with indignation. "I think you should leave."

"Flora . . ."

"I think you should leave *now*."

Gavin waited a moment longer, hoping she would see the mistake she was making, but she just stared at him with that same distant, condemning stare. Then she said, "Fine. If you won't go, then I will."

She dropped her teacup into the sink with a porcelain clatter, turned, and left the room.

Gavin was still standing there, staring at the space where she'd been, when Angus came into the room a few seconds later.

"Oy, Gavin," he said, obviously having witnessed the scene. " 'Tis best you go, mate. Give her some space, a little time. This is all new to her. She never imagined she'd find herself in this position, and she doesn't quite know what to make of it. She'll come around. She just needs to come to terms with it, is all. Takes her a while, but she will."

With a shake of his head, Gavin turned and walked out the door.

Flora was in the garden on her hands and knees pulling weeds from the rose beds when Angus came up behind her.

"Where's Matheson?"

"He's gone." And then she looked at him. "Where are the kids?"

"I brought in their bags and told them to change their clothes so they could come out here and play. They'll be along in a minute."

She tugged at a particularly stubborn dandelion until it finally pulled free, root and all.

"So what d'you mean Matheson's gone?"

She rose up, wiping her soiled hands with a towel. She hadn't bothered to go looking for gloves in the garden shed and had now ruined the manicure she'd gotten at Jen's shop. She shrugged. "He left. That's all."

She started past him, but Angus took his sister by the arm. "No, that's not all, Flora. You sent him off, didn't you? Why? Because of the kids? Because you're afraid of what they might think? They're stronger than you give them credit for. D'ye think they winna want to see their mum happy again? Robbie certainly remembers, and even Annie probably does, but poor wee Seamus has ne'er seen the way his mum's face can light up an entire room, how just the sound of her laughter can make anyone standing around her break into a smile."

Flora looked at him with tears brimming her eyes.

"I saw the way that man looked at you, Flora. I watched him eat every bite of that dreadful concoction Annie made. He could have shrugged off your kids just as easily as you just shrugged him off. I've seen plenty enough blokes do that to plenty of other single mums. Aye, 'tis grand when they've got her in bed, but when it comes time for her to tend to her kids, they're gone. But Matheson didn't do that. He came in and made an honest effort to meet us all. He spoke to your kids like they mattered, not like they were an inconvenience to his having a good time. And let me tell you, there's few men who'll do tha' for another man's bairns."

Ashamed, Flora bowed her head. Angus was right. She'd been so wrapped up in the guilt she'd felt at seeing her kids and knowing where she'd been when they arrived that she hadn't even taken into account how difficult it must have been for Gavin to have walked straight into the fray. Thoughts of Gabriel must be knotting his insides. But he'd done it. For her. And she'd responded with indignation and then finally dismissal.

"Oh, *Dia*, I'm horrible."

Ever the protector, Angus took her into his arms and held her, rubbing her back and providing her with the supportive shoulder she needed. "Now, we both know that's not true. You're just stumbling along as best you can."

"Aye. Through a minefield." She lifted her head. "I'm so confused, Angus. And I'm scared. I remember that young, carefree girl you spoke of, the same one who thought she had everything she ever needed with just her husband and her bairns to tend to. But that's changed now, and there's naught I can do about it. I'm scared of what will be if things stay the way they are, and I'm scared of moving on. I'm just so scared . . ."

"Shh, m'pet . . ."

Angus turned her, tucked her head beneath his chin, and wrapped her in his arms. "I shinna have brought the kids early without telling you first."

"No, 'tisn't that. I'm so happy to see them. It's just I hadn't yet prepared for how I was going to handle things with them and Gavin. This thing, last night, it just sort of happened."

"That's usually the way it is."

"But there's more to it, more you dinna know about yet, about Gavin's life. I dinna know if this is anything that will stick, or if it's just something that will pass. I just"—she took a deep breath—"I hate the idea of deceiving my own kids, but I certainly couldna tell them the truth of why Gavin came walking into the kitchen like he did."

"You handled it the only way you could. And dinna worry. 'Tis fine. But tell me something Flor, do you like this man?"

She blinked, then nodded. "He's a good man, Angus. He makes me feel . . ."

How could she explain to her brother how she felt when Gavin looked at her with such open male appreciation, how just the touch of his hands made her feel truly, incredibly alive?

"There's no need to put it to words, love. 'Tis written all over your face. I'm happy for you. But I'll be sorely put out with you if you forsake this without first giving it its proper chance. Don't take a peek and then shut your eyes before you know if it winna be something that would bring that light back to your eyes, that would let us see that carefree young girl again. Think about it, Flor. Just promise me you'll do that much."

When he hugged her again, Flora rested her cheek against the solid strength of his shoulder. Angus had always been there for her when she'd needed him. He'd even given up his career to come back to Scotland and help support her and the kids when Seamus died. But he deserved a life of his own, too. And somehow she didn't think he'd allow himself that until he saw that she could stand on her own two feet and accept whatever the future might bring.

Flora turned her head. It was then she saw Robbie, silently watching them from the kitchen doorway.

"Rabbie?"

Her first thought was to wonder, and then fear, how much of their conversation he might have overheard.

He didn't move to come out into the garden. Instead he just said, "We were wondering if we could go down and have a look at the beach."

"Of course," she said, smiling, wiping her eyes quickly with the back of her hand.

"What's the matter?" he asked. "Why are you crying, Mum?"

She ruffled his hair. "I'm just so happy to see you and your brother and sister, that's all. I really missed you guys."

Annie and Seamus came tearing out of the house to join them, providing a much welcome diversion. Flora hugged them all to her. "Now, let me get washed up and we'll go down to play on the shore. If you look over there in that shed, you can find some sand buckets and shovels."

After spending a couple hours on the beach with her children, Flora felt much better. At first it was difficult because the sight of the beach only brought back memories of the night before and the wonderful lovemaking she'd shared with Gavin. But like the tide that comes in to sweep away the footprints in the sand, she convinced herself it was best to tuck that memory away and enjoy some long overdue playtime with her kids.

They splashed through the waves and made a sand castle model of Castle Wrath, complete with a clamshell that was meant to be Libby and a stray crab claw for Graeme, standing high on the north tower. Angus even let the kids bury him in the sand and Flora took a great snapshot of him covered neck to toe, his sunglassed face sleeping in the sun.

Every now and then Flora would look up and her eyes would search down the shore at the stretch of houses that stood along the coast. She thought of herself playing with her kids on the shore, and thought of Gavin sitting alone in one of those houses, without his son, without even knowing where he was.

She had been so unfair to him that morning. She'd also been cruel when she told him to leave. And cruelty went against everything Flora was, everything she'd ever been.

When she lost Seamus, Flora knew only that she had to

do one thing. She had to protect her young family—shield them as best as she could. So she had secured them into a protective sort of ring, not a real ring, of course, but a made-up halo of light that she'd told them only they could see.

She had first drawn her children inside of that ring when she had to tell them their father wouldn't be coming home again. Back then it had been just Robbie and Annie—she hadn't yet realized Seamus had left her the gift of their third child. She would never forget their little faces, especially the way Robbie had drawn in a startled breath when she'd told them what had happened to their father. That circle had become her safeguard, that haven where the outside world couldn't penetrate, where the shadows couldn't invade.

It was the only way Flora had survived those first hours, those first days, those first gut-wrenching weeks. Everywhere they went, they went together, always shielded by that circle of imaginary light.

At the funeral, with its empty casket because Seamus's body had been lost to the sea, that circle had sheltered them as they stood at the side of that grave in the village cemetery, Annie on one side of Flora, Robbie on the other. Each of them had dropped in a flower, then stood to watch as shovelful after shovelful of dirt covered the wooden casket that represented his final resting place. She'd told the children not to cry, that it wasn't their father in that cold hole in the ground. She promised them that he was with the angels, with their grandfather and grandmother, too, and that so long as they remained in their halo of light, they were still with him, and nothing could ever hurt them.

She'd told it to the children so many times, through the subsequent sleepless nights and teary days, she'd made herself believe it, too.

Coming to Massachusetts had taken Flora out of that circle. She'd left the sheltered haven of her family and her home and stepped out, testing the waters of the world outside their haven. It hadn't been a bad thing. Nothing terrible had happened to her. But the moment her children came, the moment she'd stepped back inside that halo, the need to protect, to shield, and to defend her family had returned like a suit of armor.

Only she'd used that armor to keep Gavin out, too, and she shouldn't have.

Flora waited until the children went to bed that night. Angus was happily ensconced in front of the satellite television with two hundred and fifty channels at his beck and call. She had washed the supper dishes, folded the laundry, and unpacked all the suitcases.

Telling Angus she was off for a walk on the beach, Flora grabbed her wrap and headed for the door.

She found the path that Gavin had told her about easily enough and followed it along the line of the shore, climbing from her stretch of beach to a rocky headland that had her stopping to draw in her breath, filling her lungs with the salty sea air. She stood for a moment and let the night wash over her, chilling her beneath the summer dress she wore, a filmy thing with a long full skirt that swirled with the breeze around her bare legs and clung to her figure.

It was dark out and with no moon to light her way, Flora began to fear she wouldn't know which house she was looking for. She passed one where the windows were dark and the shutters closed, another where she heard the sounds of dinner party conversation and laughter coming from the open windows. Yet another had the squeals of children spashing in a swimming pool. Thinking surely she had come too far and had somehow missed it, she was just about to turn back when she heard the faint sound of a piano drifting on the breeze.

For a moment, she just stood and listened. She closed her eyes and let the music soothe her. It carried the haunting echo of her ancestry, the air of the Celt and the spirit of the Gael, but with it something more. It touched her with its honesty. It moved her with its beauty.

And it drew her like a siren's song toward the house above.

Gavin crumpled the sheet of music in frustration and tossed it aside with the others that lay scattered at his feet. He'd never had to fight so hard for every note or struggle through every bar of music like this before. He couldn't help but wonder if it was just this particular composition, or fear that he had gone so long without composing that he'd lost the gift that had been his life's blood.

But he wasn't giving up.

He took a sip of wine, swallowed it slowly, and closed his eyes. He cleared his thoughts like a blank canvas, and then tried to envision something inspiring—a mood, a place—but inevitably that inspiration became a face.

Flora.

He pictured her not as he'd last seen her with her eyes so cold and distant, but as he'd seen her in the early hours of that morning, sleeping beside him in that big four-poster bed. Her hair had been a torrent of fiery curls against the white sheet of the pillow and her face was utterly beautiful as she slept.

Slowly Gavin's fingers began to move over the piano keys, playing the notes he'd already written, gliding easily over the first stanza. Yes, he thought, this was it. It was right.

It flowed. It echoed. It thrummed with the mystery that was her.

When he got to the second verse he began to lose his direction. The notes, sounding flat, suddenly fell off. For whatever reason, it just wasn't right.

Gavin stopped playing and opened his eyes.

That was when he saw her.

For the first few minutes, he thought he must have imagined her. She stood framed in the French doors that he'd left open. A filmy cloud of white clung to her and she wore a wrap that drooped slightly off one shoulder. Her hair almost seemed made of fire.

He watched as she came into the room and stood beside the piano.

And then she said his name.

"Gavin . . . the music you were playing," she said, " 'tis beautiful."

Gavin pulled the cover down over the keys and shielded the sheets of music. He wasn't ready yet for her to see it or hear it. "It's a work very much in progress." Then he added, "Sometimes without making much in the way of progress at all."

He got up, crossing to the bar. "Wine?"

She nodded and waited while he poured her a glass of the fragrant Burgundy he'd already uncorked.

"Gavin, I've come here because"—she hesitated—"I owe you an apology. This morning, you tried to make the best of an unexpected situation, and I pushed you away. I'm sorry for that. It was unfair. It's just . . ."

Gavin sat on the couch across from her. "Flora, I understand your instinct is to protect your family. In fact, I commend you for it. But at the same time, you didn't really give me a chance with them." He looked at her. "You didn't really give me a chance with you, either."

She lowered her eyes, peering at the plum-colored depths of her wine. "I know that, Gavin. And I'd like to. Give you a chance, that is. If you're still willing."

Truth was, Gavin had spent most of the day asking himself that same question.

After leaving Thar Muir that morning, he'd come back to the summerhouse and taken out his photos of Gabriel. He'd spent the day going through them—remembering that time when he took him to the zoo, how the boy had laughed a deep belly laugh to see the monkeys swinging from the trees. For the longest time after Miranda had taken Gabriel and disappeared, Gavin hadn't been able to look at another child without feeling almost physically ill. Eventually he'd just trained his eyes to look away, to avoid any reminder that would touch that broken part of his heart. But at those times when he would chance to see a young boy riding his bicycle, or playing in the park, Gavin would wonder if Gabriel had learned to ride a bicycle yet, and if he had, who had taught him. Had he ever hit a baseball? Or gone ice skating? Those were the sorts of things Gavin had always looked forward to doing from the moment Gabriel was born. They were the sorts of things a father taught a son.

And they were the things Gavin would never be able to get back.

As usual, whenever he immersed himself in memories of his son, Gavin found himself calling Ivan, the private investigator he'd hired once he'd realized the authorities weren't doing much of anything to bring Gabriel home.

"Just checking in," he'd told him, as he had countless times during countless other phone calls. What he'd really wanted was some reassurance that Ivan hadn't given up on the case.

"It's been quiet," Ivan had said. "But I'm checking into a couple of possibilities. There's been some activity recently in Miranda's father's bank account. I'm waiting for the details. Could be something, or it could be nothing. Soon as I hear anything, I'll let you know."

Gavin looked at Flora to answer her. "I'm not saying I expect it to be easy. We both have our own demons to conquer. But I'm certainly willing to see where it leads us."

"On one condition," Flora added.

"A condition?"

"Aye. Last night," she said. "What we shared together. It canna happen again."

He blinked at her. "Flora, you can't think I was just looking to sleep with you."

"Nae, I don't. Last night was"—she hesitated—"it was exceptional, to be sure. It allowed me to remember what it is to be a woman, and I thank you for that. But I am a mother to three small children, as well. And I am, I have to be their mother first, before I am a woman."

"You can be both."

"Aye, I can. But only in a way that doesn't compromise one for the other. My kids are a part of me and always will be. That winna change. Until this morning, you've only known me as the woman, Gavin, not as the mother, too. And so I ask you to think on this. If you want to see where this leads us, then we'll begin it the way it should have begun, aye? But if you decide this isna something you want to do, or something you feel you aren't capable of taking on, then I accept that, too. There's no need for regrets, or explanations. We will simply hold our time together as a lovely memory."

Flora walked over to Gavin then and stared into his eyes. She smiled, and he could smell the scent of her, the hint of lavender kissed by the sea. She reached up and kissed him tenderly on the mouth. Then, touching a fingertip gently to his lips, she turned and disappeared back through the door from which she'd come.

Chapter Ten

Flora was elbow deep in a batch of scones when she heard the doorbell ring.

She pushed away a stray bit of hair that was falling in her eyes with the back of her hand, then frowned when she realized she'd just dusted half her forehead with flour.

The doorbell rang again.

She would have called to the kids to get it, but they had gone off exploring in the woods behind the carriage house.

And Angus, dutiful uncle that he was, had gone with them.

So it was left to her. Grabbing a towel, she pulled the sticky dough from her fingers and headed for the front of the house while the bell rang on.

"Och, I'm coming . . ."

A bouquet of flowers greeted her when she pulled open the door.

"Oh!"

"Delivery, ma'am."

"I can see that. . . ."

It was a huge arrangement made up of at least two-dozen perfect white roses, mixed together with bunches of fragrant blooming heather.

She smiled. True to her name, fresh flowers were one of her favorite indulgences.

"Thank you so much," Flora said to the delivery driver as she took the elegant crystal vase from him. Breathing in the heady scent, she turned and placed it on the table by the stairs, then stepped back to admire it. It was beautiful. The white flowers stood out against the polished oak paneling in the hall. The heather provided that touch of Scotland. It would add the perfect touch for greeting Thar Muir's first guests the following day.

Flora had immediately assumed the flowers were from Libby and Graeme. She plucked the small card from inside the fragrant blooms with the full expectation of seeing their names scribbled across it. The flowers, however, were from someone else entirely.

> *To beginning again . . .*
> *How about dinner?*
> *Tonight.*
> *My place.*
> *At seven.*
> *Bring the kids . . .*
> *And Angus.*

He'd signed it *Gavin Matheson, that guy at Table 7.*

Flora smiled at that and tucked the small card into the pocket of her jeans, turned and headed back to the kitchen.

She had just finished wrapping the dough and was tucking it into the refrigerator for baking the next morning when she heard the telltale tromping of feet and boisterous chatter that was a sure sign her children had returned.

"Mum! You winna believe what we found!"

Not surprisingly, Annie was first to burst through the

door. Her carroty ponytail tilted to one side, with more of it
hanging out of the elastic than in. Her trousers were caked
with a stiff hem of wet sand a good four inches up the cuffs,
and her jumper had run afoul of—something truly *foul*.

Dia! Whatever was that smell?

"Apparently you found a bog, Annie MacCallum, and
you loved it so much you decided to have a bit of a roll
around in it," Flora said, immediately yanking the girl's
sweater up by the arms and over her twig-tangled head. A
shower of sand and pebbles rained down on the hardwood
floor.

Flora shook her head. What had Angus been thinking allowing them to root around in the muck like that?

"March yourself straight back to the washroom, remove
every stitch of clothing you have on, and then get yourself
into the bathtub straightaway."

She turned and came face-to-muddy-face with the other
two.

Three, if you counted Angus.

Flora didn't say another word. She simply pointed toward
the back of the house.

Annie still stood in her undershirt and sand-caked jeans.
"But, Mum, I wanted to tell you about what we found!"

"Certainly you can. After you no longer smell like a
byre."

"But we found something really—"

"Annie . . . " Flora warned, putting up one finger to silence her. "You can tell me about it after you've washed."

"We found a grave," Robbie said then, grinning at his sister with purely evil sibling satisfaction.

"Rabbie MacCallum!" Annie gaped at him, filthy hands
fixed firmly on her scrawny little hips. "I was going t' tell
Mum!"

"What did you say?" Flora asked Robbie, completely forgetting about her bath orders. "A grave?"

"Aye, we found a grave, Mum," Annie said, squeezing herself between them and seizing whatever glory she could preserve. "Right there in the woods ahind the house!"

"A grave . . ." Flora looked at Angus. " 'Tis true?"

They had moved into the kitchen, and he ducked into the adjacent washroom, pulling off his shirt, then taking the clean jeans and T-shirt Flora had just retrieved for him from the laundry basket. "Aye."

"Whose grave is it?" she asked, though she was almost afraid to.

"It dinna say," Annie said.

"There wasn't any name? Any stone? How can you even be certain it really is a grave?"

"Oh, there's a stone," Angus answered, scrubbing his fingers with a nailbrush. " 'Tis old and worn and covered with moss. And the only markings on it are two letters. *R* and *H*, and a date, 1753."

Flora took a moment to consider this. "I wonder if Libby is aware of it."

"She might not be, because if Annie hadn't literally stumbled over the stone, we'd ne'er have seen it. The stone's only about as big as Rabbie's football, and the grave itself is overgrown. But once we cleared away the leaf litter and brushed off the stone, 'twas obvious what it was."

Flora was thinking about the markings. "*R. H.* Libby's maiden name was Hutchinson. So it must be one of her ancestors. We'd best give her a call."

But Libby was completely unaware of there being a grave anywhere on the property.

"I used to play in those woods all the time as a child," she said on the other end of the phone line. "My father never mentioned anything about it. But if anyone would know anything about it, it's Dugan. He has all the legal papers and surveys of the property at his office. Surely if it is a grave, it would be indicated on his paperwork somewhere. I can give him a call, if you'd like."

"Nae, dinna trouble yourself," Flora told her. " 'Tisn't as if whoever is there is going to be leaving anytime soon. I'll just ask him about it the next time I see him at the café."

"The café," Libby sighed. "How are things down at Common Grounds? Tell Sal I'd give just about anything for one of his special espressos. I don't know what he does or how he does it, but he's a true maestro when it comes to steaming a cup of coffee. None better."

They chatted a bit about the different regular locals with whom Flora had become acquainted at the café and whom Libby had known nearly all her life. It was nice just to indulge in a little "girl talk," and soon Flora found herself steering the conversation toward the man who had been on her mind for most of the morning.

"I've actually sort of met someone."

"Met? Oh . . . you mean you *met* someone . . ." Libby immediately seized on the new topic. "And who is it? Anyone I know? Don't tell me. It's one of the O'Connell boys, right?"

"Nae. Actually, 'tis no one you would know. He's only been here in the village for a few months. He's staying at his friend's summerhouse."

"So, then . . . " Libby pressed, "who is he?"

Flora took a peek out the window to make sure none of the kids might overhear the conversation. They had all moved into the garden and were playing what appeared to be a rather lopsided game of lawn tennis with the boys teamed up against Annie. Angus was watching from the hammock nearby.

She said, "His name is Gavin. Gavin Matheson."

"And . . . ? Don't even think you're getting away with just telling me that. Let's have it."

"Well . . . he's a songwriter—a *composer.*"

"Wait a minute," Libby interrupted. "Gavin Matheson . . . yes, I remember reading about him in the papers. Must be at least a couple years ago now. He had his son taken from him by his ex-wife . . ."

Flora frowned at the mention of Gavin's private heartache. "Aye, that's him."

"Did he ever—"

"Nae," Flora answered, knowing Libby would ask if he'd gotten Gabriel back.

"How awful for him. I can't imagine it."

"Aye . . ."

"So," Libby said after a moment, "tell me about him. How'd you meet?"

"You remember the problem with the key and my 'visit' to the police station? Well . . ."

Flora went on to tell Libby the story of that day, and how Gavin had come to be called her "accomplice."

"I see," Libby said. "And what does Mr. Matheson look like?"

Flora took a sip of her tea. "Late thirties. Tall. Dark. Reasonably handsome."

She could hear Libby's responding smile. "Reasonably, huh?"

"Actually he looks like a taller Joseph Fiennes. Especially when he hasn't shaved."

"Hmm," Libby mulled the image over. "So, tell me, Flora

MacCallum, how is it you've seen him before he's had a chance to shave, then?"

Flora nearly choked on the tea and coughed slightly.

"Flora MacCallum!" Libby demanded. "Details, and I want them now."

Flora checked the kids' whereabouts again before responding. They'd apparently decided against allowing Angus to loll about in the hammock since Annie was yanking one arm, Robbie one leg, and Seamus was pushing him out from underneath.

" 'Twas the night afore Angus and the children arrived. We had dinner and then we . . ."

Libby didn't need any further details. "Oh, Flora, I'm so happy for you."

"Libby, we were still in bed when they got here! Had I known they were coming, I ne'er would have . . ." Flora took a breath as she remembered that morning—how panicked she'd been when the kids had shown up and how she'd lashed out at Gavin. "I ne'er should have let it go that far."

"You had sex with a handsome man. You're young, beautiful, and certainly entitled. So why the heck not?"

"Because . . . now it's all so complicated. When it was just me and him, I felt . . . I don't know. I felt different. It was like we were dating. But once the kids came here, I realized I am not some carefree lass any longer. I'm a mother. And I've responsibilities to them . . ."

"Flora, don't do this to yourself. You've a right to move on with your life, and if this Gavin is the one, why not . . ."

"Nae," Flora cut in. "I've already told Gavin it can ne'er happen again. We started out backwards. Like we skipped straight past the beginning chapters of the story without taking the time to get comfortable with the setting."

"And what did he say to that?"

Flora looked down the hall and caught a glimpse of the huge bouquet of flowers taking up the front table. "Well . . . he's asked me to dinner. Tonight. With the kids. And Angus."

Libby sighed through the phone. "Flora, tell me you are going. I mean, I certainly don't know all there is to know about men by any means, but a guy who's already slept with a girl, and who's told things are going to have to be cooled down because of her kids, who *still* asks the girl for dinner? He's a definite keeper in my book, and not one to be taken lightly."

"I dinna . . ." But Flora knew she was only kidding herself. "Aye, I'll go. We'll all go." She watched then as Robbie tormented Annie by holding the ball high above his head, just out of her reach as she jumped about screeching out loud as she tried to get it. Flora could remember Angus provoking her in much the same way.

"I just wonder if he realizes what it is he's getting into."

Gavin glanced at the clock on the stove as he brushed the dinner rolls with butter and slid them into the oven to warm.

Quarter to seven.

Okay . . . he thought and toweled off his hands. He looked around the kitchen. Everything was ready. The stockpot was filled with water and simmering on the stove at nearly a boil. The potatoes, wrapped in foil, were baked to just the right softness, and the corn he'd picked up at his favorite farmstand was ready to steam. All that remained was the main course and the arrival of his guests.

He heard them coming as he stood out on the deck, waiting for the sun to set.

"Are these the steps, Mum?"

"Aye, Annie."

"There must be a million of 'em. Come on, Seamus! I'll race you to the top!"

William Wallace's *Braveheart* army couldn't have made a more significant arrival. Footsteps pounded. Voices squealed. It was Annie who reached the top step first, but rather than gloat at her victory, she turned and knelt with arms open and waited, encouraging her younger brother as he toddled up the stairs in her wake, stopping every third step to catch his breath and giggle.

When he finally arrived, Annie turned, Seamus's hand fixed firmly in hers, smiling her mother's same smile.

"Hullo, Gavin!"

"Hi, Annie. Seamus. Glad you could make it."

Robbie emerged from the shadows behind them, locked eyes with Gavin, then looked down. "Hey."

"Hey, Robbie." He kept it cool. "If you take your sister and brother just inside that door there, there's a telescope. A family of harbor seals sometimes hangs out around those rocks just offshore. You might catch a look at them. If you're into that sort of thing."

Robbie gave a typical eleven-year-old's shrug. "A'right."

Flora appeared next, bringing a pie and outshining the sunset behind her.

She had her hair pinned up with bits of it bouncing in a fall against her slender neck. She wore a summery dress with a long full skirt and a rounded neckline that showed off the graceful line of her shoulders. She was barefoot, toes painted pink, her sandals hooked on one finger. She was such a sight, Gavin hardly noticed that Angus followed close behind her.

Gavin went to meet Flora with a thought to kiss her, but then drew back. *Like starting over,* he reminded himself and had to force himself not to picture her as she'd been, lying naked beneath him on the bed just a couple of nights before. It was near torture to have known the touch of those lips, to have felt the softness of her skin, and now to deny himself the pleasure of them.

"You look incredible," he said and enjoyed the blush that stole over her face, had her smiling and glancing away. He didn't know how it was possible, but this woman was somehow not accustomed to male attention. It left Gavin wondering if the men in her Scottish village were blind, or just utterly oblivious.

"Thank you," she murmured, then quickly changed the subject. "This is a beautiful house, Gavin."

"It is, if you're into the contemporary sort of style. Personally, this place reminds me more of a museum. My friend Alec's wife is a California girl, so it's sort of 'Malibu beach house meets New England.'" He shrugged. "Everyone has their own tastes, and I'm certainly not complaining since they've been nice enough to let me stay here. But I much prefer a house with character, with a history like Thar Muir."

Flora smiled. "I'm sure your friend would rather have someone looking after the place than have it standing empty anyway." She peered inside the French doors. "Now, if you'll just point me in the direction of the kitchen, I'll set this pie in the oven to keep it warm."

Gavin led the way, indulging in the soft, spicy scent of her perfume.

"Hey, Mum! I can see all the way to Thar Muir from here!"

Robbie, Annie, and Seamus surrounded the telescope, jostling one another for a turn at the eyepiece.

"Kids, be careful," she reminded them with a mother's natural apprehension, no doubt envisioning the thing toppling over and crashing to the floor.

"They're fine," Gavin reassured her. "That's a sturdy telescope."

"You dinna know my three. They could barrel through an armored car if they put their minds to it."

After she'd left the other night, he'd spent a long time thinking about what she'd said. He'd thought about the hell he'd been through the past two years and the emotional armor he'd donned, starting with his divorce. It was something he'd cemented around himself after losing Gabriel. He'd been hurt. He had hurt so badly he'd sworn never to make himself vulnerable to that kind of pain again. But what he'd been left with was a kind of dark, cold, lonely shell that only brought a different kind of hurt.

Living without the tender touch of a loving hand wasn't living at all. It was just another sort of death. But now Flora had come. She braved the armor to offer him that tender touch like the first daffodil that defied winter's last grip to bloom. He'd convinced himself he couldn't bear to be around another child again, and avoided them at all costs. But how did he know unless he tried?

Gavin poured Flora a glass of Chardonnay while Angus went for one of the assortment of beers in Alec's bar.

"Is it almost time to eat, Mum?" Robbie asked as Annie took over the telescope. "I'm starved."

"Robert MacCallum, where are your manners?"

Gavin looked at him. "Actually, Robbie, that sort of depends on you."

"Sir?"

"Well, I haven't quite 'caught' our supper yet. I was hoping you might be willing to give me a hand."

He motioned Robbie to follow him out onto the deck. Annie and Seamus, of course, had no intention of missing out on anything, and abandoned the telescope to follow them.

"Angus, if you don't mind, I could probably use a little of your help with this, too," Gavin said, and they all headed down the stairs toward the water.

Alec's house wasn't built on the beach like Thar Muir, so the stairs virtually came to an end above a small cove where the tide washed in over a jumble of seaweed-draped boulders. It was deep enough for the small boat that Gavin kept tethered by way of an old iron hook fixed to one rock. Gavin turned when the kids had all gathered around him.

"So, guys, what do you say we go get ourselves some supper?"

"What do you mean, like fishing?" Annie asked.

"Sort of. Have you ever had lobster before, Annie?"

The little girl shook her head.

"Well, see all those little buoys floating out there in the water?" He pointed so Annie could see. "If we're lucky, we'll find us some lobsters at the other end of them. Think you can help me take a look?"

But Annie shook her head. "I don't think Mum would like it. I'm wearing my best dress."

Gavin thought a minute. "How about this?" He pulled off the sweater he wore over a blue chambray shirt. "This will keep your pretty dress from getting dirty." He helped her with the sweater, rolling the long sleeves back over her arms. It covered her completely, the hem of it falling well below her knees.

"Mum," Annie asked. "Can I go, too?"

Flora smiled, knowing if she refused her, Annie would be crushed. "Aye. Just be mindful of what Mr. Matheson tells you, now."

Flora sat on the steps and sipped her wine, watching as

Gavin and Angus fitted life jackets onto each of the kids, directed them to the inside seats in the boat, and then pushed off, skimming across the water toward the bobbing buoys. She shaded her eyes against the light of the setting sun and let the breeze off the water wash over her. It was a perfect night, the air was warm and the wine was good. She watched as they took up the small cages from underneath the water's surface. Twice Annie turned to wave at her.

It took them little more than a half hour before they drifted back to the landing point, each of them carrying a small bucket from inside the boat.

"Look, Mum! They're huge, like sea monsters!"

They were slick and green and clearly none too pleased at being removed from their happy depths. Gavin had banded their claws so they couldn't pinch. The children tromped up the stairs, eager to get a better look at their catch in the lights on the deck.

"Cool!"

"Wicked!"

"But I thought they were supposed to be red?"

"They will be," Gavin promised. "When they are finished cooking. I've a pot waiting for them in the kitchen."

But when Gavin went to collect all the buckets, Seamus held tightly to his, shaking his dark head with a stubborn and determined, "Nae!"

His supper had apparently become something else.

His *pet*.

Flora tried to reason with him. Even Robbie and Annie couldn't convince him to let go.

"I'm sorry," Flora, clearly embarrassed, said to Gavin. "He got this way once with one of our neighbor's chickens."

"Cluck," Annie confirmed. "He became our pet and lived in our garden . . ." Then she whispered so only Gavin could hear her, " 'Til Hamish MacNamara's dog got him. But Seamus dinna know that. He just thinks Cluck went to London to see the queen, like Pussy Cat in the nursery rhyme."

"Oh, I see," Gavin said. "Well, then . . ." He thought quickly, taking mental inventory of what he had in the freezer, grateful he'd just gone to the market that morning. "Let me see what else I can do."

And so supper consisted of tender baked potatoes, sweet steamed corn, and hastily prepared cheeseburgers, which suited Seamus just fine.

What didn't suit him, however, was learning that he couldn't keep his lobster, like he had Cluck the Chicken.

"Seamus," Flora responded when he'd said for the fourth time how he'd planned to sleep with "Lawrence" that night. "We cannot keep Lawr"—she caught herself—"the lobster as a pet."

"But *whyyyy*?"

His voice echoed around the table and Flora looked mortified. Gavin understood that no matter how well you think you've taught your child proper manners and good behavior, no matter what, as soon as they are in the very situation for which you have taught them those manners, they abandon them completely. It was just one of life's little ironies.

He remembered once when he'd had to take Gabriel with him to the studio. He must've been around Seamus's same age, perhaps a little older. They'd been having a difficult time getting the recording right, and Gavin had been concentrating so much on the temperamental singing "star" that he'd momentarily forgotten about the temperamental toddler. Until Gabriel, fascinated by the lights and gadgets on the control panel, managed to climb atop a chair and punch the PLAYBACK button just when they'd gotten that perfect take, adding a loud "Hey!" at the end of the track.

Smiling now at the memory, Gavin realized he hadn't allowed himself to indulge in memories of Gabriel for fear of how it would make him feel. But as he thought back to that day at the studio, he found himself able to appreciate it for what it had been, the happiest time of his life.

"Mumma, answer me! Why canna I keep Lawrence? *Whyyyy?*"

Flora looked at Seamus. "We canna keep him, Seamus, because he is a lobster. And lobsters live in the sea, not in wee laddie's rooms."

"But we have a bathtub. . . ."

"Aye, we do. And it is used for its proper purpose, which is bathing."

"But what about a 'quarium?"

"We dinna even know what lobsters eat!"

"I could give him my porridge," he offered. And then he added, "And my peas."

Flora took a deep breath as if she was struggling to think of a response.

But it was Gavin who took the next round.

"Hey, Seamus, do you suppose Lawrence has any brothers or sisters?"

The little boy looked across the table with a milk mustache dripping down his chin. He shrugged. "Prob'ly."

"I was just sitting here wondering that he might have a sister and even a brother, too, just like you. And they could be down in that cove right now, wanting to play a game of football with Lawrence, but the problem is, they can't find him."

Seamus furrowed his brow at that thought. He looked across the table at his uncle.

"D'you think?"

"Oh, aye," Angus agreed. "Absolutely, lad."

After another moment's thought, Seamus slid down from his chair, and bounded over to the French doors where the buckets had been set. He took up one of them, presumably Lawrence's, then motioned across the room. "C'mon, Gavin. Let's go."

Flora followed, watching as Gavin led the children back down the stairs off the deck. But instead of boarding the boat, they climbed up on an outcropping of rocks that stretched above the waters of the cove. Gavin felt his heart twinge when he reached out on instinct, taking Seamus's hand to keep him from slipping on the uneven surface. It was something he'd done countless times with Gabriel and he supposed that once the impulse became habit, it never went away—even if the child did.

Gavin helped Seamus climb the slippery rocks. When they stood where the water was deepest, one by one, they liberated the lobsters back to their watery home.

On the *woosh* of the wind, Gavin smiled a bittersweet smile as Seamus's tiny voice called out, "Bye, Lawrence! Go play football wit' your brother, now!"

After the lobsters had vanished beneath the surface of the sea, Gavin turned to Annie. "So, do you or your brothers like ice cream?"

She didn't even answer, just spun around and tore up the stairs to where Flora stood. "Come on, Mummy! Gavin said we can have ice cream!"

By the time he topped his sundae off with hot fudge, butterscotch, whipped cream, gummy bears, multicolored jimmies, and two cherries, Seamus had all but forgotten his desperation to have a sleepover with Lawrence the Lobster.

At some point during the sundae-making operation, however, Annie managed to slip away. Nose smudged with chocolate sauce, she'd been there one minute, only to leave behind an empty sundae bowl the next. Gavin didn't say anything to Flora, who was busy keeping Seamus from dumping the whole container of jimmies onto what remained of his sundae. He just went off on his own to look for her.

Gavin found Annie in the back bedroom, the same room he'd been using while staying at the house.

She was sitting on the bed, humming softly to herself, and she was holding a small framed picture of Gabriel that he kept on the night table.

Annie looked up when Gavin stepped into the doorway. "Who's this, Gavin?"

Gavin took a slow breath against a sudden tightening that wrapped around his chest. "He's . . . he's my son."

"Oh." She nodded. "What's his name?"

"Gabriel."

"Like the archangel?"

"Yes."

Annie nodded. "Why isn't he here?"

"Well, because he's with his mother and she lives far away from here. In another country. I haven't been able to see him in quite some time."

"Oh." She nodded again. "I'll bet he misses you very much. I know I miss my da. I was only four when he died. I remember him, my da. Rabbie says he remembers him better, because I was so young, but I remember him, too. He used to pick me up and spin me around. He called me his princess." She looked at the photograph one last time before placing it back on the night table. "I bet Gabriel remembers things about you, too."

Gavin sucked his breath in sharply, but managed to say, "I sure hope so, Annie."

Chapter Eleven

The Squires weren't due until around three that afternoon, so Flora took her walk early that morning in hopes of easing the nervousness that had kept her lying awake the night before, staring at the shadows cast across the ceiling while butterflies had fluttered a panic in her stomach.

This was it. Her first "official" guests were arriving that day. Everything was ready. There wasn't one detail she could think of that she'd neglected. So why was she feeling so anxious?

Because she knew she wanted so badly for Thar Muir to succeed, not just for Libby and Graeme, but for herself as well.

It *would* succeed, she told herself as she rounded the corner onto Main Street, ponytail swinging behind her. It had to. She had worked hard, had put so much of herself into the house.

As she crossed the common, she breathed deeply, filling her lungs with the summer air. It was a glorious day. The sun was out. The birds were singing and everything was green and blooming and alive. It was a perfect day to turn the page on a new chapter in her life.

She ducked into Common Grounds and dropped into one

of the stools at the counter. With a quick glance over her shoulder, she noticed that Table 7 was unoccupied, and wondered if Gavin had slept in that day in an effort to recover from spending the night before in the company of her ragtag trio of children.

Gavin was another reason she hadn't slept the night before. Flora knew spending time with her kids had only made the absence of his own son that much more palpable. She wished she could do something to ease the emptiness in his heart. Time and again she had looked at him, searching his eyes. While he seemed to have enjoyed their supper—even without the lobsters—the smiles she'd seen had been tinged bittersweet.

"Hey, Flora," Jules said as she brought her usual steaming pot of Earl Grey, this time accompanied by her mother Maria's fresh almond biscotti. "Today's the big day, huh? Ipswich-by-the-Sea's first official bed-and-breakfast opens for business."

"Aye, 'tis. I just hope I havena forgotten anything."

"Don't worry. I'm sure it will be great."

Jules's father, Sal, came up behind his daughter with a reassuring wink. "Just be sure to send anyone looking for coffee here, eh?"

Flora assured him she would.

While Jules went off to see to another customer, Flora sipped her tea and skimmed the morning edition of the *Ipswich Post*, which had been left on the counter. She was checking her horoscope when someone said, "Today's the big day, then, eh, Ms. MacCallum?"

James Dugan pushed his lawyerly bulk onto the stool beside her, lifted the cover from that morning's selection of pastries, and took the topmost one, a sweet *pasticciotti* swollen with lemon custard. When he took a healthy bite,

Flora's ingrained mother's instinct had her sliding a napkin underneath it to catch the resulting crumbs.

"Good morning to you, Mr. Dugan. How do you do today?"

"Oh, fine, fine. Weather's been grand, hasn't it? Looks to be a fine summer. Everything all set up at the house, then?"

"Oh, aye."

Then Flora added, "Actually, Mr. Dugan, I was going to stop by your office this morning to see you. I wanted to ask you about something. About the house, rather, the estate. Are you aware of any graves located on the property?"

Dugan returned a crumbly frown. "Graves? You mean like those with dead people in them? No. Not that I've ever seen. Why do you ask?"

"Well, my brother and the kids were out walking in the woods and they found something that they think could be a grave site. They said there's a stone, and that it shows two initials. *R* and *H*. We figured the *H* must stand for Hutchinson."

Dugan considered this as he took a sip of his coffee, then wiped his mouth. "Well, should be easy enough to clear up. I have the property surveys right in my office. If there are any graves, they should certainly be indicated on them somewhere. Why don't we go by and see what we can find?"

But the survey revealed no indication of any grave in the wooded area by the house, or anywhere else on the property, for that matter.

"And you're sure it's a grave?"

Flora shrugged. "Well, no, I'm not certain. I haven't actually seen it yet myself, although I don't know what else it could be."

"A pet's grave, maybe? Lover's initials? These are the same surveys on file with the town. They date back to"—

Dugan shuffled through the papers—"1850. You said the stone was dated in the 1750s? Well, any surveys of the property earlier than these would more likely be recorded with the village's Historical Society. Check with Betty Petwith, the society's president. She should be able to help you."

The Ipswich-by-the-Sea Historical Society was housed in one of the village's oldest standing houses, the Zebediah Thornhill Mansion, a seventeenth-century saltbox with the traditional central chimney and diamond-paned windows that blinked in the morning sun. There was an older woman standing outside in the garden watering the window boxes when Flora came through the front gate. She turned and gave Flora a curious smile.

"Good morning, m'dear," she said from behind the thick lenses of her horn-rimmed eyeglasses. "How are you today?"

"I'm well, thank you," Flora responded. She offered the woman her hand in greeting. "We've never met before, but I'm Flora MacCallum. I manage—"

"Thar Muir," the woman finished on a nod. "Yes. Yes, I know. Libby's mother, Matilde, was one of my closest friends." She took Flora's hand and gave it a squeeze. "Betty Petwith, dear. I'm pleased to meet you. I was just going to sit for a spell and have some tea here in the garden. It's a glorious morning, isn't it? Would you care to join me?"

Flora happily accepted the invitation.

"You know, you've done a marvelous job up there at the house," said Ms. Petwith—but, please do call her Betty— while they sat with the morning sun filtering down through the thick oaks that shaded the old house. Betty poured Flora a cup of fragrant tea from a lovely flowered china pot, then filled her own.

"Matilde would be so happy to know that Libby's turned

the house into a bed-and-breakfast. She always said the place was too big for just the two of them, and she would have hated to see it sold. It's been in the Hutchinson family for generations, you know."

"Yes, I know," Flora confirmed. "Actually I've come to see you because Mr. Dugan thought you might have some copies of any recorded property surveys here in the Society's archives."

"Oh, well, indeed, we certainly would. In fact, we have all the earliest records from the village. Did you know that the village was founded by someone who intended to land at Boston, but made a misnavigation and ended up here instead? In fact, it was the very man who built and lived in this house, Mr. Zebediah Thornhill. He liked the place so much, he decided to stay on, and I must say I personally am pleased he was such a bad navigator." She chuckled at what must be for her an oft-told tale. "Now, what is it in particular you are looking for, dear?"

Flora explained what the children had discovered in the woods near the house.

"A grave you say? Hmm. Well, that is interesting. I mean, it wouldn't be unheard of. But as Mr. Dugan said, it could also be a pet's grave or a lover's keepsake. Come, then, let us go and see what we can find in the archives."

Betty showed Flora inside the old house, stopping along the way to show her the museumlike displays that the society had created from different artifacts representing the village's history they'd collected over the years. There were old cooking utensils and spinning wheels. Garden rakes and eyeglasses that had been worn to read by candlelight three hundred years earlier. There was even an old doll made out of thick woolen stockings and the traveling trunk of misguided sea captain Zebediah Thornhill himself—he had

brought it with him from England across the ocean to the
New World and it was quite obviously Betty Petwith's pride
and joy. From the way she spoke so passionately about each
item, retelling its history with a scholar's precision, it was
evident to Flora that Betty had found her life's calling, that
of preserving her hometown for posterity.

After skimming through the museum's collection, Betty
led Flora to a door that revealed stairs descending down into
total darkness.

"We find the cellar is the most ideal place for storing the
documents," Betty said, and flipped a switch on the wall to
light their way. A progression of fluorescent lights blinked
to life above their heads. "So long as we keep it from getting
damp, the temperature stays cool throughout the summer.
But we've installed climate control to protect the documents
as much as possible. Oh, and of course fireproofing."

If ever anyone wanted to know about anything in the village of Ipswich-by-the-Sea, without question this was the
place to find it. Underneath the creaky Thornhill Mansion,
there was a maze of shelves and storage closets filled with
books, periodicals, and newspapers dating back centuries.
Countless albums containing photographs and engravings
gave a visual record of how the village had developed, and
a vast collection of family papers, including letters and diaries, told the story of this small New England landmark.

"Let's see now. Property surveys," Betty said, and went
to a tall standing cabinet where she pulled out a shallow but
very wide drawer. She thumbed through a stack of oversized
vellums and parchments, some with ragged edges, others
curling with age.

"Here we are . . . the Hutchinson property."

The first one she pulled out was the same survey Dugan
had shown to Flora that morning, the one from 1850.

The second was dated a little earlier, showing *c. 1800* across the top of the page. It had been drawn up shortly before one of the additions to the house had been completed. It revealed a physic garden and a laundering site down near the river. There was a cowshed and a tobacco barn and the boathouse that still stood down near the shore, the one Flora intended to renovate into an artist's studio. The survey didn't, however, show any marking for a grave site in the woods behind the carriage house.

"Have you any other surveys?" Flora asked. "From earlier, perhaps in the 1700s?"

Betty Petwith looked through the drawer again, but didn't remove any other sheets. "I'm afraid that anything else we might have had was likely lost in the fire."

"There was a fire?"

Betty nodded gravely. "Oh, yes. Back in 1888, the building where all the village's archives were kept at that time was actually an old converted church. The steeple was struck by lightning late one summer night and caught fire. Tragic, to be sure. Unfortunately, by the time anyone realized it, the church was consumed by flames. The damage was quite extensive, and we lost a good many of the records that had been in storage there." She removed her glasses, blinking against her myopia and shaking her head with regret. "I'm sorry, dear."

And then she held up a finger. "But there is one other place I can check . . ."

Betty went to one of the shelves and pulled down a huge, leather-bound volume. Then she took out a rolled-up plan that appeared to show the location and names of those who were interred in the village's cemetery.

"One thing our historians have always been diligent about is in recording the genealogies of our earliest families.

The Hutchinson family should certainly be included, and if they are, then we can at least check to see if there was anyone who lived at the house who had a first name beginning with *R* around the time of 1750. If there was, we can then cross reference it with the known Hutchinson grave sites in the village. I would say it's a safe bet that if there are any who aren't in the village burying ground, then that would probably be who occupies the site in your woods."

Flora smiled, thinking Ms. Betty Petwith would have made a terrific Watson to Sherlock Holmes.

The older woman paged through the huge book until she found what she was looking for. "Here we are. The Hutchinsons."

Betty and Flora spent the next hour going through all the R. Hutchinsons, and even those whose names began with other letters. But in the end, all of them could be accounted for in the cemetery plan.

"Well, dear, it seems you've turned up quite the mystery. My guess is that one of the earlier generations more than likely had a stillbirth. Odd thing, though . . ." Betty peered at the page in her book, tracing down with her finger. "At the time of the gravestone's date, 1753, records indicate the house was occupied by a reclusive bachelor, Hiram Hutchinson. In fact, he died in 1755, aged seventy-nine, without any issue. That's not to say he couldn't have been having a"— she cleared her throat—"er, *relationship* with one of the local women that resulted in a child." And then she laughed. "He very well could have been a rather spry seventy-seven year old in 1753. However, as small as this town is now, it was even smaller then, and well, people certainly would have talked. I suppose the only way to know for sure would be to exhume the site to see what, if anything, is actually buried underneath . . ."

Flora shook her head outright against the idea. "I will speak of it to Libby, but I rather doubt she'll want to do anything of the sort. I should hate to be responsible for disturbing the eternal rest of anyone—most especially a child—simply for the sake of satisfying curiosity. Whoever it is, if anybody is there, he or she has been there for some time already. I should think it can continue."

Ms. Petwith agreed. "You'll let me know if I can be of any further assistance then, dear?"

Flora thanked her for her help and was on her way.

She hadn't meant to spend so much of her morning at the Historical Society. By the time she returned to the house, it was approaching noon. She shooed the kids and Angus out of the house and down to the beach, and then set to cleaning up the kitchen from the kids' breakfast and retrieving all of Seamus's building blocks that had been strewn across the front hall. After that, she scrubbed the peanut butter from the door handles.

While she cleaned, Flora couldn't get her visit with Betty Petwith out of her mind. She kept thinking about that grave in the woods, that it might represent the final forgotten resting place of a child. It bothered her so much that when she finished cleaning, Flora pulled on her Wellingtons and set off in the direction of the woods.

She found the site easily enough. It wasn't all that far into the woods, and the children had cleared away the leaves and debris to better reveal the stone. The ground beneath the ragged marker was carpeted in a thickly leaved plant that smelled of wintergreen. It was a very quiet spot, with only the distant sound of the ocean and birds flitting through the trees overhead. Peaceful. Flora knelt beside the little stone, setting down the small posy of flowers she had hastily gathered from the gardens behind the house.

"I don't know who you are," she whispered softly, "but I hope you know you are no longer forgotten."

She said a quick prayer, got up, and went back to the house to shower and await the arrival of the Squires.

Their taxi rolled up the drive at precisely 3:08 p.m.

Mrs. Squires looked just as Flora had imagined her after speaking with her on the phone. She was plump, with a perpetual sunny smile on her face, and had a puff of hair that could be either blond or brown, depending upon the light. It was curled and teased into a grandmotherly sort of style that was so hairsprayed it virtually defied the wind to muss it. She wore a pretty sundress with a cardigan she had probably knitted herself and had sensible sandals on her feet. Her eyes alight as she got out of the cab, she stared at the house as if it were made out of gingerbread.

Mr. Squires, in contrast, looked completely out of his element. He wore a western-style shirt over a rounding girth with a Native American–style silver-tipped bolo tie. A large cowboy hat was perched on his balding head and pointy-toed boots poked out from his weathered Wranglers. He waited while the cabdriver fetched their luggage from the cab's boot, then handed the man several bills out of his silver and turquoise money clip. When he turned, he looked at the house as if he expected it to cave in on his head the very moment he walked through the door.

All right, Flora thought to herself as she pasted on a welcoming smile. So New England was *not* Mr. Squires's idea of a vacation. That much was obvious. He'd probably only agreed to it in order to appease the whim of his bubbly wife, so Flora put the task of setting him at ease at the top of her to-do list.

"Mr. and Mrs. Squires, welcome to Thar Muir," Flora greeted them as she stepped down from the porch. She had put on a pair of dressy khaki trousers with a pale blue cashmere top and the strand of pearls Libby and Graeme had given her for her last birthday. She'd swept her hair off her face and up in a decorative clip.

"Oh, George, doesn't she have the cutest li'l accent?" Mrs. Squires said in her own heavy Texan drawl.

"Hmph," was all Mr. Squires offered for a response. Until he asked, "Do we bring in our own bags at this sort of place, missy, or do y'all have a bellhop?"

Angus, bless his heart, chose that moment to come around from the back of the house. "I've got your bags, sir," he said, and hefted them all up in his arms, including Mrs. Squires's floral hatbox, which he hooked around one finger. With a glance to Flora, he confirmed, "The Turret Room, aye?"

Flora smiled at him and nodded, then turned her attention back to her guests.

"Now, would you care for some refreshment after your journey?" she asked. "We've tea, either iced or hot"—she noticed Mr. Squires's expression growing blank—"or if you prefer, we've some excellent scotch from the Highlands of my Scottish homeland."

His eyes immediately sparked with interest. "Well, now, I'm more a Jack Daniel's man myself," he said, thumbing his belt loops, "but I suppose I could give your scotch whiskey a sample."

Flora grinned to herself as she led them inside to the reception desk. While Mr. Daniel certainly distilled a worthy brew, 'twas the Scottish and the Irish who had been distilling *uisge beatha* back into the Middle Ages, long afore America was even . . . America. Flora had collected an impressive selection of some of the best whiskeys the land of her birth had to offer. Mr. Squires was in for a true revelation.

During the course of the next hour, Mr. Squires shed much of his lack of enthusiasm, along with his bolo tie. Flora claimed victory in her effort to put him at ease. While he extolled the virtues of each successive shot glass of whiskey, Mrs. Squires let slip that their trip to New England was for a second honeymoon of sorts, in celebration of their thirtieth wedding anniversary. The news gave Flora an idea. After encouraging them to take a relaxing walk down by the beach, Flora put a bottle of her best champagne on ice. Then she made dinner reservations for them at an elegant restaurant in town that overlooked the harbor—she'd been told it had an award-winning chef who did marvelous things with the local seafood. She also tucked a picnic blanket into the car, and encouraged them to enjoy that night's concert on the common, a summertime tradition in Ipswich-by-the-Sea.

Shortly before Angus was due to return from picking them up from the concert, Flora lit a half-dozen candles in glass-covered sconces and scattered them about their room, as well as around the massive claw-foot tub in their bathroom, setting out extra towels and a fragrant bottle of bubble bath. She smiled to herself as she wondered whether Mr. Squires would wear his cowboy hat with him into the tub. Then she banished the children to the family's section of the house for the night, with promises of popcorn and DVDs to keep them quiet so as not to disturb their guests.

In the end, all her attention to detail paid off.

The following morning, Mrs. Squires came down for breakfast with a youthful and romantic glimmer in her eyes.

Over their coffee and full Scottish breakfast, which Mr. Squires consumed eagerly, Mrs. Squires inquired as to whether they could extend their two-night stay to three.

And Flora, beaming from her success, was all too happy to oblige them.

Two days later, Flora stood on the porch, waving as the cab that had come to retrieve Mr. and Mrs. Squires—now known simply as George and Noreen—vanished down the drive.

The guestbook on the front table lay open with the following entry:

Thank you for giving us a second honeymoon to remember for the next thirty years. . . .
    George and Noreen Squires, newlyweds once more from Texas.

The phone in the office started ringing as Flora closed the front door.

"Hallo, Thar Muir," she answered. "May I be of assistance, please?"

"Well, I certainly hope so."

Flora smiled when she recognized the voice on the other end of the line. "Gavin."

She had missed seeing him in the past few days. After the lobster debacle, the sundae explosion all over his kitchen, and Annie snooping into his things, Flora had begun to wonder whether he would ever want to see her again.

"I was calling to inquire whether you might have availability, say tomorrow morning?"

Apparently, he did want to see her again.

Flora's smile deepened. "Well, sir, that depends on what you have in mind."

"Hmm . . . I was thinking about a sail out to this little island in the harbor, maybe even a picnic. I thought the kids might go for a little exploring, too."

It was a tempting offer. The kids would certainly love it, and Flora would love to see Gavin again.

"We don't have any other guests coming 'til Friday. I'll just have to see if Angus would mind staying in the house whilst we're away, just in case someone calls or turns up at the door. I'll ring you back in a bit, aye?"

Gavin responded likewise.

Fifteen minutes later, Flora called Gavin back.

Chapter Twelve

Hathaway Island was a rocky blister of a place that rose up from the dark waters of Ipswich Bay some four and a half miles off the Massachusetts mainland.

It had been formed fifteen thousand or so years before, when a great glacier moved across the land, forming the picturesque little bay before melting to fill in the valleys left behind. Three smaller islets, uninhabitable but for the cormorants and piping plovers that nested there, were known as Rachael Hathaway's Stepping Stones because they led away from the main island on its western shore and reached for the mainland.

Even on a day as clear as today, the island seemed cloaked in an odd sort of mist—it moved, swimming and swirling the nearer one drew to it. When the weather was unsettled, the isle could be positively ghoulish. It was a devious isle, and though Gavin had always loved the sea and had done his fair share of sailing, he'd chartered a local captain to take them out that morning, one who would know the pull of the tide and who could navigate them through to the safest landing place.

They disembarked on the north shore at a recently constructed pier. Despite, or rather because of, its ominous place in the village's history, the "witch's" island had always been a point of interest for campers and other nature lovers. The more inexperienced sailors often ran afoul of the dangerous sand ledges that lay hidden beneath the water's surface. Countless shipwrecks littered the ocean floor. So the townspeople had agreed to a proposal to build a pier at the most accessible point on the isle, one that stretched out into deeper water. It had opened the isle "officially" to the public only the week before.

Robbie and Annie were the first to leap ashore, even before the mooring lines had been secured. Flora called to them to wait, taking up wee Seamus, and waited for the captain to loop the fat ropes around the pier's supporting post.

Gavin was a little taken aback when Flora handed her youngest off to him after he had turned to help her disembark. Thickly lashed green eyes blinked up at him from above the fist whose thumb was stuck firmly in his mouth. Seamus smiled at Gavin around that thumb while his other arm snaked behind Gavin's neck in a hold worthy of a boa constrictor.

"Hi, *Gah-win*," he mumbled around his thumb.

"Hello to you, Seamus MacCallum."

Flora stepped off the boat with the help of the captain. On this lovely day, she'd worn patterned capri pants and a light blouse and the curved brim of her straw hat shaded her eyes from the morning sun. She reached to take Seamus back into her arms until she saw that Gavin had hoisted him up to sit on his shoulders. The three-year-old, accustomed to looking at the rest of the world from hip level, was suddenly taller than them all. His delight with his new perspective shone with the same brilliance as the sun on his tiny face.

"Look a'me, Mumma!" He reached both hands above his head. "I can touch the sky!"

In a moment, Flora was taken back some eight years, when it had been Robbie doing much the same thing, only the shoulders that had carried him were his father, Seamus's. The image and the twinge that memory gave her left her blinking.

"Aye, Seamus, you're very tall indeed," she agreed as she managed to swallow back her emotions. She quickly took up the tote bags she'd brought, which contained among other things their picnic lunch, bottles of sunscreen, and a jug of wet wipes worthy of a Viking explorer.

Gavin carried Seamus the length of the pier, until they were standing safely on solid ground, then lifted him off on legs that were already running as Seamus chased after his older brother and sister ahead of him.

"Rabbie . . . Annie . . . *waaaaaait!*"

During the boat ride over, Gavin had regaled Flora and the children with the story of Rachael Hathaway and the mystery surrounding her demise. He'd thrown in appropriate amounts of black magic and dashing pirates. As such, by the time they arrived on the island, the children were beyond keen to visit the ruins of her cottage first thing.

The village had created a map of sorts that showed the footpaths and various landmarks all across the isle's fifty-five acres. Robbie and Annie were wrangling with each other to be the first to lead them to a picnic spot near the cottage ruins.

When they arrived at the cottage site, there were several other sightseers already there, reading the small signs that the village had erected, which told the abridged version of the famous tale. A steadfast *Harry Potter* reader, Annie was particularly fascinated with the story of the *Ips-witch* and was determined to find some heretofore undiscovered relic left behind by her.

"Mummy, d'you think that tree there could have been planted by Rachael Hathaway? It looks very old. I bet she used to hang her striped stockings to dry on its branches. . . .

"Mummy, d'you think perhaps Rachael Hathaway used to preserve those same brambleberries . . .

"Mummy, d'you think Rachael Hathaway might have practiced her witchcraft atop this same rock?"

Her litany of "Mummy, d'you think . . ." went on without pause.

The cottage itself was little more than four crumbling rock walls with a thick carpet of green clover growing inside where once the famous witch had dwelt. A small stone circle had been marked out in one corner where overnight campers often dared one another to pass the night. And generations of names and initials had been carved into the tree trunk that now grew out of the spot where Rachael's parlor had once been.

But all Annie had to do was close her eyes and she could see it as it could have been three hundred years earlier.

She stood before the ivy-covered chimney, what remained of it anyway, and pressed her hands to the hearthstone, ducking her head to take a peek up and inside.

"What d'you think she cooked in here?"

"*Gaikit* little girls, probably," said Robbie. "In a big black pot."

Ever the older brother, he grabbed Annie from behind, frightening her into a squeal. "And you're next!"

"Mummy!"

Flora looked at her oldest and simply raised a brow. She said, much as her own mother had when she and Angus had been children, "Robert Angus MacCallum . . ."

"Oh, come on. I was only playing with her."

"Mumma . . ."

Wee Seamus was eying the chimney as if he expected it to suddenly come alive and swallow him whole. "Is what Robbie said true? Did tha' witch cook children in her hearth?"

"Nae, dearie bee. Nae. Robbie's just trying to give Annie a fright. Come on now, all of you. Enough of witches and big black pots. Let's find a spot down by the water to have our picnic, aye?"

They spent the next few hours stretched out on a wool tartan blanket on a grassy bluff above a pebbly shore where the waves lapped softly and the sun was shaded by ancient, sea-scarred trees. For such an ominous history, the island was beautiful . . . peaceful, even calming. Flora thought of Rachael Hathaway and wondered if she'd ever sat at that same spot, peering at the mainland and the village that banished her. Whatever had become of her? Had she tried to escape? Or had she truly been saved by a pirate?

Flora decided she much preferred the latter, and imagined the misunderstood lady sailing away from her island prison on the arm of her lover, instead of dying alone and forsaken.

After wolfing down their peanut butter sandwiches, the two older kids had gone off to search for seashells in the tidal pools close to the shore while Flora and Gavin watched on. Exhausted from their earlier explorations, Seamus dozed quietly on the blanket beside them.

"They grow so fast. 'Tis amazing how quickly they change."

The minute the words left her mouth, Flora caught the darkening in Gavin's eyes and immediately regretted them. "I'm sorry, Gavin. That was an insensitive thing for me to say."

Gavin shook his head. "No. Don't apologize." He looked at her. "Being with your kids these past few days has actually been cathartic. It helps to imagine Gabriel doing things like this, you know, normal kid things." He looked out at the water. "No matter where he is and who is with him."

How difficult it must be on him, the not knowing, Flora thought, the torture of weeks, months, and then years passing by. She thought of Seamus, whom Gavin had taught to play "Twinkle Twinkle Little Star" on the piano the other night, and the squeal of delight Seamus had given when he'd played it all on his own. She wondered about the things Gavin had missed, was still missing, with Gabriel.

Wanting, needing to comfort him, to soothe that loss, Flora covered Gavin's hand with hers, tightening her fingers around his. Gavin looked at her deeply, and squeezed her hand, clinging to it as if it were a lifeline. They stared at each other, neither speaking a word.

A moment later, they were interrupted by the sound of Annie's squeal.

"Mummy! Gavin! Look! I found a treasure!"

The "treasure" was a small, flat, blackened disk about the size of a quarter. In fact, that's what Gavin first thought it was, lost long ago by some overnight camper and colored black from the salt of the sea. But when he took a closer look, chipped away some of the salty crust that covered it, he realized it was not any sort of coin he'd ever seen before.

"Is it an American pound?" Annie asked, peering over his shoulder at her discovery.

"They're not pounds in America, *muckleheid*," Robbie said to her. "They're dollars."

"It isn't a dollar, though," Gavin said, trying to rub away some of the dark that colored the coin. "I think it might be a lot older than that. Annie, I could be wrong, but I think this might actually be a Spanish piece of eight."

Annie's eyes went wide with wonder. "You mean like the pirates used to have?"

Gavin nodded. "It isn't unheard of. There's a museum down on Cape Cod that houses thousands of artifacts they've brought up from other pirate wrecks. And remember, some believed that Rachael Hathaway had a pirate lover who took her away from the island prison and made her his queen."

Annie's face was positively alight. "Did you hear that, mummy? A pirate! Just like Blackbeard . . . maybe it even *was* Blackbeard, and maybe this is part of his buried treasure. Maybe there's more! Come on, Robbie . . . let's go look!"

Her excitement had woken Seamus, who wasn't about to be left out of the fun. He popped up from the blanket like a jack-in-the-box and toddled after his brother and sister. For the next two hours, they waded through the tide pools and flipped over every rock and seashell they could find. They raked through the sand with their fingers. They dug as deep as their beach shovels would allow them in search of more buried treasure.

All in all they found Annie's coin, the rubber sole of someone's sneaker, a countless collection of bottle caps, and enough driftwood to erect a small wooden fort, which Seamus set to building when he'd grown bored with searching through the sand.

As he watched Flora, who had joined the children and was standing ankle deep in the surf, Gavin admitted to a sneaking suspicion that there must be some sort of witchcraft still lingering on that isle. How else could he explain himself falling deeper and deeper under Flora's spell? With those gleaming green eyes and that fiery red hair, she was a vision. But when she was with her kids, she transformed. On her hands and knees in the sand with Seamus, helping him to stack the driftwood into a makeshift fort, her face reflected the unquestionable love and devotion she felt for her children. And that light touched everyone around her.

In fact, Gavin felt so warmed, so embraced by that light, that he scarcely realized it when he reached for her. She had stretched to grab a seashell, and Gavin moved to meet her. He took her face into his hands, touched his mouth to hers, and kissed her softly, tenderly . . .

"No!"

Something hard shoved between them.

Stunned, Gavin turned and met Robbie's very dark, very furious stare.

"Rabbie . . ." Flora's soft voice tried to soothe him.

"He kissed you," the boy accused. "He shouldn't do that. Da wouldn't like it."

"Rabbie," Flora repeated, "come here to me."

But the boy just shook his head, as if trying to shake the image of his mother in the arms of another man out of his mind's eye. "No." And then he turned. *"No!"*

Robbie bolted up the hill with Flora calling after him in vain to come back.

"Mumma . . ." Seamus's voice was trembling, tears brimming in his wide eyes as he realized something had just happened, something bad, but he had no idea what it was. "Wha's wrong with Rabbie? Why'd he run away like that?"

" 'Tis all right, sweetling," Flora reassured him. "Mummy will go find him."

Flora looked at Gavin. "Will you please stay here with Annie and Seamus while I go after Robbie and talk to him?"

Gavin nodded, feeling sick that he'd let his emotions for Flora get the better of him, to the peril of that boy's tender feelings. "I'm sorry, Flora."

She shook her head. "Dinna be sorry, Gavin. 'Tis something we've just got to work through, is all."

She looked at Annie then. "Annie sweet, please stay here with Gavin and Seamus. I'll be back with Rab in a bit, aye?"

Annie simply nodded.

While Flora got up and dusted the sand off her legs, Gavin went to join the other two. "Okay, guys, let's see how big we can build Seamus's sand fort."

He turned one last time and watched as Flora retreated up the hill after her eldest son.

Flora found Robbie bunched into one corner of the ruined cottage with his knees drawn up to his chest and his face buried deep in the fold of his arms. She said nothing, just knelt down to sit beside him, drawing his lanky form into her lap. She wrapped him in her arms and held him as she had when he'd been a wee lad.

Robbie refused to pull his face from his arms, and she knew it was because he was crying. Knowing she had caused that pain sent a sharp slice of regret deep into her heart.

Flora sat and caressed Robbie's head, not saying a word until he finally lifted his reddened eyes to hers. When he did, Flora no longer saw the face of a boy trying so hard to be a man. What she saw was boy—pure, innocent, utterly vulnerable boy.

"Don't you love Da anymore?"

She swallowed once before answering him. "Of course I love your da, Rabbie. I will always, *always* love your da."

"Then why did you do that? Why did you kiss Gavin like that?"

Flora took a breath, searched for the words that would help him understand. "Rab, you know that if I could do it, I would bring your da back to us this minute, aye? We all miss him so very much. Annie misses him. I know you miss him. And I miss him, too. Think of Seamus, how he ne'er had the chance to know him, to know how funny and wonderful your da was, how he would toss you in the air and tickle you till you wet yourself laughing."

Robbie blinked, fighting an unwilling smile. "I ne'er wet myself. . . ."

Flora nodded. "You're right. Must have been Annie I'm thinking of. But the sad truth is, no matter how much I wish I could do it for you, for all of us, I canna bring your da back to us. Sometimes life just works out that way."

"But it's no' fair . . ."

"No, you're right. It's not. But that's how it is. And there's naught we can do to change that. So we have to adjust to our new life, the one in which we don't have your da. But we still have each other. We have to remember that. If I dinna have you three after we lost your da, I don't know what I would have done. My life is so empty, so lonely without him, but I know I have you three to love and care for, and that helps me to bear the missing of him. Just as I know having your sister and your brother and me helps you."

Looking at his fingers, he nodded against her breast.

"But there are times in your life when even having me isn't quite enough. I try to be everything I can for you, Rab, but the truth is, I canna be everything your da should have been for you. No one can. Now, your uncle has tried to fill that place for you, but the time is coming when Angus will need to settle into a family of his own and stop putting off his life for ours. It isna fair to him. And when you've grown, and Annie's grown and is married with ten kids of her own"—that got at least a half laugh out of him—"and Seamus is grown, my job of raising you three will be over. You'll go off to make your own families, because that's what people do. And at that time I will really be needing your da the most. To keep me from being lonely. Only he winna be able to be there with me."

"So you want Gavin to replace Da?"

"No, no, no," she whispered against his hair when she heard his voice tremble on the question. "No one will ever be able to replace your da for me. But that doesna mean I canna find something different, something that will help me to feel less alone, something that will give me that strong shoulder to lean on that.I used to have in your da when I needed it. Remember when your grandda died and how sad I was? At least then I had your da with me, to help me. But then, so soon after that, we lost your da and then I had no one, although your uncle Angus has done his best to help me. 'Tis the same for you and Annie and Seamus, too. No one will ever take the place of your da, but if you think about it, what is better? Having no da, and only that empty shadow where he used to be? Or perhaps having someone else, someone who might help make that shadowy place a little less dark and a little less scary?"

Flora watched Robbie's face as he considered her words. "I guess having someone else is better."

She lifted her son's chin so his eyes met hers. "Rabbie, having that someone else doesna mean we ever forget your da. In fact, don't you think that since we canna have him, your da winna probably want you to have something . . . rather than nothing?"

Robbie closed his eyes as tears squeezed past his lashes. She could almost see the conflict warring inside his young heart, that of loyalty to the only father he had ever known against the idea, the possibility of anything—or anyone— else. Flora wrapped him in her arms and rocked him as he came to terms with the lash of emotions, rocking herself, too, against her own private tumult.

Daylight was beginning to fade when Flora, Gavin, and the children climbed back onto the small skiff that would return them to the mainland.

All in all, it had been a lovely day. After she'd taken Robbie aside and talked with him privately, he seemed to emerge with at least a willingness to give this new arrangement a chance. He didn't apologize to Gavin for his behavior, and Flora didn't ask him to because she knew Robbie needed to feel as if he'd been there to do his duty to his father when he'd thought he needed to. But a short while after they returned to the beach, Robbie did start helping Gavin and the other two with finishing off Seamus's sand fort. He even laughed when Gavin pretended to fall in mock battle after Seamus and Annie besieged him with seashell catapult bombs.

After the boat glided up to the harbor pier, Gavin took Flora's hand and led her up the stairs, along the boardwalk toward the village common where others had begun to gather for that evening's summer concert. Some were on blankets spread out on the grass, others in folding lawn chairs. Citronella torches had been set up around the periphery for lighting and to keep the pests at bay. Through the open front door of the café, Sal's espresso machine could be heard sputtering and wheezing.

They found a spot and spread out their picnic rug near the bandstand a short distance away from where a group of children were playing an impromptu game of whiffle baseball. Annie and Robbie ran off to watch, each taking Seamus by one hand. When they turned back to look at her, Flora waved to them, telling them not to go any farther.

A short time later, a man came to the microphone on the bandstand.

"Evening, folks. I'm sorry to say our vocalist wasn't able to make tonight's concert."

An audible lament came from the surrounding audience.

"But if you'd like, we'll be more than happy to play for you anyway."

An encouraging murmur of applause was offered in response.

"And if you recognize any of our songs, please feel free to sing along."

The man sat in a chair on the stage and took up a guitar, picking softly at the strings in preparation. Standing beside him was another man holding a flute.

They began playing a gentle airy piece that fit in perfectly with the soft, lazy summer night. The music floated through the loudspeakers that were set up around the bandstand and Flora closed her eyes, letting the sound of their songs wash over her. She didn't even realize it when she leaned back against Gavin's shoulder.

But he did.

He was staring at her in the torchlight and was completely mesmerized by her. Her face was soft, serene, her lashes resting lightly on her cheeks. He'd never seen anything so incredibly lovely.

Some time later, the musician who was playing the guitar spoke into the microphone again, while his partner put away his flute and took up a violin.

"This last song is probably less familiar to most of you. We first heard it when we spent some time in Ireland a few years back. While the music is certainly charming, the words of this particular piece tell a truly touching story of a woman who watches the sea for the return of her long lost love. I wish you could hear them. It's called 'The One I Love.' "

"Mum, you know that song!" Flora suddenly heard Annie exclaim in a voice that was easily overheard by many of the people sitting nearby.

"Annie, *wheesht*," Flora told her. "You're interrupting the performance."

"But, Mum, you could sing it with them!"

By then, word had reached the man on the bandstand that someone in the audience knew the song. He looked over at Flora with a hopeful smile. "I'm told we've an audience member who might actually know this particular song. I wonder if she'd be so kind as to sing it for us all tonight?"

Flora tried to shake her head in refusal, but the people sitting around her would have none of it. They encouraged her with words, and when that didn't convince her, they started to clap hands, a rhythm that was soon echoing throughout the whole common. Drawn by the commotion, Jules had come out of the café and was shooing Flora up with an insistent wave of her hands.

Sitting on a nearby blanket, Jen from the salon quickly joined in.

Gavin looked at Flora. "Doesn't look like you have much of a choice."

"But, Gavin, this is different than my singing back home, before people I've known all my life."

"How is it different? They are an audience who appreciate a lovely song, just as these people are. You've a beautiful voice, Flora. Personally, I think it's a crime not to share it with the world."

Flora looked at him, then rose reluctantly to her feet, approaching the bandstand. She stopped and told Annie and

Robbie to take Seamus back to Gavin on the blanket, then climbed the stairs onto the stage.

The audience applauded accordingly.

"Sorry," the guitar player said to her with a shrug. "I hope we didn't pressure you into doing something you didn't want to."

"Nae, 'tis fine," Flora said. "I'll do m' best for you."

He offered her his hand in greeting. "I'm Michael. And that's my partner, Gino."

"Flora," she said in response.

"Great, Flora. Well, we play it in A," Michael said, strumming a chord so she could hear the key.

She nodded. "That's just grand."

Flora stood at the microphone that had been set up for the missing vocalist and blinked as she lifted her eyes to the crowd. While she had been singing nearly all her life before the people in Wrath Village, she knew them like her own family. In many respects, since the death of her father, and then Seamus, they *were* her family. She'd never felt any reluctance to share her love of song with them, never worried about singing off-key. But now, standing before this sea of shadowed faces, all strangers, she felt an odd sensation of uncertainty and nervousness grip her inside.

But then she saw Gavin, and the smile on his face set her at ease.

As Michael and Gino began playing the opening notes of the song, Flora closed her eyes against the image of that sea of unknown faces, trying to convince herself they weren't watching her. She took herself into the story in the song, away over the sea to a lonely place set in ancient lands. She knew the man and the woman in this song and the longing of their hopeless love. She felt their music swell through her, let it carry her along, until it took her to the first word.

"One, I love . . ."

And with that, Flora simply began to tell the story.

Sitting in the audience, Gavin watched in wonder as Flora took each and every person sitting on that common with her into the story of the star-crossed lovers. She brought him with her, too, her voice making him feel the torment of their lost love, wrapping him in the magic and beauty like a lover's warm embrace.

He had to find some way to convince her to record that voice.

And then he had an idea.

Gavin took his cell phone out of his pocket and scrolled through his speed-dial list until he found the one he wanted.

Alec answered on the third ring. "Gavin, what's up? Anything wrong at the house?"

"No. Just shut up. And listen."

Gavin held up the phone and let Flora's voice drift into the mouthpiece.

When he put the phone back to his ear moments later, Alec said only two words.

"Call Phil."

"I am now."

Gavin punched the END button, scrolled through the list again, and hit SEND when he found the right number.

"Phil, it's Gavin."

"Yeah? Gavin who?"

"I know. I should have returned your calls. Listen, we'll talk about that some other time. I want you to hear something."

He held up the phone again, and this time he held it there until Flora finished the song and the crowd on the common broke out in a cheer.

"Interested?" Gavin said when he went back to the call.

"Who is she?" Phil's voice was filled with the hunger of someone who recognized something extraordinary . . . and wanted it.

"She's someone I discovered. Someone who's gotten me writing again. I'm writing a song for her. And I have an idea for something. Alec's with me on it."

"Then so am I."

"Good. Now all we have to do is convince her to do it. Believe it or not, she's not very confident of her talent. How fast can you get to Boston?"

"I can be on the train tomorrow."

"All right. Wait and let me see what I can pull together tonight. I'll give you a call later."

Gavin ended the call just as Flora returned to join him on the blanket.

She smiled at him, only at him, even while everyone sitting around them congratulated her and complimented her on her performance.

"That was incredible," he said. "*You* were incredible."

If not for the darkness, Gavin would have sworn she was blushing.

"I didn't sound flat?"

"Are you kidding? In fact, I was just—"

Before Gavin could finish telling her about the calls he'd made and the plans he had, Annie and Robbie came running up, followed by a handful of other children, all gawking at the newest local celebrity.

"Mummy! You sounded grand!"

Flora smiled at her daughter. "Thanks, m' love. And I see you've made some friends, too. But didn't I tell you to come over here earlier? Now 'tis getting late and we'd best be returning to the house else—" She looked around her at the sea of tiny faces. "Annie. Where's wee Seamus?"

"Robbie had him."

But Robbie shook his head. "No, I dinna. Annie was supposed to be bringing him back to Gavin, but she was too busy showing off t' everyone."

"No, I wasn't!"

"Yes, you were. You were twirlin' around like a *bawheid* while Mum sang her song."

"Mummy, he's lying. He was—"

"Enough," Flora said, silencing them. "Both of you. Now think. Where is the last place you remember seeing wee Seamus?"

They both returned faces as blank, as colorless, as hospital sheets.

"All right," Flora said, trying to think. "Sit, both of you, on that blanket and do not move until I come back. I will go and look for him."

But Gavin had other thoughts.

"Flora, don't you think we should get the police involved?"

"The police?" She shook her head. "No, I don't think we need to cause any alarm just yet. I'm sure he's around somewhere."

Flora turned and called out to Seamus.

But there was no response. People were getting up from their lawn chairs, packing up their things, and leaving the common. Car engines sparked to life. Headlights beamed.

"Flora, this isn't some remote village in Scotland where everyone looks out for everyone else. You are in a foreign country. And this is a country where children disappear every day and are never seen again."

"Gavin, if you're trying to scare me, you're doing a bloody damned good job of it. Now, please. I'm sure he's here. I'll find him."

She started to walk away to look for Seamus, but Gavin grabbed her by the arm. "Listen to me. My son was taken by his own mother and I can't even find him. Just what do you think would happen if it's a complete stranger doing the taking?"

Flora just stared at him, her heart pounding so hard in the back of her throat that she was suddenly finding it difficult to breathe.

Sweet *Dia* . . .

"Mummy!"

It was Annie who came running up between them a moment later.

"It's all right, Mummy. Rabbie found Seamus."

Flora and Gavin both turned and watched as Robbie came toward them across the common, clutching Seamus's hand.

"He was petting somebody's dog," Robbie said.

Flora put her arm around her eldest and kissed him on his head. "Thanks, Rob. You're my hero, you are."

The older boy beamed proudly as Flora hoisted Seamus up and into her arms, staring at him nose to nose.

"That was not very well done of you, Seamus MacCallum. You gave Mummy and Gavin quite a fright."

She looked over his head at Gavin, who was still standing there, staring at them as if he couldn't quite remember how to breathe.

"Am sorry, Mumma," Seamus said, and buried his face in Flora's neck. "I just wanted to see the dog. He licked my hand."

But Gavin still looked as if he'd seen a ghost.

"'Tis all right, Gavin," Flora said. "He's fine. We found him and all is well."

Gavin shook his head. "You know . . . I was beginning to think I could do this. But now I'm not so sure."

"Do what?"

"This. With you. And the kids. But what just happened, Seamus going missing like that and the fear it struck in me, the helplessness. It was Gabriel all over again . . ." He shook his head. "It just confirms something I'd told myself."

"What's that, Gavin?"

"That I would never allow myself to have another child who could be taken from me. I just can't put myself in that position again. I won't."

"Gavin . . ."

He reached down, grabbed the blanket, and stuffed it into the bag. "Come on. I'll take you and the kids home."

"But . . ."

Flora could only stand, holding Seamus in her arms with Annie and Robbie on either side, watching as Gavin turned and walked away.

Chapter Thirteen

Flora stood on the driveway and hugged Angus good-bye.

"You're sure you're going to be all right?" he asked for what must be at least the tenth time.

"Aye," she said with as reassuring a smile as she could give him. "Come on, now. Jen's sister Hallie is starting work today and will be here five days a week to help out, and Jimmy O'Connell and his sons will be here almost daily with the boathouse renovation. I'll hardly be alone. Besides, I'm a thirty-two-year-old adult woman. I have crossed an ocean. I've nearly been arrested. And I have personally given birth to three little human beings. I think I can handle the running of one guesthouse."

Angus looked at her doubtfully. "I can stay another week, you know. Just till Hallie learns the ropes. I have holiday time due to me."

"Angus, you have a job to do, too. You're responsible for the safety and well-being of an entire village." She grinned at him. "As well as the more physical needs of one as yet un-named lass who I'm certain is more than just a little put out with me for keeping you away so long."

Angus grinned right back. "Och, now. Who says there's only one?"

"Angus Allan MacLeith!" Flora punched him in the arm. "You are an incorrigible sod!"

Then she smiled at him, hugged him, and kissed his cheek. She would miss him. The kids even more so. They had each come to depend on Angus for their own individual needs. And that was precisely the problem. They had come to depend on him too much, and somewhere along the line, had stopped depending on themselves. Flora realized the time had come for her to be a grown-up again, to stand on her own two feet. The time had come for her to make her own life for herself and for her children.

"You better go now afore you miss your flight," she said.

"You'll wish Gavin well for me? Or should I have the cab stop over to his place on my way to the airport and tell him myself?"

"I'll tell him for you." And then she added, "If I should see him."

She hadn't seen Gavin at all, not since the night she'd gotten up to sing at the bandstand on the common, when Seamus had gotten lost and Gavin had all but told her he wasn't able, wasn't *willing,* to "deal with" her and her children. He hadn't spoken more than a word when he took her and the kids home that night. His good-bye when she opened the car door to leave had been filled with finality.

And Table 7 had been conspicuously empty each morning at the café ever since.

The phone hadn't rung.

No more flowers had come to the door.

He had, it seemed, made his decision about any future they might have had.

Flora just shook her head and tried to ignore the regret that thought left her with.

"Give him time, Flora," Angus said to her then, reading

her thoughts. "It canna be easy on the man, losing his son like he did."

"I'm sure it's not, especially with my three running around as constant reminders to him of what he lost. Truth is, anything a'tween us was likely hopeless from the start. We both just bring too much 'past' to complicate any 'future'."

"Gavin's a decent guy, Flor. He's got some issues to come to terms with, aye. But I'm not giving up on him yet."

The cabdriver started the car's engine to signal his impatience with the length of their farewell.

Angus bent down and kissed his sister lightly on the forehead. "I'll be seeing you at the end of the month, then, back home for the baby's christening?"

"Aye. We'll all be there."

"Good. In the meantime, call if you need anything." He looked at her closely and repeated, "Anything."

Angus ducked into the taxi then and shut the door. Flora stood in the driveway and watched him go. She waited until the cab swung onto the main road. Then, looking up at the sun shining right above her head, she took a deep breath before turning for the porch and the houseful of guests that awaited her.

Now it really was up to her.

Their latest visitors had arrived just the day before and would stay through the weekend. They were a family of four—the Wilsons from Ohio, with two young sons, Jake and Zach, ages six and eight. Her kids had all but attached themselves to the boys from the moment they'd arrived. Flora had installed them in the family cottage with offers for them to make use of the collection of sand buckets and beach toys that were stored in the garden shed.

In addition to the Wilsons, there was a young couple from

Virginia staying in the Heather Room and two middle-aged women from Oregon who had been friends since high school and were traveling the East Coast together from Washington, D.C., to Maine. They were currently occupying the Highland Room and the Tartan Room.

Flora was glad for the business. Between it and tending to her own kids, she was quite literally occupied from morning to night. By the end of the day, she was usually so tired, she dropped right to sleep the moment her head hit the pillow. A good thing, too, since then she wasn't left to lie awake, alone and thinking about Gavin Matheson.

"Mummy?"

Flora found Annie waiting for her in the kitchen, already wrapped twice round with an apron. Seeing her, Flora remembered that she had promised her daughter they could do some preserving that morning. Annie loved so much to do anything in the kitchen, the messier and stickier the better. Flora gave her expectant face a smile.

"How's m' wee bird today? Ready to help me make some jam, then?"

Two dozen jars of strawberry, plum, and peach preserves— and one dozen fresh scones—later, and the kitchen looked as if an army had just marched through. There was flour dusting the countertops, peach preserves sticking to Annie's hair, and the sink was overflowing with what looked like every pot and pan in creation.

The entire house, however, smelled like heaven.

"All right, Fiona MacCallum," Flora said when she noticed her daughter trying to make a subtle getaway. "Part of working in the kitchen is the cleaning up of it afterward."

When Annie pulled a less-than-enthusiastic face, Flora added, "Come now, with the two of us, it'll go much faster.

For starters, why don't you take these jars down for storing in the cellar and I'll start to washing the dirty pots?"

Flora was elbow deep in a sink full of sudsy water when Annie came back up the stairs sometime later. "Well, that certainly took you long enough, lass. What were you—"

When Flora looked, she noticed Annie reading what appeared to be a dusty book.

"What d' you have there, Annie?"

" 'Tis a book, Mummy."

"I can see that. Where did you get it?"

"I found it down in the cellar. It was stuck in the back corner of the shelf."

Flora dried her hands on a clean dish towel. "What sort of book is it?"

"I dinna know. I can't read the writing. 'Tis funny-looking."

"Here, sweetling. Let Mum have a look at it."

Flora took the book from Annie and peered at the scribble-covered pages. The handwriting was almost illegible, ink-smudged and written in short entries.

"It looks like it could be some sort of diary, but there aren't any dates." Flora lowered into one of the kitchen chairs.

Annie peered over her shoulder. "Whose diary is it, Mummy?"

Flora struggled to decipher the somewhat-faded handwriting and peculiar text. "I don't know. It doesn't say."

One thing that was certain was that the diary was very old. The pages had been hand cut and sewn crudely into the binding, the ink was faded and almost illegible in places, and the language used by the author was archaic, spiced with "thee" and "thine." Yet despite this, Flora soon became engrossed.

Almost immediately she knew that whoever had written the diary must have been a woman. The tenor of her words, and the feelings she expressed, were all clearly feminine in nature. She mentioned events from her everyday life, listed herbs that she used from the physic garden, and even included recipes, although some of the ingredients were unfamiliar to Flora.

Throughout the text, the author often referred to someone designated merely as *H. H* was definitely a man, and he clearly shared the writer's life in some way, but theirs didn't appear to be a love relationship by any means. Flora began to suspect that the diary had been written by a former maid of the house, although her obvious education in writing and reading should have precluded that. Flora wondered if Betty Petwith might be able to help her figure out who the author of the diary might have been. She quickly placed a call to the Historical Society.

Betty—aka "Watson"—Petwith was more than interested in seeing the diary. The added delight of Annie's possible piece of eight had her promising to come personally to the house, instead of waiting until Flora could find the opportunity to get to town.

Jen's sister Hallie arrived just as Flora hung up the phone.

Hallie was twenty-two and a recent graduate from Boston University with a bachelor's in business administration. She had intended to spend her summer as she had every summer for the past several years—working at her sister's salon sweeping up hair, putting away styling magazines, and ordering supplies—before heading out into the workforce in the fall. That is, until Flora mentioned she would be looking for someone to assist her at the house. Jen had immediately suggested Hallie, whom Flora had already met and was thinking of asking to watch the kids on occasion. That was before she knew about her business acumen. Having her to help out at the house with reservations, advertising, and occasional cleaning would be doubly helpful.

Flora realized almost immediately that Hallie was perfect for the job. The petite brunette listened and caught on quickly. And she was a whiz with the computer, offering to jazz up Thar Muir's Web site with digital photographs of each room and hyperlinks to many of the local attractions. When Betty Petwith arrived for tea, they agreed to work together on a section that would feature the history of the house and the village as well. And the kids just adored Hallie—most especially Robbie, who actually took the time to comb his unruly mop of hair, spoke in a noticeably deeper voice, and tried very hard to impress Hallie at every opportunity.

When Flora brought the tea tray out onto the summer porch with a plate of the scones and preserves she and Annie had made that morning, Betty was already nose deep in the diary.

"This is certainly fascinating reading," she said. "Fascinating indeed. You say your daughter found this in the cellar?"

"Aye." Flora poured them each a cup of Darjeeling, then tucked a slice of lemon on the lip of Betty's saucer.

"Fascinating . . ." Betty repeated, reading on. "I've seen other historical diaries, and given the language, I should think it's almost certainly eighteenth century. If only she'd thought to date her entries, we would be able to pinpoint it better. But I do think your hunch is right and she was likely a maid here at the house."

"And Mr. *H*?" Flora asked.

"Well, at first, of course, one would assume it stood for Hutchinson. But if I'm correct and this was written in the early eighteenth century, then it could also stand for Hiram. Hiram Hutchinson."

"Oh, right," Flora said. "That man you mentioned to me. The bachelor Hutchinson."

"Indeed, which is another reason I suspect this diary was written by a maid. After you left the Historical Society the other day, I did a little research on my own. Seems our friend Hiram was somewhat of the village physician, although I could never verify that he'd had any formal training in medicine. But he did seem to have a knack for remedies."

"Herbal remedies?" Flora asked.

"Well, I should think so."

Flora looked at Betty. "It would seem whoever wrote this diary also had quite an extensive knowledge of herbs."

Betty agreed. "You know, if you would allow me to, I would love to take this diary back with me to the Historical Society. I could compare some of the entries with other recorded events from that time. I could see if I can better identify just when this diary might have been written."

"Of course," Flora said. "Now, what can you tell us about Annie's other treasure?"

Betty set aside the diary and took up Annie's coin. "Well, I checked with my colleague down on Cape Cod, and Mr. Matheson's hunch was right. It certainly is a Spanish piece of eight. While there have been occasional discoveries down on the Cape over the years, this is the first known artifact of this type found along this part of the coast. I'm thinking that terrible storm last week probably churned this little guy up from wherever it's been hiding. I'm sure Mr. Matheson told you about the long-held suspicion that Hathaway Island was once used as a pirate haunt. This coin would certainly support that theory, as well as give credibility to the notion that

Rachael Hathaway was carried away from her island prison by such a flamboyant suitor. One thing I do know for certain," she added on a wink. "Your Annie is quite the treasure finder."

"You know, she always has been. Whenever I haven't been able to find something, or if one of her brothers misplaces a toy, she always seems to be the one to turn it up. Odd, that . . ."

"Oh, I don't know about calling it odd," Betty said. "Some people might just call it a gift."

After Betty Petwith had gone, taking the diary with her, Flora sat down with Hallie and went over the accounting and reservations system they used for Thar Muir's record keeping. Hallie picked it up straightaway, even suggesting a way to streamline things by merging the two into one utility. And then, when she'd finished with that, she started working on the Web site. She was young and her energy level seemed limitless, which was a good thing considering Flora's own stamina had been lagging the past day or so. She knew she'd been overdoing it, single-handedly trying to make every aspect of their guests' visits just right. Hallie's help with the technical side of things would be a very welcome addition.

Later that day, Jimmy O'Connell stopped by with pepperoni pizzas for the kids and cold beer for himself so they could discuss his ideas for converting the boathouse into another lodging for guests. This one would be more private and outfitted with an eye for the extended-stay guest, not the overnighter.

Flora's only sticking point was that they keep the original outer "shell" of the building, one that had been built out of the natural local stone and had been weathered over the centuries from the salt of the sea. That was something that just couldn't be replaced, and Jimmy O'Connell agreed. But inside, the cottage would require a complete overhaul, with the addition of insulation, electrical wiring, and modern plumbing, for a start. They discussed a warm golden maple paneling and flagstone floor, and the addition of a chimney was a definite requirement. A small kitchenette, a bathroom similar to those up at the house, and a bedroom and separate sitting room, they both agreed, would keep the place quaint, yet still comfortable.

Jimmy expected he could start the following week, and with the help of his three able-bodied sons, they could have it finished by summer's end. And since the boathouse was a distance from the main house, his construction work wouldn't prove any nuisance to their current guests.

By the time they finished, it was too late in the night back in the UK for Flora to call Libby to share the plans for the boathouse. Angus had phoned a couple of hours earlier to check in after his flight, but Flora hadn't been able to do much more than exchange a couple of words and get back to the boathouse plans.

After shooing the kids off to bed, she went around the house checking the doors and clicking on the hall lamp for the Rices, the young couple from Virginia. They had left earlier for a walk into town to have a late supper and after-dinner espressos at the café. Though she furnished all her guests with a front-door key that allowed them to come and go as they pleased, Flora still stayed awake until she knew everyone was in for the night.

The movie she'd popped into the DVD player had just started rolling the credits when the Rices returned. After asking them about their evening, Flora locked up for the night.

It was ten past midnight when she finally fell into bed.

When the alarm clock went off at five thirty the next morning, Flora didn't immediately awaken. Nor did she head off to the kitchen to begin preparing the seven o'clock breakfast for her guests. When she finally did stir a quarter of an hour later, sitting up on the side of the bed, she felt a sudden queasiness roll through her stomach.

Her first thought was that perhaps she shouldn't have eaten the pepperoni the night before. But when she stood from the bed and that queasiness doubled, nearly buckling her knees, she was seized with a different thought entirely.

There had been a few other times in her life when she had felt that same goose-bump-raising lurch in the pit of her stomach.

Three times to be precise.

The first had been Robbie.

The second, Annie.

And the third had been wee Seamus.

Flora's heart began to pound as she quickly counted backward through the days of the previous month.

And when she did, she swore that same racing heart actually stopped beating.

Chapter Fourteen

Gavin opened the door and blinked when an unexpected face greeted him on the other side.

"Robbie."

The boy looked at Gavin, then looked away. "Hullo."

"Something I can do for you?"

When he just stood there saying nothing more, Gavin took a step back. "You want to come in for a minute?"

Robbie shrugged. "Sure."

There was obviously something on the boy's mind, and the list of possibilities Gavin quickly ran through all held the potential for some degree of awkwardness.

Had Flora sent him over? And if so, what for?

Was something wrong at the house?

With Annie?

Or Seamus?

Rather than invite trouble, Gavin decided to let Robbie bring up in his own time whatever had brought him there.

"Thirsty?"

Robbie shrugged again.

"Want a soda?"

"Sure."

Gavin took two bottles from the fridge, opened them, and

handed one to Robbie. He took the other with him as he led Robbie out onto the deck.

They drank in silence, Gavin staring out at the sea, Robbie staring down at his muddy sneakers. Seagulls, looking for a meal, soared along the shore, lofting up toward the deck where they stood. Gavin took the remnants of the sandwich he'd been eating and tossed the bread crusts to them.

Finally, when he could stand it no longer, Gavin asked, "Something on your mind, Rob?"

He watched the boy put the soda bottle to his lips and drink down three healthy swallows before he said, "Sam wants me to join his baseball team."

"Really? His mom's the one that owns that salon, right? Well, that's cool." Gavin looked at him. "Isn't it?"

"Yeah. But we don't have that game back home where I come from. We have football. So"—he hesitated—"I was sorta wondering"—looking at Gavin from under the fringe of his perpetually unruly hair—"if maybe you'd want to show me how to play."

Gavin had to fight the urge to let out a relieved exhale. Of all the things that could have brought Robbie to his door, this was unexpected and definitely doable.

"Sure, Rob. I can do that. First, does your mom know you're here?"

"Uh . . . I told her I was going for a walk."

"Okay." He picked up the phone and handed it to the boy. "Give her a call. Tell her we're going to go to the ball field down behind the school for a little while. I'll drop you by the house afterward."

While Robbie called Flora, Gavin got his keys. He checked Alec's garage and found a bat, a couple of gloves, and a ball and tossed them into the backseat of his car.

Robbie came down a couple of minutes later.

"Everything set with your mom?"

He nodded. "She said it was all right so long as I wasn't bothering you."

Actually, Gavin welcomed the interruption. It allowed him to avoid thinking about other things.

Namely, Flora and that night on the common when Seamus had gotten lost.

Gavin knew he'd let his emotions get the better of him that night. That feeling, the same terrible feeling he'd had the day Gabriel disappeared, had come back like a solid punch in the gut, leaving him weak and gasping for breath. In the space of those first thirty seconds or so, he'd imagined every possible scenario, every news headline he'd ever read about a child who'd gone missing.

Hadn't he sworn when he'd lost Gabriel that he would never put himself in a position to feel that helpless again?

But he had.

He'd let himself get close to Flora's kids, and then he'd panicked at the first suggestion of trouble. It was almost as if he'd been waiting for something to happen, something that would send him back to wearing the armor he'd surrounded himself with.

He shouldn't have said what he'd said to Flora that night, how he'd been wrong when he'd thought he could "handle" being around her kids. He'd regretted the words almost the moment they'd left his mouth. But by then, it had been too late. He'd seen the effect of those words in her eyes.

She felt abandoned by him. And she believed he had forsaken her children. But that couldn't be any further from the truth. Because just as he loved Flora, Gavin also loved her kids. He'd simply done a bad job of showing it that night.

A really bad job.

Being away from them these past days had been torture. While he'd sat out on his deck chair, he wondered what they were doing, where they were . . . if they were safe. That feeling, once it was a part of someone, couldn't just be turned off or forgotten. And that was what he planned to tell Flora when he drove Robbie back to the house later.

The school yard was empty when they arrived. Gavin had Robbie put on a glove and spent the first hour just showing him how to catch with it. It took some getting used to, but it wasn't long before Robbie started to get the feel for it. He had a sharp eye and good reflexes, probably from having grown up kicking around a soccer ball. Then Gavin had him try a pitch and realized the kid had a good throwing arm as well, with dead-on accuracy.

"Where'd you learn to throw like that?" Gavin asked him.

"Back home. Me and my mates used to throw rocks at a can on the fence post. Not much else to do there."

"Here. Let's try something. . . ."

Gavin directed Robbie to the pitcher's mound, then crouched behind home plate. He held up his gloved hand. "See if you can hit my glove."

Robbie wound up and threw the ball straight and hard, right across the plate. It smacked into the leather of Gavin's glove.

Damn.

"Try it again," Gavin said.

Robbie threw three more.

A couple of kids riding down the street on their bikes stopped at the fence to watch.

Gavin waved them over, sending one to center field and the other to the batter's box.

"All right, Rob. Now, throw the ball into my glove again. Same as before."

The batter, Mikey he said his name was, tipped the first pitch Robbie threw foul. Gavin moved his glove a little to the inside, beating it with his fist.

"Right here, Rob."

The next two pitches had Mikey swinging at nothing but air.

Mikey's friend in center field was laughing.

"Can it, Billy!" Mikey yelled. "Let's see you try to hit off this kid."

Billy, Mikey told Gavin, was one of the best hitters in Ipswich-by-the-Sea. He readily accepted the challenge to hit off the new kid.

Three strikes later, he was out, too.

"Where'd you learn to pitch like that?" Mikey asked. "Billy never strikes out."

Robbie actually cracked a smile. "I dunno. Back home, I guess."

"You talk weird," Billy said. "Where you from? England or somethin'?"

"Scotland."

"Like *Braveheart?*"

Robbie nodded. "Yeah . . . I guess."

"Cool. Well, listen, Braveheart. What're you doin' Saturday? 'Cus we got a game against those bums from Westerville, and our regular pitcher busted his arm doing an ollie on the half-pipe."

"I can't." Robbie shrugged. "I already told Sam I'd play on his team."

"You mean Sam, Cassie's brother?" Mikey grinned. "He's our second baseman. So looks like we'll see you Saturday, Braveheart. Right here at the school. Ten o'clock sharp."

*   *   *

The stick was blue.

Not just a little blue, but a bright, vivid pool-water blue that left little doubt as to the result.

Flora was pregnant.

Pregnant.

And Gavin was the father.

Flora sat on the toilet seat, hands shaking, and stared at that stick, at that glaring blue line, trying to catch her flagging breath.

Oh . . .

Sweet . . .

Dia.

How had this happened?

It had been just one night, that night on the beach two weeks before. Two weeks and three days before to be exact. One night of foolish, carefree, stupidly *unprotected* sex.

That's how it had happened.

And now she was pregnant.

She was going to have a child. Another child. A fourth child.

What was she going to do?

Flora couldn't so much as consider a possible solution because a moment later, the bathroom doorknob turned. The door pushed open, revealing Annie. Flora quickly tossed the pregnancy test in the trash bucket.

"Annie! Mummy is in here just now!"

"Oh." But she made no move to leave. "Mummy? Are you okay? You're not going—to the toilet, I mean. You're just sitting on top. Are you sick?"

"No, baby. I'm just a little tired and I'm taking a wee rest. Please, just give me a moment, aye? Close the door now."

Flora watched her daughter back reluctantly out of the

bathroom and close the door. The look on her face said that Annie already sensed something was wrong.

Flora's heart was pounding in her throat and her hands were trembling when she retrieved that test stick from the trash bin.

It was still blue. Even brighter than before, if that was possible.

She took a ragged breath to try to calm the storm of emotions churning inside of her. Then she asked herself again:

What was she going to do?

What *in the bloody hell* was she going to do?

She was a widow, a thirty-two-year-old widow, a single mother of three, who was just beginning to adjust to a new life after losing her husband. And now this, another child, with Gavin, who had just told her that the very last thing he wanted was to be a father again.

Just thinking about it made Flora's head spin. And that made her stomach lurch. She closed her eyes and waited until the feeling passed.

A few minutes later, Flora stood. She turned on the tap, cupped some cold water in her hands, and splashed it over her face. She toweled dry and stared at her reflection in the mirror. But the woman who looked back at her didn't look like she had any solution to offer, either.

She just looked scared as hell.

Flora turned and left the bathroom.

"Everything all right, Flor?" Hallie asked her when she came into the kitchen. "Annie said you were sick."

"Nae. I'm fine. I just haven't eaten much of anything all day. Is that tea you're making?"

"Sure is. It's herbal. Want a cup?" When Flora nodded, she added, "How about a sandwich? I was just making one for m'self." And then, "Turkey okay?"

Flora did feel a little better after she ate some of the sandwich, but her stomach was in such a tangle she could manage to choke down only half of it. She tried to focus on Hallie's nonstop conversation about Web sites and spreadsheets and promotional brochures, but all she kept seeing in her mind's eye was that vivid blue line.

More than once, Flora nearly went to the office to pick up the phone and call Angus. Her brother had always been there for her. She knew there was nothing she could not tell him. But this . . .

No. She needed to come to terms with it first before she could tell anyone else. If she called Angus, she knew he would be on the next plane back to the States. She also knew he would take over, doing everything he could to fix the situation for her—insomuch as it could be fixed. He would give up his own life all over again in order to help her figure out hers. Flora had let him do that once. This was something she had to figure out for herself.

She just needed time, time to think. And she needed to do that thinking alone somewhere where she wouldn't be interrupted by inquisitive children.

Flora grabbed the keys to the SUV from their hook on the wall. "Hallie, do you think you can mind the kids and manage things here for me for about an hour or so? I just remembered something I need to take care of in town."

Like buying another test perhaps . . . to double-check . . . maybe some prenatal vitamins, as well.

Hallie nodded over a bite of her sandwich. "No problem. The Rices checked out and are on their way back to Virginia, very happy with their stay, by the way. All the other guests are out sightseeing for the day. Robbie's still out and Annie and Seamus are watching the *Shrek* DVD I rented. Take your time coming back. We'll be fine."

*   *   *

Gavin ducked into the pharmacy, his last stop after the market, the dry cleaners, and the post office.

He'd dropped Robbie off at Thar Muir an hour earlier and had noticed Flora's car missing from the drive. Someone named Hallie told him she'd gone into town.

And so to town was where Gavin had gone looking for her.

But he hadn't found Flora at the market, the dry cleaners, or the post office, either. When he'd stopped in at the café, Jules told him she hadn't seen Flora in the past several days.

He'd just about given up when he spotted her SUV parked outside the pharmacy.

"Don't forget your change, Ms. MacCallum. . . ."

Gavin stopped short when he opened the door and nearly ran headfirst into her.

"Oh," she said.

"Hi," he said.

"Hi."

They stared at each other, filling the pharmacy doorway.

"How've you been?" he finally asked.

The look on her face was a mixture of emotions—apprehension, awkwardness, and something else he couldn't recognize. In fact, it almost looked like fear.

Flora stared at Gavin for some time, and then she said, "I've been okay. Busy, in fact. We've had nearly a constant string of guests this past week. I should get back to the house now."

"Flora, I'd really like to talk. . . ."

Were those tears he saw brimming her eyes?

"Gavin, can we please do that later? I'd like to talk to you, too, but I really need to get back to the house . . . now."

Clutching her paper sack, she didn't even wait for him to

answer. She shoved past him in her haste to get out of the store.

And away from him.

"Damn it, Flora . . . wait!"

But she was already tearing out of the parking space and heading down the street.

Feeling like an idiot standing in the open doorway of the pharmacy with Alice the cashier gawking at him, Gavin had little choice but to go in and grab something. He picked up a package of razors and headed for the counter, until he remembered—

"Aspirin," he said to himself out loud, for the headache he was sure to have by the time he got home.

He was looking through the selection on the bottom shelf when he heard the pharmacist's voice at the front of the store.

"Alice, make sure to put in an order for more prenatal vitamins. Looks like Ms. MacCallum just bought the last bottle."

Gavin froze, hand poised in midair, inches from the aspirin bottle. He told himself he'd overheard it wrong.

He must have overheard it wrong.

Until the pharmacist added with a chuckle, "Looks like that pregnancy test she bought did its work."

Gavin felt a rush of air leave his mouth. He tried to breathe, but he seemed to have forgotten how. He blinked when his vision began to blur.

He grabbed the aspirin bottle and rose, locking eyes with the pharmacist. The white-coated, bow-tied, balding man instantly went red in the face.

"Oh, Mr. Matheson. Excuse me. I didn't know anyone was in the store. . . ."

Gavin simply nodded, went for the cash register, and

waited while Alice took what seemed like an interminably long time to ring up his purchases. He threw down a twenty to pay, and turned, thinking if he didn't get out of that store in the next ten seconds, he was going to pass out.

"Mr. Matheson! Wait! You forgot your change!"

He didn't bother to go back.

Outside, Gavin stopped, staring straight ahead. He grabbed onto a lamppost for support.

Flora was pregnant.

Gavin took a deep breath, then counted back the days. It had been just over two weeks since he and Flora had been together, that one incredible night on the beach.

And in that bed.

And on the floor in front of the fireplace.

No wonder she'd looked at him like she had when he'd come into the pharmacy. The last time they had seen each other, he told her he couldn't deal with children and would never put himself in a position to have one of his own again.

He was such an ass.

Gavin tossed the bag with his razors and the aspirin in the passenger seat and gunned the BMW's engine as he headed for Thar Muir.

When he roared up the drive, Flora was standing on the drive. Seamus and Annie had just come out of the house onto the porch to meet her.

"Hi, Gavin!" Annie said when he got out of the car.

"Hello, Annie," he said without taking his eyes from Flora.

"When were you intending to tell me?" he asked when she turned and saw him coming. "Or weren't you planning to tell me at all?"

Flora looked back at the kids without responding. "Annie, take Seamus back into the house."

"Mummy," Seamus said, looking from her to Gavin and back. "Why's Gavin so mad?"

"I don't know, sweetling. Now, why don't you go with Annie to the kitchen or find where Hallie is while I talk to Gavin and find out, aye? Hallie will give you some of those biscuits I bought at the market, the ones with the chocolate icing. Annie, you pour the milk and be careful not to spill. . . ."

Flora and Gavin stood staring at each other while Annie and Seamus went reluctantly into the house, looking back at the two of them standing on the driveway, sensing as kids did, that something was very, very wrong.

Flora waited until she'd heard the front door close before she spoke. "They dinna know anything, so please keep your voice down. They will undoubtedly be listening at the door, and this certainly isna the way I would want them to find out."

She was right.

"Then come for a walk with me."

He didn't even wait for her to answer, just took Flora by the arm and led her around to the back of the house, past the trellis where he'd first met her scarcely a month before. Somehow, it seemed like a lifetime ago.

Gavin stopped when they were a safe distance from the house. He closed his eyes and paused to take a breath before he spoke.

"I won't even ask *if* it's true. It was written all over your face when you saw me at the pharmacy. It's written all over your face right now. You're pregnant. You're carrying my child, aren't you?

Flora just looked at him, tears brimming her eyes. "How did you find out?"

"The pharmacist has a big mouth. He didn't know I was in the store. Why didn't you tell me?"

"I just learned of it," she said. "Not even three hours ago. I haven't even had the time to accept it m'self."

Gavin reined in his emotions when he saw the turmoil that was simmering inside of her. "Were you going to tell me?"

She looked at him and set her jaw. "I don't really know. You made your feelings about this sort of thing quite clear the last time we spoke." And then she closed her eyes before exhaling slowly. "Of course I would have told you, Gavin. Eventually. Just as soon as I had figured out what I was going to do."

Gavin didn't like the tone her voice had suddenly taken on. It sounded so resolute. So *final*.

"What do you mean, Flora? What are you going to do?"

"I just spent the past hour thinking about it, and I've decided I'm going to do exactly what I have always intended to do. I'm going to stay here through the summer, see to things at the house, and then I'm going to go back home."

"To Scotland?"

"Aye." She nodded. "To Scotland."

Gavin looked at Flora, and the thought of there being an entire ocean between them nearly choked him. "Stay."

"Gavin, I canna do that."

"Please, Flora. I can't lose another one."

His pain was so raw, it felt like a living, breathing, heartbreaking thing.

"I would never keep you from your child, Gavin. *Our* child. You have to know that. But Scotland is my home. It is where I was born. Where my children were born. My family is there. My friends. I need them now more than ever. Everything I know is there."

"I know that." He reached out to touch the side of her face. He saw her lip tremble and rubbed his thumb softly over it. "But I'm still asking you to stay."

Flora looked at Gavin, them shook her head. "Once the summer ends, my job here will be done. I will have no other reason to stay."

"Yes, you will."

She looked at him, waiting.

"Me. Us. All of us."

"What do you mean, Gavin?"

"I'm saying I want us to be a family—even with the worry and the chaos and not knowing what the future will bring. Do you know why I got so upset the other night when Seamus went missing? Because I was scared to death that something had happened to him. Because I love that little guy . . ." His voice broke but he refused not to finish what he had to say. "Just as I love Annie and Robbie. Just as I love you."

Flora lost the battle against her tears as a sob rocked her, buckling her knees. She dissolved against him, no longer able to bear even her own weight, and Gavin pulled her into his arms, holding her, kissing her as he buried his face in her soft hair. Now that he held her, he wasn't about to let her go.

"Be my wife, Flora. Give us both, give all of us, a second chance."

Gavin waited until her sobs quieted before he pulled back only far enough to take her mouth in a kiss. He kissed her tenderly, brushing away her tears, filling that one simple gesture with all the love he felt for her. And when he felt her wrap her arms around his neck, clinging to him, when he heard her soft sigh against his mouth, he knew what her answer would be even without her having spoken the words.

"I canna spring all of this on the kids at once," she whispered against his face when she finally broke from the kiss. "I need time."

Gavin nodded. "We'll take it a step at a time, Flora. But we'll do it together."

Three hours later, Fate wielded her hand yet again.

Flora had just put the kids to bed and was sitting in the kitchen alone, wrapped in her bathrobe, sipping a cup of tea. She was trying to sort out the best way to tell the children that she and Gavin were going to be married. They couldn't wait long, she realized, especially with the baby coming.

The baby.

Flora rested her hand on her belly, yet flat, the life nestled inside but a seedling.

They would be flying back to Scotland at the end of the month for the christening of Libby and Graeme's son. They would be home, with all their family and friends around them. It would be the perfect time, the perfect place . . .

For a wedding.

The phone rang. She'd expected it would be Gavin calling, and in fact had waited up for him. They had so much to talk about, so much to decide.

What she hadn't expected were the words she would hear him say when she picked up the phone.

"Flora . . ." His voice was thick, breathless.

"Gavin, what's wrong? Has something happened?"

"They've found him. They've found Gabriel."

Flora gasped. She covered her mouth. Tears immediately swelled in her eyes. "Gavin, oh *Dia*. How? When? Where is he?"

"I don't know that right now. Ivan, my private investigator, left me a message. I just got it. I can't reach him. I don't even know where they are. All I know is they're bringing him home to New York. They'll be flying in the day after to-morrow." She heard his voice break beneath the wave of emotion that had to be threatening to drown him.

"Come with me, Flora," he said to her then. "Come with me to New York. Be there with me when I get my son back."

Chapter Fifteen

They were on the train out of Boston's South Station by ten o'clock the next morning.

Flora's first call after hanging up with Gavin the night before was to Jen, who was more than happy to take a couple of days off from managing the salon to come and stay at the house with the kids. She would even bring Cassie and Sam along with her to keep the kids company. Hallie would handle the business end of Thar Muir, checking out the Wilsons later that morning, taking any new reservations, and otherwise holding down the fort until Flora returned.

Gavin finally reached his private investigator in the early morning hours. He was in London, and he had Gabriel with him. It was then Gavin learned the specifics about his son's recovery.

After two years of living on the run, Miranda had apparently decided she was tired of looking over her shoulder and wanted to go home. So she had . . . to Britain. Knowing she would easily be noticed coming and going from her parents' South Kensington town house, she'd rented a flat in South London, leasing it in the name of her Brazilian boyfriend.

Ivan had set up surveillance and then waited for the moment to present itself.

It did less than a week later.

Miranda had left Gabriel in the care of her boyfriend one afternoon. He'd had to go out to use the pay phone on the corner and brought Gabriel with him. While the Brazilian was arguing in Portuguese on the phone, Ivan had swept in. He'd quickly explained to Gabriel who he was, that he worked for Gavin, and then showed the boy his father's photograph. Then he asked Gabriel if he wanted to go home.

Gabriel agreed, apparently as tired of life on the run as his mother.

He'd ducked with Ivan into a cab, leaving the Brazilian still barking into the pay phone, none the wiser.

Because Gavin had a valid American passport for Gabriel, which Ivan had with him, they were able to avoid the governmental red tape and bring Gabriel home almost immediately. Flora would never forget how Gavin's face had lit up when he'd spoken to his son for the first time in over two years.

"Hey, buddy. It's Dad."

She didn't know what Gabriel said in response, but when Gavin ended the call a short time later, there were tears brimming his eyes.

Gavin was quiet, understandably so, during the three-and-a-half-hour train ride down the New England coast to New York. Flora spent most of the time watching him pace the train car's center aisle like a lion in a cage, placing calls on his mobile to his attorney, the courts, even a therapist in preparation for Gabriel's return.

Their flight would arrive at JFK the following morning, leaving Gavin and Flora the entire day and night to wait . . . and wonder.

Flora could only imagine what Gavin must be feeling after all the time that had passed, to know that he would soon see his son again. There was so much they needed to discuss—their plans to get married, their future—but for now that was secondary to the more immediate issue of Gabriel's impending return. Once he was back with Gavin and the courts had sorted through the issue of his custody, then they could concentrate on the life they would build together.

The train pulled in to Penn Station just before two o'clock. As soon as she got a clear signal on her mobile, Flora placed a call to the house. She recognized Annie's voice on the other end of the connection.

"Hallo, Thar Muir. May I be of assistance, please?"

Flora smiled to hear herself being mimicked by her seven-year-old.

"Good morning, Fiona MacCallum."

"Mummy! Are you in New York?"

"Aye, sweetling, I am."

"Have you seen the Statue of Liberty? Is she very pretty? Is there really a giant gorilla climbing on top of the Empire State Building like Uncle Angus said?"

"No, Annie. I'm still in the train station, trying to find my way out. How are things there?"

"Oh, fine. Sam and Robbie are playing ball outside. Seamus rolled in the mud, so Jen and Hallie are trying to convince him that he must take a bath, and well, you know how that goes. So I get to answer the phone. How'd I do, Mummy?"

"You did grand, Annie. Very grand, indeed."

"Shall I get Jen for you?"

Flora heard a sound over the phone then that she recognized as her youngest son's trademark shriek, the one he always gave in protest to his bath.

"Nae, Annie. It sounds as if Jen and Hallie have their hands quite full at the moment. Just tell them I called to check in. You've got my mobile number should wee Seamus prove too much of a challenge for them, aye?"

"Aye, Mummy. I do."

Flora smiled. "That's m' girl."

"Mummy?"

"Yes, Annie?"

"Will you bring me one of those pizza-sized biscuits home from New York with you? You know, the ones Aunt Libby told me about?"

Flora had already spotted the very ones in the bakery at the train station. It was a big round cake of a cookie, covered half in chocolate icing, half in white. Annie would be in biscuit heaven.

"I certainly will, Annie dear. But only if you're on your very best behavior for Jen and Hallie whilst I'm away. And you can tell the same to your brothers, too. Especially that wee ornery one."

Annie laughed. "Oh, they've gotten him into the water now! He's splashing all o'er the place."

"Okay, pet. You best go and help them with wee Seamus. He'll listen to you."

"Okay, Mummy. I miss you!"

"And I miss you, dearie be. We'll be back just as soon as we can."

Flora was about to disconnect the call when she heard Annie's voice summoning her again from the earpiece.

"Mummy?"

"Aye, Annie?"

"I almost forgot. When you see Gabriel, will you tell him something for me?"

"Aye. What's that?"

"Tell him I canna wait to meet him."

Flora smiled into the phone. "Okay, Annie. I certainly will do that."

And for that, Flora decided as she ended the call, Annie would get two pizza-sized biscuits brought home to her.

The streets outside the train station swarmed with people and cars, busses and delivery trucks, all buzzing on their way to somewhere else. Flora, lost in the midst of it, had to stop on the sidewalk and stand still for a moment, just to give herself time to take it all in. She'd never seen anything like it—the vastness, the incredible pulse—in her life. There were probably more people standing in that one city block than in the whole of Wrath Village.

In fact, she was sure of it.

"There's the Empire State Building," Gavin said to her, and Flora looked down the street, trying to find the famous landmark among the jungle of other tall high-rises.

"Where, Gavin? I dinna see it."

Gavin smiled softly at her and put his finger under her chin, lifting her gaze heavenward. "It's there."

The building, all glass and steel and stone, stretched above her head and reached straight into the clouds. She could barely see the tall spire that topped it.

"Oh . . ."

While she gaped at it, Gavin quickly hailed them a cab. Moments later, they were speeding along Seventh Avenue.

Flora nearly pressed her face to the cab's window as shops and tall buildings flashed by. The collision of colors and noises and smells left her feeling as if she had to catch her breath.

"How are you?" she asked Gavin, taking his hand and linking her fingers with his.

"Anxious. Impatient. Elated. Worried." He looked at her.

"Should I go on? I'm sure I can come up with at least twenty more."

Flora smiled at him. "'Tis going to be all right, Gavin. You'll see. He's coming home. Everything else, the details, the what has been and what's to come, will all sort itself out once he's here."

"Until I see him standing right in front of me, I think I'll still wonder if I'm dreaming." Gavin looked at her deeply. "In case I forget to say it later, thank you for coming with me. I couldn't imagine doing this alone."

But Flora just shook her head. "My place is with you. Today, and from now on."

The cab had turned down a side street and rolled to a stop before a tree-lined brownstone with a warm brick facade and a bay window. Cast-iron grillwork and stone balustrades traced in character. When Flora looked up, she felt her mouth fall open as she stood on the sidewalk and stared. "This is . . . *your* house?"

Gavin grabbed their bags from the sidewalk and paid the cabdriver. "It is, although it's been more of an investment than a home the past few years. I bought it for a song." And then he smiled. "Literally. My first major purchase after one of my compositions went platinum. It was built in the 1880s, and when I bought it, it hadn't been touched since the twenties. Still had the original cloth-covered wiring and coal-burning furnace. Needless to say, it cried out for restoration. I loved living here, but Miranda always hated the place, said it just smelled old. That is, until the lawyers got involved. Then suddenly she was fighting for it."

Flora followed Gavin up the wide stone front steps and waited while he fished the keys out of his pocket, unlocking the front door after punching the security code into the adjacent keypad.

"I've no idea what we're going to find in here. It's been a while since I've been here, although there is a super who's been looking after the place, having it cleaned and taking care of any repairs."

They crossed into an entrance hall that was paneled in warm oak, graced by Victorian ceilings and elegant crown moldings. There was a sweeping staircase that gave access to the upper floors, and a checkerboard marble floor spilled underfoot, stretching all the way to the back of the house.

"It's beautiful," she said.

It was like stepping into a different world. Outside, the twenty-first century raced and blared through the city streets in stark, glaring neon and shiny chrome. But once Gavin closed the door behind them, that world seemed to vanish, somehow leaving Flora feeling just like Alice stepping through the looking glass.

Gavin dropped their bags at the foot of the stairs and went into the front parlor to open a window and pull dust-covers from the furniture. Flora wasn't surprised at the taste-ful selection of antiques revealed underneath the cloths, especially the rosewood grand piano that highlighted the front corner. Anything else would have been starkly out of place in this elegant room.

Flora watched as Gavin absently trilled his fingers over the piano keys and she wondered at the many songs he must have composed while sitting there with the city sunlight fil-tering through the windows behind him. She could just see him with his pencil stuck behind one ear and his coffee cup perched beside him, composing some beautiful ballad while the city buzzed by outside.

"I know we just got here," Gavin said to her then. "But how would you feel about taking a walk? I'm too restless to just sit around watching the clock, waiting for tomorrow morning. I need to get out, do something."

So they strolled Fifth Avenue hand in hand, peering in the store windows, stopping at the corner market to pick up a few things—a bottle of wine, tea leaves for Flora, coffee beans for Gavin. They bought "I ♥ NY" T-shirts for the kids, and Gavin couldn't resist buying a New York Yankees ball cap for Robbie. But while their jaunt through the city seemed random to Flora, Gavin had a definite destination in mind.

"Tiffany's?" Flora asked when he stopped before the revolving door of the famous jewelry store.

"Just humor me."

Inside, a labyrinth of glass display cases sparkled with diamonds, gems, and gold, simply awaiting the shopper's pleasure. It gave new meaning to the term "bling bling." Gavin seemed to know exactly what he was looking for.

And it didn't take him long to find it.

He stopped at a display case where an elegant single band made of a complete circle of diamonds sparkled and caught the light. The salesman told them that particular style of ring was called an eternity band.

"Gavin, no. 'Tis too dear," Flora said as she admired the stunning ring he'd insisted she slip over her finger. It fit as if it had been made for her.

"It's meant to be dear," he said, ignoring her protest as he made arrangements with the salesman for its purchase. Then he pulled her against him, saying before he kissed her, "After all, it's meant to last an eternity."

After they left the jewelry store, Gavin hailed them a cab and directed the driver to a downtown address. He'd already called Phil, who'd agreed to have everything ready for them when they arrived.

They exited the taxi before a turn-of-the-century stone high-rise. Waving to the doorman, Gavin led Flora inside and they took the elevator up to the twelfth floor, emerging into a marble-appointed lobby. The lettering over the reception desk read *Studio MGI.*

"This is where you work, isn't it?" Flora said. When he nodded, she asked, "What does MGI signify?"

"Matheson for me, Grayson for my partner Alec, and I'Onorio"—Gavin looked toward the door that had just opened across the lobby—"for this ridiculously overdressed man here."

He looked every bit as Flora would imagine a record executive should look: tailored suit, gold cuff links, perfectly styled, close-clipped hair. He had Italian dark looks and perfectly white teeth that flashed an easy smile.

The old friends greeted each other with handshakes and shoulder claps before turning to Flora.

"Flora, this is Phil I'Onorio. He co-owns the studio with us. Phil, this is Flora MacCallum."

Gavin didn't introduce her as his fiancée. They had decided not to share the news of their engagement with anyone else until they had told the kids first. And they wouldn't tell the kids until they had all of them together, Gabriel included.

"Ms. McCallum, it is a pleasure."

"You've got the—"

"In my office," Phil answered even before Gavin could finish his question. "Why don't you take Flora into one of the studios? I'll meet you there."

Gavin led Flora down a side hall that was lined with framed gold and platinum records and past a series of closed doors. They stopped at number seven. The choice, and its corresponding table where they met for morning coffee at Common Grounds, brought a smile to Flora's lips as Gavin opened the door to let her in.

Couches and armchairs stood in the corners, and it looked more like a comfortable den than a recording studio, except for one whole wall taken up by an electronics console. It was covered with buttons and dials and slider switches.

"I leave the technical side to those who know it better. Most of my work is done on the other side of the glass," Gavin said. He flipped a switch to light up a second room, separated from that one by a huge window. Wallpapered in egg-crate foam, it had a grand piano, a set of drums, and a single microphone hanging down from the ceiling.

"Want to have a little fun?" Gavin asked. "Let's record you singing something for the kids. We can burn it onto a CD for them."

They moved into the other room and Gavin sat behind the piano, limbering up his fingers on the keys.

"What should I sing?" Flora asked, peering at the microphone as if it were a boa constrictor ready to swallow her whole.

"What did you used to sing them to sleep with when they were babies?"

Flora thought a minute. "Annie's favorite was always 'All the Pretty Little Horses'."

Gavin nodded and then started playing the notes of the well-known lullaby on the Steinway.

Flora closed her eyes and listened to the opening stanza of the song, remembering how she had rocked her carrot-haired little cherub in her arms each night. She could still see her, her wee Annie, with those glimmering eyes staring up at her, gripping Flora's pinky finger with her tiny fist.

Bearing this memory in mind, Flora began to sing as she had to all of her children, as she would to the one she carried now.

Gavin smiled to himself as Flora finished the song and he played the closing notes. "That was beautiful."

"Yes, it was, Gavin," agreed a voice over the intercom.

Flora turned. Phil and another, younger man sat behind the recording console on the other side of the glass. She hadn't even noticed them come in.

Flora blinked. "You heard me sing? Oh, we were only supposed to be doing that for fun. It was for my kids."

Gavin came up beside her, resting his hands on her shoulders. "Flora, I want you to hear to something."

He nodded toward the control room. Phil gave him a thumbs-up and said something to the man seated at the controls. A moment later, her voice began filtering through the sound system.

All her life, Flora had gotten up to sing whenever the fancy had overtaken her, usually at a ceilidh at the village hall or when there was a bairn who needed soothing. But in all that time, she'd never really listened to herself.

It was a startling thing, to say the least.

As she listened to the playback, really listened, she couldn't stop the smile from stealing across her face.

Well, at least she hadn't embarrassed herself.

She nodded when the recording finished. "That was nice. The kids will love it."

"Ms. MacCallum . . ." Phil said.

"Flora," she corrected.

"Flora, I'm willing to bet it's not only your kids who would love to hear you sing. Gavin shared an idea of his with me, that of recording a collection of nontraditional lullabies. I think it's a marketable project that will appeal to a varied audience. It could be a first step for you, to see if singing professionally is something you might like to do. But we need one thing to make it happen. We need your voice singing it."

Phil hit the PLAYBACK button again and Flora's voice sang out. "I've been around the music business for a lot of years. Your voice has a quality I've rarely heard before. It speaks of your Scottish heritage, but with a clarity, a sweetness that wraps itself around whoever listens. I don't see this collection as merely drawing a children's audience, but their parents, too. Something they can even relax to over a glass of wine at the end of their working day. I know talent, and I have a knack for turning it into a success, Flora. I could open a whole new world to you that you never dreamed existed."

He certainly was persuasive.

"I don't quite know what to say," Flora said.

Realizing that he was swaying her, Phil simply smiled and adjusted the already perfect knot in his silk necktie. "Well, 'yes' would probably be a good place to start."

After they left the studio, Gavin took Flora to his favorite Italian trattoria in the West Village, where they shared a spaghetti supper and discussed ideas for the recording project. It seemed almost like a dream to Flora, the idea that she might one day hear herself singing on the radio. And Gavin was determined to make that dream a reality.

When they arrived back at the town house, Flora went off to have a quick shower while Gavin put the kettle on for tea.

Gavin was seated at the piano, playing softly as she came back downstairs. The low lamplight glowed from overhead, and Flora lowered herself onto the upholstered bench beside him, sipping her tea as she closed her eyes and listened to him play.

It was a beautiful piece, one she'd never heard before. It drifted gently like the waters of a Highland loch and echoed with the distinct air of her Scottish homeland. When he finished, she opened her eyes and looked at him.

"That was so beautiful, Gavin. Was it something you wrote?"

"Yes, it is." He looked deeply at her. "I wrote it for you."

She blinked at him, not quite understanding.

"One day," he told her, "not too long ago, I was sitting alone in a café, nursing my twelfth cup of coffee and wondering if I would ever write another song. I was beginning to fear I'd lost my muse completely. And then this angel walked in. She was lost and needed help finding her way. I was lost, too. And when she appeared, the music came with her, music I'd never heard before. It was *this* music."

Gavin set his hands on the keys and played Flora's song again, letting its sweet sound wrap itself around them both while Flora rested her head against his shoulder.

The gift of his song touched Flora deeper than anything she'd ever felt before. When he finished playing, Flora reached for him, touching her hand to his jaw, which had roughened since he'd last shaved early that morning. She looked at him with emotion glistening in her eyes and touched her lips to his, kissing him as she melted into the warm circle of his arms.

Gavin moved his mouth over hers, sliding his tongue against hers in long, sensual strokes. Their first time together had been a mad, turbulent coming together of two people who had desperate need of physical and emotional release. It had been wild and free. It had been hectic. This time, when he took her, it would be slow. He would feel every stroke of her hands. She would taste every texture of his kiss. He would savor her with every measure of the feelings he had for her.

Flora traced her fingers down along Gavin's jaw, over his neck, trailing down his arm to one hand. She clasped his fingers in hers and held him, then lifted his hand with hers and slid it inside her robe, freeing him to cup her breast.

As Gavin took her, filling his hand with her, Flora slid her own hand back along his arm and curved her fingers around his neck.

Gavin could feel her pulse beating strong beneath his fingers as he caressed the fullness of her breast. He felt her breath quicken as he thumbed her nipple, and she pressed herself closer to him, seeking more. He felt a shock of pure sexual need shoot through him, going straight to his groin.

He moaned and reached for her, all of her, lifting her over his legs until she straddled him on her knees on the soft velvet seat of the piano bench. He pushed aside the folds of her robe and ran his hand over her breast, covering her nipple with his mouth and suckling her, rolling his tongue over her as she arched against him. Flora reached back with her hands to steady herself and struck the piano keys with a fervent, jarring chord that echoed in the silence of the room.

Flora could feel the stiff fabric of Gavin's jeans, which was all that separated her from him. She moved her hips over him, seeking release from the tension filling her, seeking him, and felt a tingle of pleasure as the harsh fabric and his hardness met her soft, slick center. She felt his teeth nip lightly at her breast then and gasped as a shock took her.

Gavin could think of no better inspiration than to make love to the woman he loved right there on his piano, to remember that lovemaking each time he sat down to write another song. But not this time. He would save that for another day, another fantasy. He wanted Flora in his bed, lying beneath him, naked and beautiful and open for him. He wanted to take the entire night to explore her with his hands and his mouth, to know every contour, every sensitive, breath-stealing place. He pulled his mouth away from her, then urged her to stand as he rose from the bench beside her.

But Flora wasn't ready to retire upstairs just yet.

She stood before him and loosened the sash on her robe, letting it fall to her feet in a wisp of silk. And then she stood still before him in the low lamplight, as beautiful and as perfect as a sculpture. Her hair, damp from her shower, curled around her shoulders and fell down her back, glimmering like molten fire in the light. Her eyes drank him in; her breasts rose and fell with each breath she took. Her hips flared softly from her waist and Gavin found himself trembling just to behold her.

He didn't take his gaze from hers as he came before her and swept her up and into his arms.

She smiled at him with a look that could have curled his toes, and then made good work of his neck with her mouth as he crossed the floor and carried her up that graceful sweeping staircase to his bedroom.

A massive sleigh bed filled the center of the room and Gavin noticed that Flora had already turned down the coverlet, and had even found a few candles to light around the room. He laid her gently on the bed. Then he stood above her, drinking in the sight of her naked as he hauled his sweater over his head and then yanked off his jeans. He wanted her skin . . . against his skin. And he wanted her body . . . against his body. And he wanted it now.

Gavin, impatient to feel her, stretched beside Flora on the bed and drew her over him as he fused his mouth to hers. She dissolved against him, all fluid limbs and soft, heated skin, flattening her hands against his chest and tangling her soft legs in his.

"Do you have any idea how incredibly beautiful you are?" he breathed against her ear and kissed her again, devouring her mouth just as hungrily as she was devouring his.

Flora sucked in her breath when she felt Gavin roll her beneath him and then bury his face in her breasts. She arched her back against him, seeking his mouth on her. She wanted him to touch her, to taste her. Wanted it more than she had ever wanted anything in her life. Knew if she didn't have it, she would surely scream.

"Gavin, please . . ."

Gavin breathed in her scent and dragged his hands down, over her breasts, spanning her waist as he pressed a kiss to the flat plane of her belly. He lifted his head and contemplated her navel, and it astounded him to realize that a tiny life—the life he and Flora had made—lay nestled safely in her womb. It would grow there. It would become their child. The thought of it, and the revelation of the depth of his love for her, left Gavin measuring out his breath.

He moved his mouth downward, nibbling at the angle of her hip as his hand slipped to lift one knee, and he slid his finger down into her. She shuddered and gasped, raking his hair with her fingers. And when he covered her with his mouth, she cried out as he parted her and loved her with his mouth and tongue and fingers. Her breathing hitched, grew sporadic. Her hips lifted from the bed to better meet his mouth. When it came the power and intensity of her climax rocked them both and left Flora melting into the mattress like the wax pooling in the candles.

She hooked her leg around Gavin's waist and urged him to lie back beneath her. Her eyes shone with the fire of a stoked and burning desire while her hair tumbled around her face like wildfire.

She had ignited.

Gavin lifted his hands and filled them with her breasts, stroking them, caressing them. Flora lifted her hips and slid herself over the length of him, taking his hardness fully, deeply.

Gavin let the feeling of being consumed by her overtake him. When she moved her hips, rocking over him, he felt his entire body go taut. He watched her above him, her body limned by the candlelight, her eyes closed, her head thrown back, exposing her slender neck. She was so beautiful, like an angel come to earth. Her hands spanned his chest as her movements grew quicker, and he met her thrusts, then slid his hand between them, his finger against her, bringing her to climax again.

Gavin gripped her hips and pulled her over him, driving himself deeply inside her as he surged, reaching his orgasm with a muffled curse. He brought her down against his chest and held her there as wave after wave carried them along. He stroked her hair, pressed kisses against her forehead, and fell asleep with her draped over him.

And when he stirred hours later and found her still there, tucked against him curve for curve, Gavin silently thanked whichever saint it was who had brought him this saving angel.

Chapter Sixteen

When Flora awoke the next day, the bed was empty beside her.

The sun shone brightly and the sounds of the city traffic drifted inside from an open window. Flora lay for a moment with her head tucked against the pillows. She heard music coming from downstairs. The soft, easy piano trill of a Bach concerto was playing on Gavin's stereo system.

Her robe was still down where she'd left it the night before, by the piano, so when she finally roused herself from bed, she slipped Gavin's shirt, which she found draped on a chair, over her head. She walked on bare feet down the stairs, following the music; when she reached the bottom, the checkerboard marble floor was cold, chilling her toes. She looked in and found the front room empty, echoing with the stereo.

Tracing back through the kitchen, she spotted Gavin with a coffee cup balanced on his knee sitting in a garden off the back of the house. Birds flitted happily through the trees overhead. He wore a V-neck with the sleeves pushed up to his elbows, and his jeans were comfortably faded and worn. His bare feet propped his legs at an angle from the patio table's edge. The sunlight filtered down through the leafy branches, lightening his hair and burnishing it with bronze. Flora stood for a moment, knowing he hadn't noticed her, and drank in the sight of him.

"Good morning," she said when he finally turned and saw her.

"Good morning to you," he answered, smiling. "Sleep well?"

"Aye. Too well, it would seem. 'Tis late. I never sleep till nine. Why didn't you wake me?"

Gavin took the hand she offered him. Setting the coffee cup on the ground, he pulled her to sit across his legs. "Tell me, when's the last time you were able to sleep in, without having to wake for kids or chores or bed-and-breakfast guests?"

Flora thought about it. "Well, let's see . . . Robbie's eleven, so I would say at least that long."

Gavin nodded. "I figured that. So I decided to indulge you."

She wrapped her arms around his neck, giving him a sunny smile. "Well, thank you very much, Mr. Matheson. But you were more than welcome to have slept in with me."

He smiled, shook his head. "Couldn't sleep. Been up since before five, pacing the floor."

"Thinking about Gabriel?"

He nodded. "Just not sure what to expect. Two years is a long time, and I don't know what he's been told about me, about why he went away. I've met other parents—believe it or not, there's actually a support group for us 'left behind parents.' You wouldn't believe what some of their ex-spouses told their kids, things like the other parent didn't want them, or even worse, was dead. And then I think about what Gabriel's been through. He's had no home. No real stability." He shook his head. "After the mess his parents have made of his life, how can he ever feel that he can trust either of us again? I know he came willingly with Ivan, and I know I have already been granted custody of him, but deep down inside, am I really any different than she was in taking him back like this?"

Flora put two fingers to Gavin's lips, silencing him with a soft *shh*. "You're very different, Gavin. You were motivated by love for the son who had been taken from you. She was motivated only by her own selfishness and misguided vengeance."

Gavin nodded. "You're right. I just hope somehow I can help Gabriel see that."

"You will. It'll take some time, but children are very astute creatures. They can tell when something's real, or when it's not. Just be honest with him, and everything else will sort itself out. You'll see."

"When I hear you say it like that, it makes me feel like it really will be all right." He looked deeply into her eyes. "Thank you, Flora. For being here. With me."

"I wouldn't want to be anywhere else in the world." They sat together for a few quiet moments, just listening to the summer sounds of the city. Across the way at an adjacent building, on an upper floor, a woman was hanging some laundry on a line to dry. Flora watched her, following her as she took out a watering can and drizzled some water over her petunias. When she spotted them curled together in the garden below, she smiled and waved. Flora waved back, then reluctantly slid from Gavin's lap.

"Now, let me just jump in the shower and then I'll see about fixing us some breakfast."

But no sooner had Flora stepped through the glass doors, letting the steamy water cascade over her, than she felt a pair of hands snake around her waist and capture her from behind.

"Oh!" she said as she felt Gavin nuzzle her neck. "Ohh . . ."

One hand cupped her breast while the other slid around to stroke between her legs. Her body instantly came alive. She felt the warmth of his wet skin sliding against her as he pulled her to him and the hardness of him rousing. Flora flattened her hands against the shower wall as Gavin teased and stroked her, kissing the back of her neck, caressing her breast while rubbing his fingers against her until she was gasping.

He turned her then and captured her mouth with his, his tongue delving, exploring her. He lifted her, opened her, and then was filling her.

"Gavin!"

Flora clung to Gavin's shoulders, while bracing them both against the cold tile wall. She clutched his shoulders as the water rained down over them, between them, trickling down their faces as their bodies slid against each other, moving as one.

Gavin gripped her tightly, tore his mouth away from hers, and bit at her shoulder. With a strangled moan, he thrust once, twice, and then pulled her against him as he took his release deep inside of her. The water showered down. They were both breathing hard and stayed locked to each other until slowly he eased Flora down to stand before him.

He lathered her shoulders, washed her hair, and then together they dripped a path across the floor, falling into the bed wet and sticking to the sheets.

It was nearly an hour later before they rolled out of the nest of pillows and blankets and tangled limbs.

They had planned to meet Ivan at his office at one. Flora

dressed with care, wearing a soft floral skirt and the green cashmere shell that Libby had given her this past Christmas. It buttoned up the front with tiny pearl buttons. Her hair had dried in a tangle of red while they'd romped among the sheets, so the best she could do was twist it up at the back of her head and secure it with a tortoiseshell comb.

Gavin wore neatly pressed khaki trousers and a button-down chambray shirt, his damp hair combed back from his forehead.

They still had nearly an hour, so they ducked in to the corner patisserie for croissants. They sat at a small table set out on the sidewalk and shaded by a flowering cherry tree. Flora sipped a decaf café au lait and watched the people walking by while Gavin, constantly checking his watch, feigned reading the newspaper.

At precisely twenty-five minutes to one, Gavin paid the check and hailed them a cab.

The offices of Ivan Roth, PI, were located near the South Street Seaport on Manhattan's Lower East Side, in one of the former brick warehouses that had been rehabilitated into offices and shops. Even with the fresh paint and sparkling storefront windows, the smell of the daily fish market hung in the air. They followed the cobbled street to the corner. As they buzzed the door to gain entrance, Gavin took Flora's hand, twining his fingers with hers.

They climbed a narrow flight of stairs to the frosted glass door. Gavin didn't knock, but turned the knob and led Flora into a small reception area. The woman sitting behind the desk smiled in greeting.

"Hello, Mr. Matheson."

"Hi, Tess," he replied. He was too busy trying to see inside the adjoining office to ask her how she was, or even make any introduction for Flora.

Tess smiled at Flora and then said, "I won't keep you. You can go right in."

As soon as they passed through the doorway, Gavin spotted him.

The two years had matured his features. Gone were the short child's nose and pudgy-cheeked, gap-toothed grin. Now his eyes, which Gavin had always remembered as a lively blue-gray, had a weary look to them as he blinked at his father. His face was a little thin, and pale, no doubt due to his having been spirited away and kept inside, away from any eyes that might notice him. His hair, once blond, had darkened to a dirty sand. He wore it a little long, falling over his eyes.

"Gabriel," Gavin said, and felt tears burn in his eyes as he crossed to him and took him against him, locking his son in his arms. He had begun to wonder if this day would ever come, if he would ever see his son and hold him again. He didn't ever want to let him go, and his stomach tightened as he fought to get a grip on his emotions.

When he finally pulled away, Gavin looked into his son's eyes. "I've missed you so much, Gabriel."

"Name's not Gabriel," the boy answered in a voice that was concise and now accented slightly British. "Name's Andrew. Andrew Marsh."

The words stung. Andrew was the name Miranda had wanted for Gabriel when he was born, but Gavin had adamantly refused it because he knew it was the name of a former lover whom Miranda had never quite gotten over. Marsh was Miranda's maiden name. She'd given Gabriel a new identity, and in doing so had apparently all but wiped Gavin out of his son's life.

Gavin hunkered down in front Gabriel, looking him eye to eye. "Do you remember me?"

Gabriel looked back at him, stormy eyes studying Gavin's face while he contemplated his response. Then, finally, he nodded. "You're my father."

At those three words, Gavin nearly lost the fragile grip he had managed to get on his emotions. He felt a knot catch in his throat and bit down, swallowing hard. "Yes, I am. I'm your father."

"Why'd you take me from Mum?"

Gavin had expected the question. In fact he and Flora had discussed it that morning and agreed it would be best to tread lightly in order to preserve Gabriel's tender feelings. *Be honest with him.* Gavin heard Flora's words from that morning echo through his thoughts.

"It's a complicated situation, Gabriel."

"Andrew," the boy corrected.

"Andrew," Gavin breathed out heavily. "Do you remember anything about the time when you were a little boy? Back when you lived with me here in the States?"

Andrew thought about it, blinking fixedly, then finally he nodded. "Airplane. You used to play Airplane with me. I remember you would hold me up high in the air above your head."

Gavin smiled, thinking back on Gabriel wearing his denim overalls, giggling out loud with his face to the sun.

Where was that carefree little boy now?

"And you would open your arms as far as you could for the wings. And we would fly. We would fly all over the house, up the stairs, and out into the garden. I remember that, too."

They both fell silent then, contemplating the shared memory.

Finally Gabriel said, "Mum said you didn't want us anymore. That you were going to court to get rid of us, that you wanted to divorce us. Didn't you want me anymore?"

Gavin shook his head. "Parents do not divorce their children. Husbands and wives divorce each other when their marriages are broken and no longer work. But parents are parents as long as they live."

"But if it was broken, why couldn't you just fix it? I once broke the head off one of the figurines my grandmother likes to collect and Mum just used some special glue and put it back together. You couldn't even tell it had been fixed. It was one of our secrets, Mum and me, and Grandmother never knew."

So they had been with Miranda's parents, at least some of the time, just as Gavin had always suspected. Gavin shook his head against the thought. It no longer mattered. Gabriel was home.

"Sometimes some things just can't be glued back together like that. Sometimes there are too many broken pieces. No matter how you try to fit them back the way they were, they just don't go. Do you understand what I mean?"

Gabriel nodded. "Another time I dropped a glass vase. It went everywhere, like in a million pieces. We even found bits of it across the floor and under the refrigerator."

"Right. Gluing that together never would have worked. There were just too many broken pieces. Your mum and me, our marriage was like that, too. So we decided it would be best if we just didn't stay married anymore. But that didn't mean I wanted you out of my life. Not ever. I've been looking for you for the past two years. But you never stayed anywhere long enough for me to find you."

He nodded. "Mum and I lived in a lot of places."

Gavin tried to steer the conversation toward more pleasant ground. "I'll bet you saw a lot of interesting things, too."

Gabriel shrugged. "Yeah. Some of it was cool. I liked Venice and the canals. And the pyramids in Egypt, too. But after a while, it wasn't so much fun to have to leave again and go somewhere else. We only stayed a couple places where I could make any friends. I miss my friend Adi the most."

"Oh, yeah? Where's Adi from?"

"He lives in Poland. In a town called Lublin. He lived in the flat above us."

"Well, maybe sometime I can take you back there to see him."

His eyes sparked at the suggestion. "We could?"

"Sure. Once we get everything here figured out."

Gabriel nodded. Then he asked, "Would you take me to see Mum sometime, too?"

Gavin stiffened. "We'll have to see about that."

"Because she stole me?"

"Did she tell you that?"

"No. But I overheard Grandfather talking to Mum once. He was yelling at her and he said something to her about making a bed because she'd stolen me."

"Do you mean making *her* bed?"

"Yeah, that's what he said. And then he said we were nothing more than fugitives. I asked Mum later why he'd said that and she said it was like a game, a big game of hide-and-seek. We were the hiders and you and the police and the men who worked for you were the seekers. And she knew you'd come for me someday and you'd find me," he said then, as matter-of-factly as if he'd just said it was expected to rain later that day.

Gavin stared at him. So that was it. It was all a game to her. But then, to Miranda, it would have been a game. Her whole life had been one game after another, first with her parents and later with him. Only this game had put Gavin through a living hell for two long years. Gabriel as well.

Ivan Roth motioned to Gavin from the door of the adjoining room. "Gavin . . . a word?"

The private investigator who had brought Gabriel home looked more like a schoolteacher than a private investigator. He had thinning hair of a nondescript color and the sort of bland face no one would ever really notice. He could be anywhere in age from late thirties to early fifties. That, combined with his medium build and medium height, was a large part of the reason for his success. He could easily disappear in a crowd, blend in to the background, and move about unnoticed.

Gavin nodded, then turned back to his son. "Gabr—" He corrected himself this time. "Andrew, I'd like you to meet someone. This is Flora."

The boy glanced at Flora and gave her a small smile. "Hullo, Flora."

"Hullo, Andrew," she said, offering him her hand. "Pleasure to meet you."

"I'm going to go with Mr. Roth for just a few minutes," Gavin told him. At Gabriel's worried look, he said, "Everything will be okay. I'll be right in here. Just call out to me if you need me for anything."

Gabriel nodded.

Flora waited until Gavin had gone and then joined Gabriel on the sofa.

"So, Andrew, do you like sports?"

He nodded. "I like football. Me and my friend Adi used to play in the park near to our flats."

"Well, you know, my son Robbie loves to play football, too. He's eleven. And my daughter, Annie, she plays sometimes, as well. In fact, she's almost the same age as you."

"You have two children?"

"Nae. Actually, I have three. My youngest, Seamus, is just about three years old. He tries, but he doesn't quite yet know how to play."

Gabriel nodded.

"You know, they lost their father, too."

He looked up at her. "Did you take them from him?"

Flora shook her head. "Nae. Their father was in an accident and he died."

Gabriel furrowed his brow then and frowned. "Oh."

"Would you like to meet them sometime? They are always keen to meet new mates."

He nodded again.

"That's grand," Flora said.

Gavin soon came back from the other room.

"We should go now."

His tone instantly told Flora something was wrong. He looked angry, even worried. When Flora caught his attention and gave him a look as if to say, "What's wrong?" he just shook his head.

"We'll need to get Andrew some clothes and probably a few other things. Would you like that, Andrew?"

The boy nodded and got up from the sofa to follow his father.

As they headed for the door, Ivan called after them, "I'll be in touch, Gavin."

Gavin didn't even acknowledge him.

.

Later that night, after they'd had supper and Gabriel had taken a bath, Gavin tucked him into bed, in a bedroom that was still papered with the crayon and finger paint drawings he had made in preschool. The sight of his old room, which had been left untouched, and especially the well-loved, tattered teddy bear who'd been patiently awaiting his return, seemed to put the boy a little more at ease.

It had been an emotional day for both father and son as they sought to adapt to their new reality. Time and again, Flora noticed Gavin just staring at Gabriel, as if trying to memorize his every feature. He seemed to want to make up for all the time they'd lost in that first day, asking Gabriel everything from his favorite foods to what sports he liked to play.

Gabriel, however, was no doubt dealing with his own turmoil, and spent most of the time just silently watching everything else going on around him.

That afternoon was the first step in what would be a long process of coming home.

Gavin and Flora were sitting in the kitchen, talking over a late-night tea. They talked about what they would do next, once they got back to Massachusetts. They had to plan for their wedding, something Gavin seemed intent on doing as soon as possible. But beyond that, they would have to allow Gabriel and his adjustment to being back with his father dictate what came next.

Gavin had just gone to check that his son was still there, sleeping in his bed. When he returned a few minutes later, he said, "Apparently, Ivan didn't exactly have the cooperation of the local authorities when he took Gabriel."

"You mean Andrew."

Gavin shook his head. "He's Gabriel to me, Flora. I just can't think of him as anything else."

"Well, unfortunately, you may have to. To him, he's Andrew, and I think to force a different name on him now might hinder his adjustment to life here. Too much change too quickly might cause him to feel troubled. Give it a little time. Perhaps he'll want to take his true name again after a while. Now, what's this about Mr. Roth?"

"Ivan said he had been getting nowhere with the authorities in the UK. He knew where they were, but Scotland Yard insisted neither Miranda nor Gabriel had re-entered the country. Of course, they could do this because Miranda somehow purchased forged papers giving them new identities. I also spoke with my lawyer, and even though she broke the law in taking him, there will still have to be a hearing to redetermine Gabriel's custody. It'll be here in New York, and Miranda will be asked to appear."

No wonder Gavin had looked upset after he'd spoken with Ivan Roth. To have come so far, and after getting Gabriel back, did he really have to fear that he'd lose him again?

"When will this hearing take place?"

"I don't know. I'll have to wait to hear from the courts."

"What do we do until then?"

Gavin looked at her. "We go back to Ipswich-by-the-Sea spend what time we have with Gabriel . . . and pray I don't lose him again."

Annie must have been watching for them at the window.

She was out of the house and standing on the top step of the porch stairs when Gavin parked and got out. She shaded her eyes against the midday sun to try to see inside Gavin's car.

"How's m' wee bird?" Flora said to her when she got out on the passenger side and opened her arms to gave her daughter a hug.

"I'm fine, Mummy." She gave Flora only a halfhearted hug, too busy craning her neck to see around her mother. "Where's Gabriel?"

Flora smiled. "He's in the car, Annie. Let's try not to smother him the moment he comes out, aye? Oh, and for now, his name is Andrew."

Annie looked at her mother. "Oh, you mean sort of like my name is Fiona but everyone calls me Annie?"

"Aye, dearie be. Sort of like that."

Annie nodded. "A'right." She looked toward the car where Gabriel had just come out and was standing looking over the house from ground to roof. Ever the social butterfly, she skipped right over.

"Hi, Andrew!"

"Hullo," he said to the buoyant little girl.

"I'm Annie. Although my real name's Fiona. Just like you're Andrew, but your real name's Gabriel."

He looked at her and nodded. "Uh, yeah . . ."

"Heya, Andrew, do you like skim boarding?"

"Ehm, I don't know what that is."

"Oh, it's grand fun. See, you take this flat board, sort of like a surfboard but flatter and smaller, and you slide it across the water right when a wave comes in to the shore and then you run and jump on the board and glide as far as you can go. My brother Robbie has glided the farthest so far out of all of us. He's down at the beach right now with my brother Seamus and our friends Sam and Cassie. I told them I'd wait for you while they went down to the shore. D' you think you'd like to try it?"

"Sure, but I don't have a swim suit."

"That's all right." She took his hand to lead him toward the stairs. "I'm sure Robbie has a spare one you can borrow. It might be a little big, but I think it'll still work just fine."

Andrew turned and looked at Gavin. "Is it all right if I go?"

"It's okay, Gavin," Annie assured him. "Jen is down

watching all of us, and Hallie is here at the house. We'll take good care of Andrew."

Gavin smiled at her, then nodded to Gabriel. "Go on with Annie, then," he said. "I'll be down to join you in a little while."

After Annie and Gabriel had gone, Gavin waited while Flora checked in with Hallie, quickly going over any business she'd seen to while they'd been away—new reservations, supplies that needed ordering, and so forth.

The business was definitely on its way. They were now fully booked for the July Fourth weekend with a waiting list of three and had definite interest from a prospective bride for a wedding and reception weekend at the end of September. If she decided to book with them, it would close out Thar Muir's inaugural season perfectly, Flora thought.

Leaving her bag by the door, Flora and Gavin slipped off their shoes and headed down the path for the beach.

When they got there, Andrew was already surrounded by the others, busily trying to answer the questions being fired at him from Robbie, Sam, Cassie, Annie, and even Seamus.

"How old are you?"

"Do you have any brothers? Sisters?"

"Do you have a dog? We've never had one, but Mum says maybe someday."

"What's your favorite ice cream flavor?"

Jen sat on a blanket beneath a colorful beach umbrella, paperback open on her knee, watching on as the kids alternated taking a glide on the two boards they shared among them. Annie's delighted squeal carried on the breeze off the water as she took her turn and tumbled into the waves. Robbie laughed, then took a turn himself. The sun was shining and the water glistened on this perfect summer afternoon.

Gavin sat, pant legs rolled above his ankles, and watched

them, enjoying the sight of Gabriel playing with the others. Flora's kids and their friends had drawn him in immediately, and soon he was running and playing along with them. They even convinced Gavin to give the skim board a try, exploding with laughter when he lost his balance and tripped fully clothed into the surf.

When Jen got up and went into the house for a fresh jug of lemonade, Gavin, dripping with seawater, went to join Flora on the blanket.

"You know," he said to her after he'd toweled off his hair, "I realize I've been so caught up in getting Gabriel back and settling all the details, that I never really asked you how you're feeling about this."

She smiled. "Of course I'm thrilled about it, Gavin. How could I not be?"

"I know that, but I'm talking about us. About our plans for the future. This changes things a bit. We started out with three, and then"—he smiled, placing his hand on her flat belly—"a fourth. Now suddenly there's a fifth, with a situation that brings its own set of complications . . ."

Flora simply shook her head. "I'm not Miranda, Gavin. Gabriel is your son, and as I love you, so do I love him. It's just the way it works with me. I will welcome him into our lives every bit as much as you welcomed my three into yours."

Gavin turned back to look at the kids so that Flora wouldn't see how deeply her words touched him. He smiled, watching as Gabriel took his turn on the skim board. Seamus ran after him, trying to catch up as he glided over the water. It felt so good to see him doing normal kid things, rather than imagining the very worst. "He's never going to want to leave here."

Flora agreed. "You know, I've been sitting here watching

them together and thinking. Why don't you and Gabriel move here to Thar Muir? It would give him the opportunity to get to know the kids. It would give all of us the chance to get to know each other. That way we can sit them all down together and tell them about the wedding as a family." She squeezed his hand. " 'Yours.' 'Mine.' Those things don't exist any longer, Gavin. Now they are simply 'ours.' " She placed a hand against his face, adding softly, "They are *our* family."

And when she touched her lips to his and kissed him, Gavin felt as if he'd just fallen in love with her all over again.

Chapter Seventeen

The childrens' reactions, when Gavin and Flora sat them down to tell them that they were getting married, were a true mixture of emotions.

Seamus clapped his hands.

Annie asked if she could be a bridesmaid.

Gabriel shrugged.

And Robbie didn't say a word. He just stared at Flora for a long moment, nodded, and then asked if he could go to his room.

Flora followed him there a few minutes later. He was sitting on the side of his bed, lying on his back with his hands linked behind his head on the pillow. He was staring up at the ceiling in stony, expressionless silence.

"Rabbie, aren't you happy with this news?"

"Aye, 'tis fine."

"'Tis fine, but . . . ?" Flora knew there was something more, something that was troubling him. "You dinna care for Gavin?"

"Aye, I like him fine. He's nice to us. And Andrew's fun to play with." He looked at his mother. "It's just something that Uncle Angus told me."

"Oh. And what's that?"

Robbie sat up on the bed and looked at her as if to say, *Well, if you're going to make me tell you . . .*

"When Da died, Uncle Angus told me it was my responsibility to be the man of the house. I was to watch out for you and for Annie. He told me it again after Seamus was born. But now, with Gavin to marry you"—his voice thickened a little as a mix of emotions swept through him—"you winna need me anymore. To be the man, I mean."

Flora felt her mother's heart twinge. Her sweet, sensitive, firstborn child. She smoothed a hand over his hair and then stroked her thumb softly against the side of his face as she cupped his chin, looking deeply into his eyes.

"Oh, Rab . . . don't you know I will always need you to be the man around the house for me?"

"Nae. Not now that you'll have Gavin."

"And who says there should only be one man? I've had you and your uncle Angus both since we lost your da, aye? You've been there for me in different ways when I needed someone, or when I needed the strength to face something difficult. And for that matter, who says it need be only a man at all? I've Annie, too. And wee Seamus. I dinna know what I'd do without any one of you. You're all of you my strength, and the more of you I have with me, the stronger I am. The stronger we all are."

Robbie swallowed hard, nodding at his mother. Fighting tears, he looked down. He thought for a few minutes, then blinked and looked at her again. "Will I have to call him 'Da'?"

Flora had already prepared herself for the question. "Nae, of course not. You'll call him Gavin, and Annie and Seamus will do the same. 'Twas your da who gave you to me, and nothing and no one will ever change that. Gavin certainly is not meant to replace your da. You must always know that."

Robbie nodded. "I'll call him Gavin, then."

"That will be grand, Rabbie." She took his hand in hers then, noticing his badly chewed fingernails. "I am counting on you to do something else for me, as well."

"What's that?"

"D' you remember how you felt, how lost and alone you were after your da was gone? Everything seemed sort of confused, aye? Like it was upside down and turned inside out?"

Robbie nodded.

"Well, although Andrew has his da, his life has been very troublesome these past two years while he's been away. He hasna had a real home, no real friends, has only gone from place to place. And now he no longer has his mum either, who despite her problems, is the only one he has known for a long, long time. So you can imagine how he must be feeling, aye?"

Robbie looked at her. "Lost?"

Flora nodded. "I'm hoping you might be able to help him a bit, if you would . . ."

"But how?"

"Just be a friend to him, Rab. Be like a big brother for him. Andrew . . . Gabriel . . . whatever he decides his name should be. He's been through a difficult time with more difficult times to come. Just like we were all there for each other during our own troubles, we must all help Andrew to be strong now, aye?"

Robbie thought about it, then sort of shrugged. "But I dinna really know what I could do for him. I don't know an'thing about him."

"Well, that will take some time. But I do know one thing that might help you." She smiled. "I know that he loves to play football."

"*Our* football?" he asked, his eyes already sparking with interest.

"Aye, Rab, *our* football," Flora confirmed. In other words, what Americans called soccer.

Robbie leaned over the side of the bed and retrieved his scuffed black and white football from its usual place on the floor. He spun it in the air and caught it, spun it again. Then with a glance at his mum and a small smile, he rolled off the bed and headed for the door.

Flora glanced at the clock ticking on the desk beside her and figured it would be probably another hour before Gavin arrived in New York.

His attorney had called him two days earlier to inform Gavin of the hearing in family court that was scheduled for later that week. The judge would review the case, update Gabriel's status, and decide whether to void Gavin's custody of Gabriel or uphold it once and for all. Miranda had been summoned to appear, but thus far they'd heard nothing to indicate that she'd be there to make her case heard and fight for her son.

Gavin hoped that she wouldn't appear and the hearing would be nothing more than a formality. If that happened, by the time he returned later that night, Gabriel would be theirs and the uncertainty of his life for the past two years would finally be on its way to becoming a memory.

As she sipped her tea and munched on a cracker to stave off her morning sickness, Flora peered out the kitchen window, watching as the kids played football on the back lawn. And she smiled.

It had been little more than two weeks since they'd brought Gabriel home. In that time, he had gone from a quiet, cautious child with guarded eyes to a boy who laughed, who played with the others, and who seemed to have begun to feel some small sense of security in their life at Thar Muir. The weather had been perfect for summertime play, and his cheeks had acquired a healthy glow. He'd even asked to have his long hair cut in the shorter style that Robbie favored.

Of course, Annie constantly "mothering" him, doing everything she could to make him feel welcome, certainly helped. She seemed to know intuitively how he was feeling, and if she ever saw him looking frightened or lonely, she would immediately devise some game or pastime for them.

But that wasn't to say there weren't times when thoughts of his mother, or memories of the past two years, reappeared.

He occasionally woke in the middle of the night with a sort of hunted look in his eyes that had him sitting bolt upright on the bed, eyes flitting wildly about the darkness. Twice Flora had found him bunched up beneath the kneehole of her desk with tears in his eyes. The first time, he'd refused to come out and had stayed there for nearly an hour. Even Annie hadn't been able to coax him out. But the second time, he'd allowed Flora to take him against her and hold him, rock him, and stroke his hair as she sang softly in Gaelic to him.

It would take time, but Flora held on to the hope that he would come to find reassurance in the safe and secure home she and Gavin were creating for him and the others.

Flora gave another glance at the clock. She didn't even want to think of all the things she had left to do before they left for Scotland the following week.

She had to pick up Baby Fraser's christening gift from the engravers. Gavin and Flora had gotten him a sterling silver quaich, inscribing it with an ancient Gaelic blessing.

They would toast to the health and happiness of the new life with it in the tradition of the Scots.

In addition to that, she had to find some time to sit down with Jimmy O'Connell and go over the progress on the boathouse conversion. He had almost finished stripping it down to its shell, and would begin routing in plumbing in the coming week. Flora wanted to take some pictures to show Libby and Graeme, so they could finalize the interior design of the finished suite.

And Flora still had to look over the list of songs Gavin and Alec had compiled for their recording project. Alec had come back to Ipswich-by-the-Sea early the previous week and he and Gavin had worked long days, sometimes into the night, making contacts for song permissions while putting words to Gavin's new composition, which he'd titled simply "Flora's Song." If all went as planned, they could begin recording in early fall and finish by the new year, well before the baby was due, which was sometime around Valentine's Day.

She still had to go for the final fitting on the dress she'd chosen to wear when she became Gavin's wife. They would marry in Scotland, two days after the christening, in the village church with Annie and Libby as her attendants. Gavin had asked Gabriel if he would stand as his best man. So, as soon as Hallie arrived for work, Flora would take a quick drive into town, stopping at the engravers. And if she took Annie with her, they would probably even have time to stop for the fittings on their dresses, too.

The sound of the front door opening a short while later pulled Flora from her thoughts, telling her that Hallie had just arrived. Flora tapped on the kitchen window and motioned for Annie to come inside so they could leave. The little girl held up her hand to indicate she'd be right in. Flora nodded, grabbed the car keys and her mobile, and started for the front of the house.

"Heya, Hallie," she said as she rounded the stairwell. She grabbed her purse, too. "If you don't mind, I think I'll take Annie and go to—"

Her words fell off when she noticed that it wasn't Hallie who'd come in. Instead there was a young woman wearing a faded jean jacket over a long denim skirt. She was small, with delicate features, and she stood just inside the entrance hall, peering in the doors on either side. Her short, spiked hair had been dyed a subtle shade of burgundy, and her eyes, heavily made up, were at that moment scrutinizing every detail of the front hall.

Until they settled on Flora, blinked once, and stayed there.

"Heya," she repeated. Her accent—and her resemblance to Gabriel—immediately gave her away.

Flora faced Gavin's ex-wife and struggled not to reveal the fact that she recognized her, while wondering why she was there, in Massachusetts, instead of at the hearing in New York.

She must have come for Gabriel.

As casually as she could while standing there, Flora used the side of her hip to flip open the mobile. She ran her finger over the numbers and pressed what she hoped was the speed dial for Gavin's mobile. She left the phone open at her side, although she was unable to see if the call had connected.

"Ehm, welcome to Thar Muir," she said. "May I help you?"

When the woman didn't say anything, just continued to stare at her, Flora asked, "Were you . . . looking for a room perhaps?"

"No. Actually, I'm lookin' for my son, Andrew."

Flora knew she had to stall Miranda somehow. She shook her head as if she didn't quite understand who she was talking about. "Andrew . . . ?"

"Marsh," Miranda finished for her. "Look 'ere. I know he's here with you, and I know that Gavin isn't. I know he's down in New York right now, trying to take my son away from me for good. But if he thought I'd be stupid enough to show up there in his Yank court with his Yank judge, he's mistaken. I don't need a court to tell me what is or isn't mine. I gave birth to that boy. Now just give Andrew over to me and I'll be out of here."

Flora took a slow breath, trying to remain calm. "I think this is something you should discuss with Gavin."

Miranda's expression darkened. "Well, I don't think you're anyone to be telling me what I should or shouldn't do. You don't know anything about me, or my situation. Now just *give—me—my—son.*"

She took a step forward, threatening her, but Flora stood her ground. "I think you should leave now."

"Oh, really? Well, I think not."

Miranda pulled her hand from the pocket of her jean jacket, revealing a small silver pistol cradled in the palm of her manicured hand. "That's the nice thing about this country. You can buy a brilliant little piece like this almost as easily as Chinese takeaway." She cocked the hammer, narrowing her eyes on Flora. Then her voice lost its easy tenor. "I'm not going anywhere without my son."

Flora stared into the eye of the pistol that stared unblinking back at her. She looked at Miranda and saw the wild gaze of a woman standing on the edge of reality and quickly slipping past it. She thanked God the kids were still in the backyard playing.

Until she heard the sound of the kitchen door opening, and remembered . . .

Annie.

Any moment, she would come bounding in.

Flora pleaded with Miranda. "It's my daughter. Please, dinna hurt her. She's naught to do with this. Just let me talk to her a moment and I'll have her to go back out."

Miranda stared at Flora and frowned, clearly displeased. She nodded a moment later.

Flora turned just as her daughter made it through the kitchen.

"I'm ready to go now, Mummy. . . ."

Flora smiled at her. "Annie, dear. I was mistaken. Hallie's not here yet, so we've a little while longer afore we need to leave. Why don't you take your brothers and go down to the boathouse for a wee spell? Tell Jimmy I asked you to, aye?"

From where she stood Annie could not see Miranda, or the gun she still held. Flora gave her daughter what she hoped was a reassuring smile. "All right, love?"

"But, Mummy . . ."

"Go on now, m' wee bird. I'll bring down some lunch in a while, aye? We'll have a picnic in the boathouse."

Annie stared at her a moment, her brow furrowed with confusion. No doubt she wondered why Flora would send her down to the boathouse when only that morning she'd forbade her and the boys from going anywhere near it while the contractor was at work there.

"Go on . . ." Flora repeated and held her breath, praying her daughter would listen. "Just go there and wait for me to come down."

Annie blinked. "A'right, Mummy," she finally said and turned, albeit reluctantly. Flora held that breath a moment longer, waiting until she heard the sound of the back door open and close once again.

She exhaled in a rush. And then turned back to Miranda.

Her first thought was to appeal to the other woman's sense of motherhood. "Miranda, please. Think of Andrew. I know you have had your difficulties with Gavin, but just think of what all of this has done to your son already. Think of how what you're doing now will surely affect him as well. You're his mum. . . ."

Miranda smirked. "Oh, aye, I'm his mum all right, but that's something I never wanted to be. Stretch marks, sagging breasts, a mewling brat to deal with. It was Gavin's fault I got pregnant in the first place." She shook her head. "Bloody bugger. I only married him because he promised he would help me break into the business. He was going to write me songs and make me a star. 'Soon, Miranda,'" she mimicked in Gavin's American accent. "'Just give it time.' Then I found out he'd given me one in the oven, and that ended any chance I had for my career right there. He left me at home to change dirty nappies and spend my days with spit-up dripping down my back while he went out to the studio every day to write music for other people, to make *them* into the stars. Saddled me with that kid and then even tried to take him from me, too. But I showed him. I left and there wasn't a bloody thing he could do about it."

"Mum?"

Flora and Miranda turned at once to see Gabriel standing in the doorway.

Flora had been listening so intently to Miranda's rambling, she hadn't heard him come in. She looked into his eyes, wondering how much of his mother's hurtful words he had heard. They were as vacant as a window that looked out onto the night.

At the sight of her son, Miranda's voice immediately changed. Her face brightened and she gave him a sweet, falsely mothering smile. "Andrew, love, look! Mummy's here. Are you surprised? I've come to get you, to take you home. Come to me now, and we'll go."

But the boy didn't move from where he stood. "Mum . . . why are you pointing a gun at Flora?"

"Gun?" It was as if Miranda suddenly remembered she was holding it. She looked down at the pistol in her own hand and then smiled, even laughed. "Oh, love. Mum was just playing a little game with the housekeeper here."

"Flora," Gabriel said.

"What's that, love?"

"Her name. It's Flora. And she's not the housekeeper. She's going to marry my dad."

Miranda's penciled brow arched. "Indeed?"

Something in the woman's face changed then, became dangerous. Flora saw her tighten her fingers around the butt of that small pistol as she turned a sharp smile on her. "Well, isn't that interesting?"

Gabriel looked at Flora. She knew he had no idea that what he'd revealed had just escalated the situation from bad to worse. Flora simply looked back at him and smiled, trying to think of a way to put herself between him and Miranda without startling the increasingly unstable woman and causing her to do something . . . drastic.

"Andrew," Flora said, choosing her words carefully, "why don't you go into the kitchen and see if you can find a bag to take your things with you . . ."

He looked at her, obviously confused.

All Flora could think of was to get him as far from the firing end of that gun as possible. " 'Tis fine, Andrew. Dinna worry. I'll explain everything to your da when he comes back tonight."

Gabriel looked at his mother. "Mum?"

"Go on. Listen to this"—she smiled—"to Flora now. You'll need your clothes with you. I'll just wait here with your father's *friend*."

She waited until he'd gone into the kitchen, then said, "So . . . you're marrying Gavin, are you?"

Flora nodded.

Miranda stared at her a moment, looking at her closely. Then she narrowed her eyes and shook her head, as if to shake the notion straight out of her spiked head.

"What do I care? It's not like I want the bugger back. Go ahead and marry him. You'll see, just like I did. He'll never be home. He'll just get you pregnant and then leave you to take care of his brats while he . . ."

She caught the movement of Flora's hand as she instictively covered her belly. Miranda immediately stopped herself, narrowed her heavily mascaraed eyes. "Unless you're already pregnant."

Flora said nothing. She could only imagine that to Miranda, the idea of his having another family, another child, would mean she was losing whatever leverage she imagined she had over Gavin.

"Two years!" Miranda began pacing back and forth in front of her. "Only took him two years to give up on Gabriel. Just found himself someone else to replace me and to replace his son, all while I was left to roam from place to place, living in poverty."

She wasn't making any sense, and Flora suspected that Miranda was losing whatever grip she had on reality. Her movements were becoming erratic. She was misinterpreting events and facts, turning them as if it were Gavin who had created the situation she now found herself in.

Flora risked a quick glance at her mobile and saw the call timer ticking away the seconds. Whoever she had dialed, hopefully Gavin, was still listening in.

But even if he was, he was nearly two hundred miles away. And Miranda was here, two yards away, holding a gun.

Flora heard the back door open again and prayed it wasn't Annie returning from the boathouse.

"Flora, you here? I've got that song list for you to go over, if you can and . . ."

He came around the corner and froze. "Miranda?"

"Cheers, Alec."

Alec Grayson came to a standstill beside Flora when he noticed the gun still clutched in Miranda's hand. "What the hell's going on here?"

Miranda just shook her head. "I should be asking the same question. Song list? So am I to assume that in addition to becoming Gavin's wife and the mother to his *new* child, you're also going to record his music?"

Flora knew that at that moment she stood on very uncertain ground. Everything Miranda had ever wanted was being visited upon Flora, like a laundry list of lost opportunities. They were opportunities that to Miranda's distorted thinking had been denied her by one person.

Gavin.

"Miranda, I'm sorry" was all Flora could think to say.

"You're sorry! Well, save your pity. I don't want it." She began pacing again, waving her arms, the gun still clutched in her fingers. One movement, one slight tightening of her fingers, and it could go off. "I should be the one applauding you, my dear. Because you apparently managed to do whatever it was I couldn't.''

"Miranda," Alec said then, interrupting her, "put the gun down and let's talk about this."

Smiling, she spun on him. "I don't think you're in any position to tell me what to do now, Alec. You and that bastard. You never intended to let me record even one of your pathetic songs, did you? Just who do you both think you are? How dare you take my career away from me?"

Alec frowned at her. "Do you want to know why Gavin never pulled any strings to have you recorded, Miranda? Because he didn't want to have to tell you. You cannot sing."

Miranda's eyes widened and sparked dangerously.

Flora knew exactly what Alec was doing. He was trying to divert Miranda's attention and her anger to him in order to protect her and the baby.

"What do you know, Alec Grayson?" Miranda wailed. "You're nothing but a pathetic, untalented nothing. A lyricist! What a joke. You've been riding on Gavin's coattails for the whole of your career."

"Well, at least I didn't have to get myself pregnant to do it."

"Bastard!"

But Alec only pushed Miranda further, goading her. "Whatever you might think of me, Miranda, at least I didn't use an innocent child for my own selfish purposes."

Flora chanced another glance at her mobile and saw that the call timer was still ticking away the seconds. She glanced at Miranda, who was wholly focused on Alec now, standing only an arm's length away from him, shrieking at him, arguing her case against his accusations.

Flora took a step back, and then another, until she was shadowed by the sweep of the staircase. Then slowly, cautiously, she lifted her hand to her ear still clutching the mobile.

"Gavin," she whispered. "Please tell me you're there."

"Flora, my God. I'm so sorry. Are you hurt? Are the kids okay? She's lost it. I had no idea. Just try to get her on the phone. Let me talk to her."

Before Flora could respond, she felt the phone being wrenched out of her hand.

"What do you think you are doing!" Miranda raged. "Trying to call the police?"

Flora shook her head. "No. 'Tis Gavin."

Miranda's face changed, becoming almost composed. "Gavin," she repeated calmly and then put the phone to her ear. "Is that true? Are you really there?"

Flora glanced at Alec while Miranda listened to Gavin's response on the phone. Alec motioned with his head toward the back of the house, telling Flora to run, to flee, but she shook her head and mouthed, "Gabriel."

She had no idea where the boy had gone, but she wasn't leaving that house without him.

Gavin hadn't felt so helpless since the day Miranda disappeared with Gabriel.

He'd been on the train when Flora's call rang in, and he'd answered expecting to hear her soft voice. In his worst nightmare he wouldn't have expected that the voice to greet him would be his ex-wife's.

He'd listened to the conversation and knew Flora was trying to feed him information about the situation by what she said to Miranda. When Gavin realized that Miranda had pulled a gun, his blood froze in his veins.

Clinging to that phone and praying the signal didn't drop, Gavin exited the train on its next stop. He waited at that station, getting on the next train heading back in the direction of Boston. He pleaded with a fellow passenger for the use of another mobile and placed a frantic call to the Ipswich-by-the-Sea Police Department.

What the hell was taking them so damned long to get to the house?

His only solace was in knowing that Alec was there with Flora. If he couldn't be there himself, he trusted no one else more than his friend. He knew Alec would protect Flora and the kids with everything he had.

"So, Gavin," Miranda said to him, "I see it didn't take you long to replace me and Andrew with someone else."

"Gabriel," he corrected her. "My son's name is Gabriel. And I never sought to replace him. You know damned well there hasn't been a day in the past two years that I haven't tried to find where you'd taken him. You may think that you were hurting me by hiding him the way you did, and you did hurt me, but you hurt him far, far more. He cannot sleep a peaceful night's sleep without waking, fearful that some faceless, nameless stranger is going to snatch him out of his bed."

"Well, that's precisely what you did, isn't it?" she raged at him. "Had some stranger grab him in the street!" She scoffed out loud. "What do you want him for? You have your new lover, your new life."

"No, Miranda, why don't you tell me what you want him for?"

"What did you say?"

"You heard me. You never wanted Gabriel. You just said as much to Flora. You wanted your career, or what you thought was your entitlement to a career. You were only using me. Did you think I didn't know that?"

Gavin let out his breath. Goading her wasn't going to get

them anywhere. He tried appealing to her more calmly. "Miranda, can't you just for once do something for someone other than yourself? Just turn around, walk out of that house, and let Gabriel spend whatever remains of his childhood in a stable, secure environment. Find the life you want and end this unnecessary war. Now."

Miranda fell silent. For a moment he actually began to think she might consider it. Until . . .

"Oh, I'll end it all right, Gavin."

And then he heard the phone fall to the floor.

"Miranda!"

He heard her voice again, but it sounded far away, echoing now. "Andrew Marsh! I've had enough of this. Come to Mummy. Now!"

"Miranda . . ." Gavin tried again.

"Get back, Alec. I mean it. Don't come near me."

"Just give me the gun, Miranda."

He heard Flora. "Gabriel, no. Go back!"

"Get away from my son! Andrew, come here."

And then a fourth voice broke in.

"Ma'am, this is the police. Put down the gun and slowly raise your hands above your head."

The next thirty seconds seemed to last a lifetime. Gavin heard footsteps and the sounds of a scuffle. A scream. Someone yelled out, "No!"

And then the phone thundered in his ear with a single deafening gunshot.

Chapter Eighteen

"Flora!"

But no one could hear him from where the phone had been dropped to the floor.

Gavin's heart was drumming in his throat as he disconnected the call and then frantically punched Flora's mobile number into his phone.

It rang, going unanswered. He leaned his head against the train window while the New England countryside whizzed by outside.

Answer the damn phone . . .

When Flora's cheery voice mail message picked up, urging him to leave a message, Gavin folded his phone closed.

He tried not to imagine what could have happened, who could have been shot, even as he knew it could be any of the people he loved most in his life.

Flora.

Gabriel.

Alec.

Dear God. What if Robbie, or Annie, or Seamus had suddenly come running into the house?

Gavin would never forgive himself if anything happened to any one of them.

He squeezed his eyes shut and seized a desperate, ragged breath.

He tried again. This time, the call answered on the third ring.

"Gavin?"

His voice broke when he heard the familiar voice on the other end. "Alec. Thank God. What . . . who . . . ?"

He didn't breathe until he heard the answer.

"It's all right. No one was hurt."

"Flora?"

"She's right here."

Gavin looked up and thanked God as Alec handed over the phone.

"Gavin?"

"You're not hurt?"

"No. Police Chief Barrett only fired a warning, to divert Miranda's attention so that Officer Faraday could disarm her. They're taking her out now."

"The kids?"

"They're fine. Robbie, Annie, and Seamus were out in the boathouse and—"

Gavin heard a chorus of voices behind her then. "Mummy! What happened? Why are the police here? Who's that woman?"

"Shh," Flora calmed them. "Everything is fine. Just a moment, let me talk to Gavin."

"Where's Gabriel?" he asked.

"He's here. He's with me. I've got him."

"Can I . . . talk to him?"

"Of course."

A moment later, he heard a muffled "Hullo?"

"Gabr—uh, Andrew, listen to me. I'm on the train. I'll be back just as soon as I can."

"All right . . ." He could hear the fear in his son's voice.

"Don't be scared. Just stay with Flora. She'll take care of you until I get there. Everything's going to be okay now. I promise you."

Gavin waited for a response, but all he heard was the sound of his son's uneven breathing.

"I'll see you soon," he said.

Just when he was about to disconnect the call, he heard his son's voice come over the receiver.

"Dad?"

"Yeah, Andrew?"

"I think I'd rather be called . . . Gabriel . . . again."

Gavin took a breath, closed his eyes. "You got it. Hey, Gabriel?"

"Yeah?"

"I love you."

He heard the boy push his face against the phone. "Yeah. Me, too."

Gabriel handed the phone back to Flora. He looked up at her from where he had his face pressed against her side. "He said he'll be home soon."

Flora smiled to herself as she stroked his hair.

Home. God, how she had always loved the sound of that word. But never more than she did right then.

She looked up when she heard the sound of someone clearing his throat.

"Officer Faraday."

"Yes, ma'am. Uh, we're taking Ms. Marsh down to the station. I was wondering if you had a few minutes to answer some questions for my incident report."

"Ehm, actually, can it wait? I really need to be with my children just now." She looked down at Gabriel and smiled. "All of them."

Faraday nodded. "That's fine, ma'am. I can talk to Mr. Grayson for now, get his side of the story. We'll hold Ms. Marsh at the station until charges can be brought."

Flora smiled. "Thank you. Come on now, Gabriel. What d' you say we go out and join the others?"

Flora had sent the three of them back to the boathouse after they'd come running into the midst of the commotion, with the police handcuffing Miranda and Gabriel watching on in stunned silence. She had no idea now what she'd even said to them, but whatever it was had sent them racing out the back door, taking Hallie, who had just arrived for work, with them.

Flora found her children sitting with Jimmy O'Connell and Hallie in the now nearly empty shell of the half-renovated boathouse. The looks on the faces that greeted her had her saying immediately, "Don't worry. Everything is fine now."

The questions erupted even before she finished speaking.

Who was shot?

Who was that woman?

Why were the police there?

Was someone arrested?

Were they filming a movie?

For a half second, Flora actually considered using that last question as an explanation for the almost unbelievable reality of what had taken place up at the house, even as she knew she couldn't.

She sat down on a concrete-dusted upside down construction bucket and explained everything to them. And then she thanked the kids for having listened to her by staying in the boathouse. She didn't even want to consider what could have happened had they come running up to the house while Miranda was ranting.

Flora wasn't quite ready to go back up to the house and answer Officer Faraday's questions, so she took the Thermos cup of iced tea Jimmy O'Connell offered her and stayed sitting on the bucket while the kids, armed with rubber-headed mallets, were set loose on the last section of plastered wall that needed demolishing in the boathouse. She laughed at Seamus, who waited until his brother and sister and then Gabriel had all crashed their hammers through the wall before doing so himself, as if to make certain it really was allowed. After waiting, he lifted his hammer high and let out with a child's roar before banging it hard against the wall, only to have it bounce out of his hands and drop to the floor.

"Here, Seamus. Let Mummy show you."

Flora took up the hammer and let it sink into the wall. Just that one simple physical act helped to relieve some of the tension that had tied her stomach in knots. When she pulled the hammer back, it brought a whole section of the plaster wall crumbling down with it.

"That's how you do it, m' wee lad," she said to Seamus and handed him the hammer to try again.

"Mummy, look!" Annie was pointing at the newly opened section of wall. "There's something there."

It looked like a small wooden box was tucked inside the cavity of the wall. Pushing the plaster aside, Flora reached for it, brushing away the plaster bits and dust to reveal a small carved, latched chest.

The carving across its lid consisted of a set of initials.

R.H.

"Mummy," Annie said with wonder, " 'tis the same letters as the stone. The gravestone we found in the woods."

Flora sat back on the bucket and inspected the box. It was very old, with tarnished hinges.

"D' you think 'tis the same person, R.H.?" Annie asked.

"Aye, so it would seem."

"Is the box locked?" Annie peered over her mother's shoulder. Seamus and Gabriel, even Robbie, pressed in on all sides to see.

"Aye, it appears to be," Flora answered. "I hate to try to break it open, considering it's probably very old."

"I have something that can spring that," Jimmy O'Connell said, and fished through his toolbox until he removed a slender, crooked-looking rod about the thickness of a barbecue skewer.

He slid the end of it against the locking mechanism, added a little pressure, and then turned it slowly.

A moment later, the lock sprang free.

Jimmy grinned. "I've had to pick a lock or two in my day."

All four children surrounded Flora as she opened the latch and lifted the box's lid.

Inside were several small books—journals—all written similarly to the one Annie had found in the cellar. Dried sprigs of herbs, rosemary and something else, were strewn inside the box. Several long silk ribbons had been carefully looped and tied. There was also a folded and discolored piece of parchment. Written on the outside were again the same initials: *R.H.* Inside the parchment they found a single curling lock of hair.

Hair that was nearly the same fire red as Flora's.

"Well, I guess we now know what color R.H.'s hair was," she said, and carefully folded the lock of hair back in its protective envelope.

"Mummy, wait. There's something else at the bottom of the box."

Flora turned just as Annie reached inside and took out

what appeared to be an article of clothing. She held it up, letting it fall its full length revealing a pair of long women's stockings.

They were red-and-white striped, faded from age, but there was no doubting it.

Annie's eyes went wide. "Mummy! The initials on the box, and on the gravestone. R.H. 'Tis the witch, Rachael Hathaway. And these are her stockings, red-and-white, just like Gavin said!"

Betty Petwith was at the house within the hour, poring through the contents of the box and the collection of journals as if they'd just discovered the Holy Grail.

And what they revealed seemed to put an end to what had been a centuries-old mystery in Ipswich-by-the-Sea—the fate of Rachael Hathaway, the famous "Ipswitch."

They were all in the dining room—Flora, Gavin—who had just returned—the children, Alec, Hallie, Jimmy, and Betty—enjoying a hastily thrown together luncheon of cold cuts, cheese, and crackers while Betty scrutinized the journals.

"According to these diaries, which appear to have been written by Rachael Hathaway herself," Betty revealed with a grin worthy of the Cheshire cat, "Hiram Hutchinson, the reclusive bachelor/doctor, wasn't quite the bachelor we thought he was after all. Shortly after she was cast out to the island by the other villagers, Hiram, who was apparently less than inclined to believe the dark accusations against her, sailed out to the isle one night alone to rescue Rachael from what had certainly become a death sentence. He knew she would never survive out there alone. Unbeknownst to anyone else, he brought her here to his home and here she stayed, living as his companion, sharing with him her knowledge of the healing properties of herbs to help him heal and cure the very people who had banished her."

"But why would anyone hide a pair of socks and some old books in the wall of a boathouse?" Robbie asked out loud.

"You wouldn't believe some of the things I've found hidden under floorboards and walled up behind plaster," Jimmy O'Connell said.

"It's folklore, really," Betty said without even taking her eyes from the journal she was reading. "In fact, the practice of deliberately concealing articles of clothing dates back to the Middle Ages. Most often, they're found near an entrance or an exit point: doors, windows, chimneys even. Odd bits of clothing are often found along with other things from the time period, such as coins or documents . . . or as in this case, diaries. It's believed to be some sort of charm or superstitious ritual of protection for the household and its inhabitants."

She looked up from the journal with a knowing smile then and added with a wink to Annie, "Some might even call it a form of witchcraft. Considering the lock of hair, I would tend to believe it was Hiram who concealed the box in the wall sometime after Rachael passed away."

"But what about the piece of eight that Annie found out on the isle?" Flora said then. "We thought that it offered proof Rachael had been carried away by a pirate lover."

"I'm more inclined to believe there was a pirate on the isle, but obviously according to these journals, he wasn't Rachael's lover. No, he was just a very clever pirate. Think about it. An island purported to be the prison of a witch? No one would dare go near the place. Where better to hide away if one is a pirate on the run from the authorities? Obviously, considering the finery the townsfolk found in that cottage when they went back to build the lighthouse all those years later—the furnishings and the crystal goblets—he'd become rather fond of his island haunt." Her eyes sparked with a speculative light behind her horn-rimmed glasses. "And considering Annie's discovery of the coin, doesn't that just leave us to wonder what else he might have left behind on that isle?"

Epilogue

"So, are you ready, m' wee bird?"

Flora stood with Annie at the back of the small stone church, the same stone church where she had been christened as a child and where she had married Seamus as a young bride. Later, all three of her children were christened there. It was, would always be for her, home.

She was home.

Standing beside Flora, Annie was a pretty miniature of her mother, wearing a crown of heather and roses in her strawberry curls. She wore a soft dress of filmy white set off with a wide ribbon sash. In her white-gloved hand, she held a basket of rose petals that in moments she would scatter along the aisle.

"Yes, Mummy," Annie answered with a beaming smile. "I'm ready."

"Well then, so am I." Flora bent to kiss her daughter softly on the cheek. "Off wit' ye, then. Right ahind Libby. And then I'll be coming right after you."

Flora watched as Annie slipped around the corner of the

church's nave where Libby waited. The trio of musicians at the front of the church took their cue and began to play.

Looking up at the small, crudely carved wooden cross that hung on the wall above the doorway, Flora said a silent prayer to the memory of her parents and another to the memory of Seamus, before she turned to where her eldest son awaited.

Robbie looked so nervous and like such a little adult, standing in his fitted tailcoat and knotted ascot tie. His usually unmanageable hair was gelled back neatly. Flora curved him a smile filled with motherly pride.

"Ready to give your mum away, then?"

"Nae," he said. He straightened his back and then offered Flora his arm. "But I'll walk with you down the aisle."

The dress Flora had chosen was a simple design, pale ivory silk with small capped sleeves and an empire waist that draped over her slender figure gracefully. She wore elbow-length gloves and her hair, woven with a strand of pearls, was pinned up in a crown of fiery curls. She felt as if she were moving through a dream.

They walked together to stand beneath the arched doorway of the main chapel. Everyone standing in the pews on the other side turned to face them.

The first person she saw was Angus, standing beside Graeme, who was holding his baby son, now her godson. Angus smiled at Flora and she blinked away tears. She mouthed a "thank you" to him, and he nodded to her, blowing her a kiss down the aisle.

As Flora and Robbie started toward the front of the church, the musicians began playing Gavin's song—instrumental now, but Flora would sing the lyrics Alec had written when she recorded the piece later that fall. They would record it in the house Gavin had bought for them, a former hunting lodge built back in the Victorian age that stood on the outskirts of the village. Gavin planned to have an entire wing of it converted into a recording studio so that Flora could be at home with the kids, living in the village where she was born, instead of in a studio an ocean away.

Flora could hear Robbie quietly counting his steps—one, two, one, two—as he walked her down the aisle to where Gavin, Seamus, and Gabriel awaited. The sight of them, and her sweet daughter standing beside them, brought the tears that Flora had struggled to contain. The frightening events of the previous week were fading into a hazy memory. Miranda was still in custody, now in Boston, as she awaited her day in court to face the charges brought against her. They considered her a flight risk, and so bail had been denied. Additionally, they had learned just that morning that the courts in New York had upheld Gavin's order for sole custody of Gabriel, putting an end to any threat that he would ever be taken from them again.

As they arrived at the end of the church aisle, Gavin stepped forward to meet Flora. Flora bent to hug Robbie, who joined Seamus and Gabriel while Flora and Gavin turned and stood together at the altar.

Bathed in candlelight, and surrounded by the villagers she had known all her life, her new family, and friends from home as well as from far away, Flora again took the vows of a wife. And as the reverend declared them man and wife, she closed her eyes and smiled, thanking the heavens above for this, her second chance.

Read on for an excerpt from

Spellstruck

by Jaclyn Reding
Coming in early 2007 from Signet Eclipse

On the Massachusetts coast just north of Boston lies a village called Ipswich-by-the-Sea. There a misty harbor gives way to narrow, tree-lined streets whose three-hundred-year-old cobbles lie littered with autumn leaves. At the end of one such street stands a sturdy red saltbox behind a picket fence threaded with sunflowers in splashes of yellow, orange, and red. A stone pathway welcomes guests through its open gate, shaded by a massive poplar whose leaves were said to whisper in the breeze. The wooden sign that hangs over the door reads the name "IpSnips" in dull gold lettering.

Jenna Wren's salon is where most of the women in Ipswich-by-the-Sea come to at times when they might find themselves in need of a little "healing." Healing is something the women in Jenna's family had been doing in various forms for generations. Some had practiced as midwives. Others had worked as wise women, as teachers, even doctors. Still others, such as her mother, dispensed their healing from their kitchens—brewing, baking, and preserving. Jenna's gift was in making women feel confident and enabling them to realize the good in themselves both inside and out.

At IpSnips women could forget the carpool, the soccer practice, the groceries that needed buying. They could step into another place where they would be listened to, where the stresses of their careers were a world away, where that urgent fax couldn't possibly reach them. Whether it took twenty minutes or two hours, each client left IpSnips feeling physically, spiritually, and emotionally reborn.

IpSnips was the place where Jenna Wren practiced her craft.

Jenna sat in her cozy kitchen, sharing a bottle of Chardonnay with her younger sister, Hallie. It had been a vexing day and Jenna was also sharing stories about the clients she'd seen that day. Hannah Greer's husband Jim had used her grandmother's hand-sewn quilt as a painting drop cloth and it had taken Jenna quite some effort to convince her not to cut off all her glorious blond hair in an effort to punish him.

And then Jenna'd had a run-in with Jack.

"Why is it men have to be so . . ."

"Obtuse?" Hallie offered. "Thoughtless? Asinine? Infuriating beyond belief?" She grinned over the soft light of the scented candles Jenna had lit around the room, sparing the utility bill their late night girl's gab session. "Because Mother Nature left out that sensitivity gene when she tossed in the other ingredients. Too bad she couldn't have left out the penis instead. It's all they're motivated by."

"You've got that right," Jenna replied, topping off her sister's wine glass and then her own. "I mean, I tell myself every time this happens that I'm not going to resort to old arguments anymore, but then he does something like not show up, not call to say he's going to be late, not care that he's got his kid nearly wetting himself, waiting for him, and all my good intentions vanish like *poof!*"

As she snapped her fingers the cork she'd just plunked into the neck of the wine bottle suddenly popped back out, landing on the table beside them.

Jenna glanced at Hallie and shrugged. "Whoops."

It was what one might call an *occupational hazard* for a practicing witch.

Magick, spellcraft, witchery—whatever anyone chose to call it—was a thing of genealogical significance to the Wren women, stretching all the way back to their Celtic roots. Theirs was a hereditary witchcraft, passed from mother to daughter to granddaughter, and they practiced as solitary "hedge" witches who revered the earth, dispensing their craft within the bounties of nature. It wasn't a New Age craft, like that of the Wiccans, but an age-old art, something to be respected, and more so than that, something to be *protected* at all costs. It was as much a part of their lives as breathing, yet it was rarely spoken of directly and never spoken of outside of the private feminine circle of their family.

"That always happens when you've had too much wine," Hallie said, picking up the cork. "Mother is the same way— she calls it 'Magick gone Amuck.' Although she swears she conjured the perfect recipe for her raspberry 'fertility' chutney after drinking a bottle of her favorite Madeira."

"Yes, well, Ingrid Bellhorn and her three sets of twins are certainly testament to that," Jenna laughed. "Hmm," she said, twirling the stem of her wineglass before her. "Perfect recipe . . . maybe someday we should try coming up with the recipe for a perfect man. One who doesn't use heirloom quilts as drop cloths, and one who shows up when he says he will."

Hallie giggled, the wine and the moonlight stealing

through the kitchen window making her game for a little harmless fun. "Okay . . . so, a recipe for the perfect man, huh? What would be the first ingredient?"

Jenna grabbed a pen and paper from the counter.

"Hmm," Hallie thought, "First, I'm thinking a really big—"

"—heart," Jenna finished, shooting her sister a cautionary stare. "So he can love the woman who claims that heart utterly and completely."

Jenna drew a heart in the very center of the page, then drew in an arrow *à la* Cupid for good measure.

"Okay, okay," Hallie agreed. "Then add two cups of 'tall.' He has to be six feet at least. We don't want to have to stare down at him in our heels."

"Right," Jenna agreed, writing "6' " beside the heart she'd drawn. "Hair color?"

"Black. No, blond, and not that dirty beach sand color either, but gleaming with a dash of brilliant gold. Like the gods of Olympus." She sighed, envisioning her creation while Jenna went on scribbling across the page. "And his eyes, they just have to be green. Like emeralds. Gold and emeralds . . ."

Jenna finished adding to the list. "Anything else?"

"Yes," Hallie piped in. "Money. A heaping bowlful of it."

"Okay . . . fine, he should have at least a stable income, but what about his inner qualities? What about responsibility? What about reliability?"

"Yeah, yeah," Hallie agreed. "Responsibility and reliability. Blah. Blah. Blah. But give him good taste, too. No ballgames for dates and he must know the difference between a bottle of good wine and a can of beer." She took a sip from her glass, then added, "Oh! And he must love the woman of his heart to distraction. He cannot sleep or eat without thinking of her. He sees her in his dreams. Everything he does reminds him of her."

Jenna laughed, enjoying the indulgence, the sisterly ridiculousness of their game while she wrote Hallie's latest "ingredients" on the page.

"Okay. This is good. But we can't forget the most important quality of all," she said then. "Above all else, he must have—"

The front door creaked open down the hall, and the creak was immediately followed by the clicking of doggie claws on the hardwood floor. Their mother had returned from her nightly walk around the common.

"I'm back," she yodeled. "Did you see that moon? What a glorious night for a walk!"

Ogre, a growth-challenged little terrier who, despite his fierce name, would just as soon run for his life whenever confronted with the neighbor's cat, Arnold, scampered into the kitchen a full minute before his matriarch.

Eudora "Nanny" Wren came bundling into the kitchen, cutting a formidable figure, cloaked in black with her polished wood walking stick levered before her. Her hair, once as black as Jenna's, had become shot through with gray over the past decade, rendering it a true salt-and-pepper mantle. When it wasn't wound up in its usual bun, it fell easily to her hips. She wore spectacles—wire-rimmed, round, and looking like they had been crafted at least the century before. And she always wore lipstick, no matter if she were only going to the front door to meet the package delivery man. Age and childbirth and a fondness for dark chocolate-covered-cherries had rounded her once eye-catching figure, but Eudora didn't care. She'd been a widow since the day her Sam, for whom Jenna's son was named, had been taken from her—he was a fisherman lost to the sea in one of the most terrible storms in New England's history. A widow she would stay until the day she joined him.

Eudora's shrewd eyes took in her daughters' expressions and the near-empty bottle of wine, then asked, "What are you two up to?"

Jenna quickly turned over the paper they'd been writing on, knowing her mother would never approve of their undertaking, even if it was only for fun. "Oh, just having a glass of wine and complaining about men. You know, normal girly stuff. Want to join us?"

"I would," the matriarch sighed, tossing Ogre a bit of cheese from the cracker platter the girls had been nibbling from. "But if I have wine this late at night, I'll wake with a headache fierce enough to stir the dead." She chuckled to herself then glanced at the clock. "It's getting late. You two should be abed as well. I trust Cassie's already tucked in for the night?"

Jenna nodded. "Hours ago. You must have worn her out with all that baking today. Didn't even put up a fight."

Eudora grinned. "She's a sweet one, that child. And canny as can be. She'll be a true Wren some day. That's for certain."

She took up her walking stick and headed for the back door. It opened onto a stone pathway that ran through the garden to her own cottage the next property over. Cricket-song chirped from the night scene outside.

"Are you coming, Hallie? You've work tomorrow, no?"

"A'yea," Hallie conceded, nodding to her sister. "Our last weekend before Flora closes *Thar Muir* for the season. We've got Betsy Berringer's wedding tomorrow, with the bridal party staying on till Tuesday, then that will be it till next spring. All in all, I'd say the B-and-B had a triumphant first season."

Hallie got up, grabbed her jacket, and whistled for the dog to follow. Ogre started forward, then skidded to a stop when he heard Arnold's distant scratchy meow coming from somewhere not so far away. The dog instantly began to shiver.

"Come on, you coward." Jenna scooped him up, tucking him under her arm and rubbing his one folded ear. "We'll protect you here tonight."

She walked her mother and sister to the door, and stood watching as they vanished into the darkness that cloaked the garden between the two houses. She glanced up and caught sight of the moon, full and fat and ringed in a mist, hovering over the treetops. A true New England autumn night.

Her mother was right. What a moon indeed.

Jenna closed the door, putting Ogre on his pillowed "throne," an old laundry basket Cassie had done up with cushions and curtains and ribbons. She took up the wine glasses, washed and rinsed them in the sink, and put them on the dish board to dry. Then she circled the room, checking the windows, extinguishing the candles.

She was tired. It had been a full day at the salon and tomorrow showed every sign of being just as hectic. Betsy Berringer's bridal party was due in at nine for hair and makeup. And then Marjorie Cummings was coming in at noon, a treat to herself for her fortieth birthday. Jenna made a mental note to include a gift of her "Youth Springs Eternal" vervain and rosemary bath sachet to help ward off any birthday gloominess.

As she reached for the last candle, Jenna remembered the impromptu "recipe" she and Hallie had been crafting. She also remembered that last quality they'd forgotten to write down before her mother's return had interrupted them, the one that would complete their makeshift concoction for the "Perfect Man."

"Honor," she whispered out loud to the dancing flame of the candle. "Above all else, he must have honor."

Jenna turned to retrieve the paper, intending to burn it in the candle's flame. It was never a good idea to leave any spell, howsoever makeshift it might be, written loose. All spells, she had learned from a very early age, must be kept in a proper *grimoire*.

But when she looked on the table where she'd left the paper, turning it facedown she remembered, she saw that it wasn't there.

It wasn't on the chair.

It hadn't fallen to the floor either.

The paper, in fact, was nowhere to be found.